BAD GIRLS

BAD GIRLS

Mary Flanagan

JONATHAN CAPE
THIRTY BEDFORD SQUARE LONDON

First published 1984
Copyright © 1984 by Mary Flanagan

Jonathan Cape Ltd, 30 Bedford Square, London WC1B 3EL

British Library Cataloguing in Publication Data

Flanagan, Mary
Bad girls.
I. Title
813'.54[F]   PS3556.L3/

ISBN 0-224-02248-2

Printed in Great Britain by
Ebenezer Baylis & Son Ltd
The Trinity Press, Worcester and London

For Arione

Contents

Cream Sauce

Lydia may not have been the world's greatest cook, but she was almost certainly the slowest. She was a fantasizer and a drunk. Moreover, she was addicted to opera. Now imagine what mealtimes at 99 Copenhagen Crescent, NW3, must have been like: tantalizing aromas accompanied by interminable waits, Callas at full decibels, the ever-present bottle of Bordeaux, the not infrequent failures which must, out of sheer physical necessity, be consumed. Her family suffered patiently.

Perhaps patiently is not the word. Perhaps their resignation grew out of causes less saintly. Elliot, for instance, was unaware of time. Of course he was unaware of time, he was a historian. How could he understand the way time siphoned off one's vital energies? While Lydia battled mundanities he lived in his study, in his mind, in the world of spirit. Eternal vistas spread themselves before *him*. Consequently, Elliot was contemptuous of other people's bad humour. Rosie and Danton, seven and ten, were engaged alternately in their charming and vicious pursuits. The world, as it should do, enthralled them, and they showed no symptoms of introversion. It occurred to Lydia that R. D. Laing would have approved of their ungovernable individualism. She supposed, wearily, that upon this she was to be congratulated.

The three of them were continually, passionately, occupied. For such types the arrival of dinner at ten thirty p.m., did not constitute disaster or even discomfort. Video games, the collapse of the Byzantine Empire, Kermit the Frog, Plato's dream, or the healthy release of aggression through punching, kicking and hair pulling assure constant diversion. Actions and ideas succeed each other in a wonderful flow, each melting into the next, all things gorgeously merging to create escape. There is no waiting, for time has ceased.

Lydia sensed that only she was trapped in the disparate, in the continual performance of petty but obligatory actions which are dispensed with only in certain dreams; banal processes which must be got through and which served to keep the others afloat in their selfish personal happiness: the sorting of laundry snatched up, worn, and discarded without a thought; telephone calls to the dentist, the gas board, the plumber; the organizing of the myriad details involved in transporting two small beings from one point to another and back again; the picking up and putting away of ever-reappearing objects; the hopeless watching of a billion dust particles resettling upon a hundred scratched surfaces. Details that never meant anything. Details that required the pushing of oneself forward through time, that were a constant reminder of time. Details that made one tense, tense, tense.

'I need a loving man.' Lydia stirred the roux with one hand and refilled her glass of Medoc with the other. It was eight thirty.

She had begun life as a reasonable enough person. She had a brain, an engaging manner, and an abundance of finer feelings. But she was half-educated. The ground had been tilled and the seeds planted. Initial growth was well under way. Then, with marriage, cultivation had abruptly ceased. The result was a leggy vegetable entanglement, clamouring and competing for the limited nourishment available. She read when she could – novels and Shakespeare – and listened to opera. But everything she read and heard became somehow mixed up with dreams of the past and impossible plans for the future. How sad, how desperately sad, to be an undisciplined woman with a head full of notions. Even though some, she felt sure, were brilliant, they were, like everything else, disparate. They could not be marketed as a world view, neither could they be a world. Besides, synthesis was Elliot's department. He had staked out his territory there years ago.

It was eight forty. Danton was practising the trumpet. Rosie began to scream. She screamed and screamed and would not stop screaming. Something shattered and she stopped screaming. But Lydia could not leave the sauce, it was the critical moment. She had only just added the hot fish stock. Besides, screams could mean anything. More than likely they were screams of delight. Lydia had drunk a bottle and a half and had entered into that state where nothing mattered but the music and the memories and the *velouté* which she stirred slowly with a wooden spoon, as in a dream.

It was a quarter to nine. In any proper London middle-class household, the children would have been asleep long ago, tucked up in bed after their tea of fish fingers or cornflakes or Sainsbury fruit yoghurts – followed by the obligatory satsuma. Here the kiddipoos watched X-rated films and jumped on the bed while awaiting their Cordon Bleu repast. And what for? Whatever for, Lydia wondered, when sausages and eggs would have suited them better. It would come to that for them all if she weren't careful and failed to curb this lust for culinary elaboration, these endless preparations which began at six and continued, often, for five hours. And this after a day of details and tension and the nightmare intimacy of family life.

'I need a rich man.'

She had been forced to let Mrs Gladstone go. Since Newton and Schreiber had put back Elliot's book until the autumn (what *were* they supposed to live on now that the meagre advance had been gobbled up?) and the bank was getting ratty about the overdraft, she had been doing all the housekeeping herself. The accumulation of tasks and trivia doubled.

Elliot was a terrible business man, his beautiful mind the prey of perfidious publishers who held back his royalties to gain themselves a few pounds extra interest at the bank. A Philistine Dutchman with a Swiss contract owed him thousands, but was Elliot bothered? Did he wake in the night consumed by anxiety and visions of deprivation? Not he. He worked on and slept on, too convinced of his own worth to stoop to bitter recriminations, let alone a lawsuit. His complacency was inhuman. He held to his theory (a cyclical, metaphysical, transcendent, and somewhat obfuscating view of history) and kept turning out his four-hundred-page books some of which, to everyone's surprise, sold.

The children grew up hyperactively. All three were having

fun. But she, Lydia, had no fun, no theory, no privacy, no precious time. She was the semi-educated wife of a semi-famous man.

'"Being your slave, what should I do but tend upon the hours and times of your desire . . . "'

Elliot came into the kitchen holding an empty glass.

'Um — what?'

'I said I have no precious time at all.' She arranged the mussels around the fillets of sole.

'Excuse me, Liddy, you've had since six, I believe.' He took a handful of freshly sliced mushrooms, tilted back his fine big head (so full of brains), and ate them. He was always taking her freshly sliced or freshly grated or freshly chopped whatevers and flagrantly devouring them. It infuriated her, especially when she was forced to weigh and measure all over again.

'I usually start at six. That's when I'm allowed a glass of wine. You know that. How's the fall of Constantinople?'

'Fitting in fantastically.'

'Confirming all presuppositions?'

'Why not?' He reached for her pile of dainty pink shrimp. 'Sole Dieppoise tonight, I see.' She stayed his hand.

'Sorry, Lid. They taste better when they're stolen.' He smiled. For a split second she liked him.

'Why was Rosie screaming?' she asked.

'Was she screaming?'

'There was some horrendous crash.'

'How could I tell above Cavaradossi's howls of agony?'

Lydia was in a Puccini phase and had been listening to nothing but *Tosca* for the past three nights. Her life began at six p.m. The world-without-end hour. It began with the first glass of Bordeaux, with the first act of *Così Fan Tutte* or *Rhinegold*. Then she took possession of her personal domain: the kitchen, symbol of slavery, sanctuary, scene of liberation. Cooking, that blessedly inexact science, was the sole activity that sustained her. She actually looked forward to it through days of accumulated details and disparate, obligatory actions. It was her only art. As she drank and half-listened and half-remembered, everything inside her began to melt like butter in a bain-marie. She beautifully fell apart, a kind of automatic pilot took control of the dinner and left her fancy free to roam through love and art and endless possibilities. There were moments of peace. Nothing else in her life quite did that for her. No wonder she sought to extend her evening's allotted span through over-elaboration, and to master even more arcane dishes.

Elliot poured himself a glass of wine and picked up the newspaper. Oh no, he was sitting down at the kitchen table. He meant to rest his big brain by feeding it yet more information. And when her back was turned he would come and steal the shrimp. She hated the intrusion, but what could she do? People want to be in the kitchen. It's warmth and mother and life itself.

'Everything takes place here now,' Lydia thought. 'The drawing room as scene of the action is finished. Even the bedroom, maybe, is finished. Dramas are written about kitchens, whole tragedies and farces played out in them. People double the size of their kitchens, allowing them to engulf lounges and dining rooms; they move divans into them, set up stereo speakers. We've done the same, and at my insistence. I've opened up my theatre of operations and let in the world, damn me.' She remembered with a shudder the dinner parties she once gave, especially after Elliot's first book was published and there was such a kafluffel. All those acquaintances swanning about, gossiping, making half-hearted offers of help, not listening to the Wagner or the Strauss, taking up her precious time. What nuisances they were and how nervous they made her. How she would long for an endless February night like this, cold outside, safe inside, alone with her cooker and her preparations. Well, all artists wished to be left alone.

It was nine fifteen. Slowly she beat the *velouté* into a mixture of egg yolks and cream then returned it to the pan. She looked through the steamy window above the sink. The moon was rising behind the branches of a bare lime tree at the end of the garden. Maria was singing '*Visi d'arte*' as the sauce maintained a slow simmer in the bain-marie. ('Slow simmering is the secret. Allows the sauce to mature. Others skip the process, but it's essential. Let it imperceptibly thicken. Slower the better.') The previously poached sole and mussels were warm in their dish. Around her lay the numerous pots and utensils: gratin dish, sauté pan, hachoir, mandoline, chinois, various pöelons. The shelves were lined with ramekins, tians, flan rings, marmites, diables, and carving boards of all sizes and depths of wear. High above them stood preserving jars of fruit conserves, plums in eau-de-vie, mustard and dill pickles, piccallili, green beans, jugged hare, and earthenware jars of preserved goose and pork. Copper moulds and timbales decked the walls. The wooden spoon collection was formidable. Bulging from a shelf of their own were the fat greasy cook-books whose authors were her intimate friends – Elizabeth, Julia, Louisette, Robert, Maurice, Arabella. The whole scene swam in a warm and fragrant vapour. Just for a moment life was beautiful.

'"A supernova explosion was sighted by Chinese astronomers in 1054."'

Lydia started. She had become lost in a recipe for hare with chocolate, which she had never tried and was calculating might be right for next Tuesday, simultaneously entertaining a recollection of Sidney, who had been her lover thirteen years ago. She had forgotten that Elliot was in the room.

'Dear God, he's going to edit *The Times* for me, I know it. I can feel it coming, he's in that kind of mood, his nearest approximation to expansive sociability.' She began to snap her way through a mound of haricot vert.

He read to her of the bomb, the Beirut massacres, and education vouchers, explaining for the hundredth time the way in which they all verified his theory of historical recurrence.

What a gifted exploiter he was. Could he let nothing be without forcing it to confirm his beautiful concept? Could nothing simply ramble loose, straying in its own pleasant anarchy? He was a mighty hunter was old Elliot. The moment he spied a vagrant thought, a vagrant person or event, bam! it was caught fast in the snare of, zip! it was under the net of his World View. He was inescapable, he was naive, he was strong. He did not fret over electricity bills or train schedules or supermarket queues or holes in tights or nosebleeds or one lost mitten. What did details that consumed a thousand precious moments matter to him, snug as he was in the armour of his Idea. In his quiet way he was quite a deadly person, really.

'I need a charming man.' It was nine twenty-five.

Rosie ran into the kitchen emitting little ceaseless piccolo shrieks that were enough to shatter the ear-drum.

'Danton's murdering me, he's murdering me! Oh help, help! Mummy, Elliot! Eek! Eek! Eek!'

She fell to the floor, clasping Lydia's knees, kicking and yelling as Danton beat her determinedly with a bunch of daffodils. Elliot continued to read aloud from a review by John Carey.

'Children!' Lydia shouted. 'My flowers, my sauce, ouch goddammit, my foot! *Will* you stop. Rosie, let go of me, *let go*!' She snapped a tea-towel at Rosie, who was crouched between her legs and the warming drawer, and tried without success to rescue the daffodils. Danton escaped her and ran from the room with a lunatic giggle. She managed, now in a rage, to catch hold of Rosie by the back of her jumper. As she reached out to slap her daughter's bottom, her head struck the overhead dish drainer and dislodged three saucers, two breakfast cups, and a plate which had been left her by her aunt. They shattered all over the floor as the saucepan toppled into the bain-marie.

'"The error arose in the determination of the structure of a gene of a tumour-causing virus in chickens." What turkeys these scientists are.'

Rosie howled. She ran to her father and clung to him in brilliantly simulated terror. Lydia seized the last two plates from the dish drainer and hurled them on to the floor.

'What is it, sweetie, what is it, my pet? There now, there now, what's upset my diddums so?' Elliot put down the paper at last and was caressing the inconsolable Rosie. 'Dear me, Lydia,' he was a little sharp, 'what's going on? Is all this really necessary? *Must* you be so nervous?'

'It's grief. It comes from grief.' She was down on her hands and knees, picking up the pieces, weeping and brushing her lank hair back from her face. 'Don't you remember? I mean, you're meant to be the Intellect. You read me that article', she wiped her nose on the back of her hand, 'that said how women retain the effects of every loss, every hurt.' Elliot sighed. 'That something inside them never forgets and never gets over any of it. The American psychologist — God, you read it to me, what *was* her name? It's all grief, unexpressed grief! And the sauce is ruined, I'll have to start it again. Anyway, I've stopped now. Look, I'm not crying, I'm not nervous, I'll start again. I'm sorry, sorry, sorry. Oh Rosie!'

She tried to embrace her little girl, but Rosie was having none of it and wriggled indignantly away. A moment later she heard her laughing with Danton over a game of 'Operation'.

Elliot took up the *Guardian*, ignoring his wife's pathetic chagrin. 'If only you realized, Lydia, how contagious your hysteria is.'

'I'm sorry. I'm nervous. It comes from grief.'

He did not ask her over what it was she grieved. 'And you, remember? You told me yourself, Elliot, that there are ions or something in the brain, and these ions migrate, the sodium and the potassium – '

'Yes, yes.'

'And when they migrate from the brain to the bloodstream you've got manic depression, that's what you've got, and women are 400 per cent more prone to manic depression than men, and it's all the fault of those bloody ions.'

'Perhaps if the children were fed a bit earlier. It doesn't necessarily imply rejection, you know. Just because you had tea with the terrier for ten years ... ' He continued reading, this time in silence.

'The children are like that all day,' she started to say, but was defeated by his total lack of response. She turned the record over, got a fresh pan from the cupboard, and started the sauce again. It was nine thirty.

Interruptions, interruptions. Everything in life, even love, even children, was an interruption. All she wished for, like any artist, was to be left alone to wander inside herself, growing and rambling without restraint. Surely all souls must yearn for this simple, precious freedom.

As the butter melted she opened another bottle of wine. Elliot, without glancing up, held out his glass for a refill. Lydia looked with hatred at his composed, concentrating features.

'"I have no precious time at all to spend, nor services to do till you require."' She poured his wine.

Of course she spent too much money on it and on the ingredients for these fancy, unappreciated dinners. The over-draft, the mortal mortgage, the unpaid royalties, the bill from

Berry Brothers and Rudd. What horror. But she could never give up the wine. She couldn't even switch to a Rioja or a Côtes du Rhone. Only Bordeaux really did it to her, took her where she wanted to go. It was her passport to privacy. Still, no more Margaux, she must make do with Good Ordinary Claret next time. Perhaps add Perrier. But not tonight. Tonight she was too nervous. Tonight the ions were migrating.

She checked the potatoes. They were fine. Vegetables must appear as a separate course. ' "One doesn't want them floating about the plate and getting mixed up with the sauce." ' Of course that meant more dishes to wash and only maddened her in the morning.

'I need a *young* man.' Like Sidney, oh like Sidney, her lovely, her only New York Jew. Once more she sought his fugitive image: brown-eyed, olive-skinned, so unlike her fair, Protestant Elliot. She had met Sidney at the British Museum at a time in her life when she had not yet begun to be nervous. Their romance had been brief, but every so often she dreamed of him – big, rich dreams full of space and the washed light that follows a thunderstorm. They had walked by the river near Hammersmith and sat on the wall outside the City Barge, their legs dangling and touching above the low tide. They had talked and talked. Everything was funny. There was so much to say. He had been young, he had been charming, he had even had a little money. He had also died in an automobile accident, a true American death. Thirteen years. Automatic pilot switched on, and she was strolling with Sidney through endless vistas, past Florentine villas and sunny rounded hills delineated by cypress. They lay down to rest in fields and gardens, and he covered her with his long, olive-skinned body. They walked down the dark Paris street holding hands. They went into an old hotel and registered at the desk. He embraced her in the tiny lift . . .

' "If Gladstone's Home Rule Bill of 1893, which was passed by the Commons, had not been defeated in the Lords we should have no Irish problem today." Just as I've always said. You see, Lid, in the twelfth century, when Henry II invaded – '

Hell. No more sullen silence. Like a child or a cat he recovered from everything, forgot everything.

Lydia tried to find her way back to Sidney — Sidney beside the sea, great black gnarled rocks and a wild wild sky.

'"Like as the waves make towards the pebbled shore, so do our minutes hasten to their end."'

'Oh yes.' Screams split the air. Seven-year-old screams. Not even Elliot could ignore them.

'I'll go,' was his munificent response. It was ten to ten.

No use. The fantasy was wrecked. In a moment she would be summoned to cope with catastrophe. She played Act Two of *Tosca* for the third time, drank another glass of wine, straight down, and began to mix the salad dressing. The call came like the voice of doom.

'Um, Lid, I'm awfully afraid that — '

'Oh Christ!' She flung down her oven glove, spilling the olive oil and the wine vinegar.

'They've been bathing Avril. The floor is rather a mess.'

'But *they* were meant to be in the bath. What the hell is poor Avril doing in the bath?'

'And your make-up as well. Now try to be calm.'

She pushed past him on the stairs, blinded by tears and exerting every effort to repress the desire to tear his eyes out. She rescued the dazed and sodden sheep-dog who was redolent of Badedas and Floris Lily of the Valley. The rug was soaked through (water was, no doubt, already seeping into the living room ceiling, the fourth time in two months). The writing was on the wall, and in her lipstick. The chaos was indescribable. Rosie had hidden under the bed in fear of further recriminations, and Danton manfully faced his mother alone. Lydia tried to check the torrent of abuse which was about to break from her. She knew what Elliot would say, how he would look, but out it came, transforming her into that termagant they all secretly knew her to be and which Sidney had never seen and never would see.

'I'm trying to listen to music, you wretched little ingrate. You know it's my only pleasure. Why do you try constantly to deprive me of it? Why do you abuse and thwart me like this and rob me of my privacy and of every little precious moment?'

'I suppose you'd better just send us to Dr Barnardo's.' Danton looked her straight in the eye.

'There's another place I've considered sending you.'

'That's enough of that.' Elliot stood in the doorway, looking, for him, almost angry, defending his children, as usual, from the mad woman he had taken to wife.

'Oh my God, the sauce.' The mess must wait, otherwise they would be eating at midnight. Lydia fled to save the supper. She was just in time. But as she mopped up the spilled dressing, she saw in despair that Elliot had eaten all the shrimp.

She heard the three of them laughing upstairs. Tosca was stabbing Scarpia. The timing buzzer went off. Grimly, she carried on with the salad, hopeless of finding her way back to Sidney, certain that the bathroom atrocity would be left to her entirely, and that she would be on her hands and knees up there well after one a.m. while the others slept.

'Din-dins' she shouted at ten thirty-five in her best approximation of cheerfulness, determined to put everything right. There was no reply. She went to Elliot's study, barely able, by now, to focus on him. He was bent over his desk, copying something out of a large volume.

'Dinner's ready.'

'Great. Be there in a moment.'

'Where are the children?'

'Asleep, I think.'

'Asleep!' She checked their bedroom. They were passed out on top of each other with the television and the E.T. radio both going, unwashed, unfed, and still in their clothes. What kind of mother was she? She returned to absorbed Elliot.

'Couldn't you have kept them awake?' Her voice trembled.

'Hm?'

'Awake. The children.'

'Are they? They were so quiet I thought they were asleep.'

'Oh Elliot, they *are* asleep, and dinner is ready. God, I work so hard and for what? No one cares, no one appreciates the squandering of my precious time. I'm being slowly ground down to nothing. I need a holiday or I shall go mad. Can't we go to the sea? What about Normandy or Sicily. Elba, maybe – '

'Lydia, they were very upset after what happened. I did my best to cheer them up, but they're beginning to live in fear of your rages. Besides, they'd had no supper.' If she were the grist, Elliot was the mill.

'But I was making the supper. Supper *is made*.'

'Why not give them tea at six and put them to bed?'

'That's barbarous.'

'Anyway, I've come across a most interesting passage in Jung. It absolutely confirms what I was saying about Uniting Symbols and the motif of circle and square in the early Renaissance. Remember?' She didn't but said she did. 'Well he's writing here about Revelations. Listen: "While the circle signifies the roundness of heaven and the all-embracing nature of the pneumatic deity, the square refers to the earth. Heaven is masculine but earth is feminine. Therefore God has his throne in heaven, while Wisdom has hers on earth, as she says in Ecclesiasticus – "'

'Amazing, Elliot. You'll fit it in fantastically, I'm sure. But dinner.'

'Just want to finish copying it down. Use it in chapter eight. With you in a moment, Liddy. Smells wonderful. "In the same way that Sophia signifies God's self-reflection – "'

There was her real child. She went back to the kitchen. The buzzer was going, had been going, no doubt, for the past five minutes. The sauce was not ruined entirely, but it was spoiled. She would have to pass it through the chinois, and that meant yet another article to wash up in the morning. She began to cry, knowing she must proceed, even though she was now hopelessly drunk. The food would be cold – or at best dismally glazed over from too long a sojourn in the warming drawer – and there would be only her and Elliot to eat it. Tosca was again stabbing Scarpia. The music induced in Lydia's mind a hazy notion which she began to act upon, hardly realizing what she was about. It was as though she had gone on to automatic pilot for good.

She opened the cabinet under the sink, the common repository of homely poisons (Mrs Gladstone had kept it very well stocked), and removed the following items: window cleaner, disinfectant, Harpic, lemon-scented cleansing powder, Flash, spray furniture polish, liquid foliar feed, and a fresh green sink scrubber. She passed over the washing-up liquid since it might so incriminatingly bubble. No, she was not about to tidy up;

she was proceeding with dinner. Elliot's eating the shrimp had been the last straw.

An experimental squeeze of creamy pink window cleaner confirmed that it would most probably integrate without curdling the sauce (would it now become an Aurore rather than a Parisienne she wondered?). Just a little bit of everything, one must be so careful to balance the flavours, only a dash of disinfectant. She sifted together a mixture of Harpic and cleansing powder and added it to the sauce, whisking constantly, of course. She could almost think of Sidney now. She removed from the oven the glazed earthenware gratin dish which held the sole and placed it on the tiles next to the cooker. She poured on the sauce, now of a lovely amber hue imparted by the foliar feed. Over the whole she grated the crunchy green sink scrubber. The effect was delightful. She returned the dish to the oven for five minutes to reheat, and leaned against the work top, watching the clock and sipping her Medoc. '"Whilst I, my sovereign, watch the clock for you . . . "'

When the buzzer sounded, she opened the oven door and took out the dinner. The sauce had curdled slightly, probably the window cleaner after all, damn. It must be reintegrated. She would have to *faire une liaison* by adding a *beurre manié*. Nope, it was too late now. She couldn't face it. Must go forward, pushing against time.

'*A table*,' she shouted. There was no reply. He never heard the first call, engaged as he was in millennial processes. 'Elliot, darling!' Oh most exasperating of creatures. Mortal enemy. Best of men.

Lydia slipped on her oven gloves, picked up the Sole Dieppoise, minus shrimp garniture, and took it to the table which had not been set. She hesitated, turned round, and went back to the cooker.

'Elliot, it's ready.' Everything was quiet. The music had stopped. She could hear the clock ticking. It was eleven fifteen. She took the dish once more to the table and stood with it in her hands. Was he coming? She walked back to the cooker. She put down the sole then picked it up. A horrid skin was forming on the top. Too late to *vanner la sauce*, there were footsteps overhead. She knew she was going to panic, something one must never do in the kitchen where timing is of the essence. And she was well aware of what miracles could be accomplished by keeping one's head and using a small quantity of plain water. But it was too late. Too late for dinner, too late for everything.

'What should I do, being your slave . . . what should I do?'

Lydia took the dish back to the table. Again she hesitated and turned towards the cooker.

'What should I do . . . what should I do . . . '

Wild Garlic

For Leslie Barbara

I

'You see how he tortures me by not eating. There, he's doing it now – pushing his plate away. Didn't I tell you, Louise?' Zelda laughed. 'And all because he thinks I ought to increase his allowance.'

Rupert rose from his place at the head of the table. 'It's not that, Mumsie, and you know it isn't. May I go upstairs now?'

'Of course, darling. But first give me a cuddle, my big, clever thirteen-year-old. You won't have some more cake?'

'Not now, thank you.' He put his arms around Zelda's neck and buried his face in her soft brown hair.

Louise admired them. They were wonderful together and very alike. The doorbell rang.

'I suppose', Zelda kissed him again, 'that's Oliver and Phyllida come to see the snakes.'

He strained a little to get away, but she held him still.

'So that's the last we'll see of you this evening, right? Never mind. Kiss your grandmother and your godmother before you leave.'

Alice, tipsy from four vodkas, interrupted her conversation with Nicholas long enough to deposit a bright red kiss on Rupert's cheek.

'Happy Birthday, Darling.'

Rupert came round to Louise. She put down her fork (she was always the last to finish) and opened her arms to him feeling his body thin but strong against her rather lumpy one.

She hugged him too hard, a bad habit of hers, but he and his mother filled her with an enthusiasm she found difficult to control. It occurred to her that he might not like her being so overt. After all, he had not seen her for three years. But he returned her embrace fully, with nothing, that she could detect, of formality or resentment. Then he ran off, letting the door bang behind him.

'Nicholas, whatever made you give those dreadful snakes to Rupert?' asked Alice.

'They're beautiful,' Nicholas snapped. He could do any-thing with his grandmother, and she particularly enjoyed his being brusque with her. 'He *likes* them. They're an imagina-tive present. And they cost ten pounds a piece. You see I'm not mean like some people.'

'My dear, you're becoming terribly mercenary.' Alice tinkled her ice-cubes.

'That reminds me, Mum.' Nicholas turned to Zelda. 'May I borrow £3,000?'

'Whatever for?'

'A motorbike.'

'Would you like it now or may I have my coffee first?'

'Then what about £350 for a three-piece suit?'

'Oh darling . . . '

'But I *need* it!' Nicholas banged the table.

Louise was not sure if he was serious. She found him arch and difficult since he had turned sixteen, a deal-maker and a discomfort-causer. They had got on well when he was little, but now he treated her as most men did.

'Louise, you see what I have to contend with. They expect me to be father and mother both at once: make the rules, break the rules. Dispense the money, provide the love. It's terribly difficult.' Zelda looked helpless but not at all distressed.

'Darling Zelda, you're not firm enough.' Alice sighed. 'You've always been indulgent like your father. He was a Pisces too.'

'Oh mother . . . '

Louise stared at her plate and pushed some birthday cake around with her fork, listening to the three of them squabble, she guessed amicably, and trying to smile when appropriate. No use. She couldn't keep up. So she played with her food, gradually re-tuning her ear to the Lacey's London English, straining to understand the fatuities of their blood-kin conversation. The way they talked — it was mysterious and it was nothing. It was, above all, conservative. They followed the same rules they had always followed, adopting high tones for trivialities and passing off the big things as bagatelles. She wondered if they ever meant any of it.

'And as to Phyllida's staying the night — '

Nicholas feigned astonishment. 'Crafty old bat! Alice, however did you know that? Wasted as a grandmama, she is. Pity. MI5 has need of women like her.'

' — in the same bed!'

'It's nothing to do with me,' drawled Zelda. 'They arrange it all themselves.'

Louise always marvelled at Zelda's moral lassitude. That she made few judgments and exerted less will was evident in her movements, her clothes, and the pastel messiness of her house. Even the surroundings exuded the air of limp grace so especially hers.

The big dining room in which the birthday supper was going on looked to Louise as if it might not have been cleaned in the three years since she had last sat in it. Zelda's whole establishment was like that — dusty, disordered, and completely inviting. You came in and wanted to collapse in a corner right away, hopefully to have an intimate chat with the lady of the house, who probably would have forgotten she invited you. Louise thought of her own room back in Philadelphia, a cell in her father's sprawling apartment. Compared to Zelda's environment, it was like the pair of sensible shoes she had bought to help her cope with the English climate. She envisaged the solid desk, the single bed, the filing cabinet, the orderly bookshelves; like an office, all neat and hard with good reproductions in expensive frames. Zelda, of course, thought nothing of Blu-tacking her Braque to the wall and letting cobwebs collect at the corners. Nor was it unusual to find treasures under the bed or mixed up with the laundry. When you rescued the fragment of Roman sculpture, the bit of Alexandrian faience, or the vase (in which pallid celery had usually been rotting for a week) from the precipice of the kitchen work top and presented it to her in awe and astonishment, she would frown at first as if trying to think whatever could be distressing you. Then recognition would flood her face, and she would laugh and say something like, 'Oh yes, lovely, isn't it? Richard's uncle, the art historian, the one who wrote the book, I never can remember the title, oh you know, well anyway, he gave it to us as a wedding present. At least I *think* it was he. Just put it down anywhere, lovey, and I'll take care of it later. Better still, why don't you keep it.'

Keep it?

She had married young and very well. Alice had been delighted but Zelda seemed unaware of the glory of her connections. She took them all for granted and was not a snob. She did nothing and so had time for everything, had no patience but infinite tolerance. She never tried. She let everything go and was unconscious of the way she made people adore her.

Only with her boys was it different. She hovered over them with a fierce love, fighting for rights and money with their perpetually absent father who made films (he had won an award) and had a house and a mistress in Argyllshire. Richard and Zelda, separated for four years, still argued punctually, once a week, over the telephone. The whole arrangement intrigued Louise. It was glamorous, puzzling, sexual.

'But we *are* being so boring,' Zelda interrupted her mother. 'Louise has just flown the Atlantic, and she's exhausted.' She gazed at her old friend with kind eyes and held out her hand across the table. 'I'm so pleased to see you,' she said, and she did mean that. 'Mother, do you know, Louise just got her PhD. It's really exciting, isn't it?'

'My dear, how thrilling! Now that calls for a drink. Nicholas, darling, fetch the brandy. You are clever, Louise. If only Zelda had finished her education – '

'Mother, you were ecstatic when Richard proposed, and couldn't wait for me to leave Cambridge. Nearly wet your knickers in anticipation of half-term.'

'Pure invention, *and* gratuitous vulgarity. Zelda, you are without conscience. Louise knows, and I reiterate it now, that I was opposed to the marriage from the beginning. And oh how justified my trepidations were!'

Nicholas regarded Louise with a gleam more interest and asked her about her thesis.

'Mmmmmmmmm, difficult to explain. Very specialized. You really want to know? Just a little, please — ' she stayed Alice's hand. Brandy, nearly all spirits, made her ill. She would have a sip though, just to be nice; they were being so enthusiastic for her. Nicholas pressed for more information, ignoring his grandmother who was now criticizing Zelda's appearance.

'Lady miners! That's steep. Did you really live with them, then, tape their breakfast conversations and bathroom activities?'

Louise had hoped to avoid this. She hated talking about her work. Five years of sweat over this thing was enough. Five years of psychoanalysis, too, and consequent interruptions, deciding in pain to stop, then in greater pain to go on.

They told her she should publish; they seemed very aroused by the thing. But Louise had been sceptical. It wasn't that wonderful. Better wait on it. Wait, think, decide. Do what was right, without haste and with the way safely marked.

'Used tapes, listened for hours. Edited. About 50,000 words.' Louise spoke in shorthand whenever she was in a hurry to get past a topic. Nicholas clearly wanted to hear more of these singular females. Louise wanted to forget them. She wanted to forget everything. She tried to re-route him, then to derail him completely, but he came straight down the line. She must at least keep him off the subject of her new job.

Alice was bullying Zelda into having her hair cut, and Louise took the opportunity to break in.

'She's beautiful just as she is.'

'But so scruffy. Louise, you mustn't undermine me, expecially when your hair has been done so divinely.'

Louise reached instinctively for her thick bob — her best feature, if she could have been said to have one.

Zelda sweetly brought the conversation to an end. 'And now if you'll excuse us, mother,' she pushed back her chair and looked at Louise, 'we want to talk privately. Louise, come into the little room. By some miracle there's a fire.' They went out hand in hand, leaving Nicholas to bicker with his grandmother. By the time she left, he had got twenty pounds out of her.

Louise and Zelda, alone for the first time in three years,

brought out all the old things, family, psychoanalysis, books, school friends, Louise's thesis, Zelda's peculiar husband, the rosy progress of their son and godson, ending with tears and *La Bohème*.

'I always think it will be strange, you know – seeing you again after one of our great gaps. But it never is.'

'No. We go right on as if nothing had intervened.'

'As if we'd just put the phone down yesterday. Ah, this aria . . . ' Zelda hummed a bit. 'It's amazing, really, that we should be room-mates for only a year then friends for ever.'

'I've never understood why.'

'Oh Louise, it just *is*.'

'But we're so different. Everyone who looks at us knows.'

'Not at all. We like the same things. We have good taste. You're just more intelligent than I – don't shake your head like that, Louise – more industrious and practical.'

'Me!?'

'Well, you, at least, *do* something. You write, you research, you speak languages, you have objectives, you have a brief-case. You were the cleverest girl in our class. Everyone said you had a beautiful mind.'

'Well, I haven't.'

'All right, all right. But *I* have a lover, did I tell you? He's very young.'

'Really?' This was better. She adored Zelda's private life. 'How young?'

'Eighteen.'

'Only half your age? I thought you meant *very* young.'

They laughed, but Louise's voice rose abnormally high. Her lovers, when she had them, were forty-five-year-old statisticians with names like Chuck.

'I am fond of you, Loulee. You're so comfortable.'

Louise went upstairs to the toilet, the one downstairs having been in need of repair for six weeks. Hours had passed since the birthday supper, but the children were still up. She stopped short outside Rupert's room. If she had not been so dark, she would have blushed at what she saw there. Eight beautiful eyes stared back at her, quietly, unperturbedly, with only a faint annoyance. She knew she was an intruder, but felt paralysed, ashamed of her obvious need to look longer. Then

Rupert released her with a smile, and she was able to move away. No one said a word. And she heard no sound as she went to the loo, passed the door again – this time deliberately without a glance – and went downstairs, feeling noisy and clubfooted.

'Well that was peculiar.' Louise forced a laugh and sat down on the floor next to the fire, her back against Zelda's chair. She knew she could trust her to make light of the incident.

'Why, what were they up to, the little beasts?'

'Something pretty exotic, I'd say. Rupert and another child – a girl, beautiful, with long hair – his friend, I guess; what's her name? Phyllida. Rupert and Phyllida were lying on the floor together – or rather, wrapped up together, entangled in each other – '

'They do that.'

' – with snakes in their hair and round their necks, writhing snakes?'

Zelda laughed out loud and Louise began to smile.

'It was bizarre, I mean, taking me by surprise and all. But the most peculiar thing was the other two watching. Her brother – I suppose he's her brother – sitting on the bed and Nicholas standing over them with his arms folded. Not doing anything. Not saying a word. Very serious. Just watching. I felt really intrusive, believe me.'

'Nonsense, Louise. Children are always doing odd things. They're so close, still, to the Unconscious.'

'And you don't mind. You let them.'

'Let them what?'

'Do "odd things".'

'Oh, you mean what mother was talking about.' She refused to be surprised or defensive. 'Phyllida probably did stay the night once, but I've no idea what they get up to really. I think they're rather beautiful.'

'Oh, I agree, I agree. My dear, they're exquisite. I'm just thinking of our more – how shall I say – strictured-structured upbringing.'

'Well that's all past, thank God.'

'Yes. Thank God. Yes. It must be nice. I meant to – like they are, at their age. So – unfettered.'

'Yes.'

'I'm envious.'

There was a sudden rushing and bumping on the stairs, a charge of bodies, giggles and scuffles in the tiled entrance hall, then the slamming of a door. Two quick pairs of feet ran away down the dark road. Rupert looked in. He was panting and smiling.

'Would Auntie Louise like to see John-Paul and John-Paul the Second?'

'He means the snakes.'

Louise jumped up. 'Oh she would, my dear. She certainly would.'

II

Breakfast was long and late.

'You'll stay with us a while, won't you, Loulee,' Zelda entreated. 'You won't rush off to meetings and lectures. You will take time for frivolity and not insist on *seeing* everything like you usually do.'

'If I show any symptoms, if I look as if I might be going to, stop me.'

'But I don't know whether I can. Your virtue will almost certainly get the better of you. You'll feel compelled to go in quest of knowledge. You'll get tired of swanning around with me and miss being energetic. You're more than part Puritan, Louise.'

'I know.'

'Why are you like that, do you think? What kept you from becoming degenerate like the rest of us?'

'Believe me, I'm really embarrassed about it.'

'You're a hard-working American. Isn't that funny.'

'I'm also nuts.'

She had five weeks. Five weeks not to work and not to worry. She pleaded with herself to make no plans. Louise, she said, don't even read.

'I will see Alex though.'

'Alex? Oh yes, by all means, see Alex. You *must* see Alex.'

They shivered, despite the electric bar heater that burned under the dining room table. A Schubert sonata came from another part of the house, growing loud or soft whenever the boys entered and let in a draught. Outside it was March-cold and a gale was blowing off the river. Through the French door Louise could see the tangled garden with its clumps of snow-drops and three or four flattened daffodils. 'Of all the damn dumb times to go to England,' her father had said. He didn't, he couldn't understand how it was exactly the right time. She was going for Rupert's birthday, and for the spring.

Zelda leaned back and ran her long fingers through her hair. 'Last day of term today.'

'That means the boys are — '

'Home. For over a month.'

'Great. So they'll be running in and out all day with footballs and bicycle pumps.'

'There's been some terrible talk from their father, about visits and wanting me to pay the fare.'

Louise remembered Richard well. She had been Zelda's bridesmaid, and at the wedding he had danced one perfunc-tory dance with her. Since then, she had seen him twice.

'Bastard.'

'He used to be nice.' Zelda couldn't hate anyone. She was sweet, genuinely sweet.

She had got tickets for Covent Garden that evening — orchestra stalls as a special treat for Louise. It was to be just the two of them with Rupert left in the care of callous Nicholas.

'You won't be lonely now?' Zelda stroked his dark hair.

'Oh Mumsie,' Rupert pushed her playfully away. 'I'm hardly a baby.'

He opened the door for them, kissing them both as they left. Off they went in the ancient Rover, Louise in an expensive trouser suit, intended to smooth out her too prominent curves, and Zelda like some hybrid iris in her fluttering printed silks. They returned at midnight to find six adolescents playing new wave rock on the landing and jumping up and down on the beds. After shooing them off Zelda made Horlicks, and she and Louise stood in the wreckage of the kitchen talking until three.

It felt right. It felt full of relief to be there again with Zelda and her handsome family, even as an outsider. But Louise was that wherever she went. At least it was nice to be cushioned, for a while, by what was around her, to live at a different tempo, to talk trivialities, to hear real noises – shouts, laughter, music, quarrels, dogs barking – instead of central heating, refrigerators, air conditioners, garbage disposals, or her father, when he was in town, creeping past her door at seven a.m. after being out all night with some twenty-year-old. It was good, and it was painful.

The boys were on holiday from their expensive school. They were growing up articulate and confident. Louise watched them, fascinated by the most trifling aspects of their lives. Rupert particularly. Rupert was special. Nicholas already ran after the world, wanting big, new, important things, and learning, like his father, to manipulate. She could sense his basic contempt for her. But Rupert was still a little boy. There was something old-fashioned in his nature, or so Louise thought. She imagined boys like him had stopped being produced, that they existed only in Victorian novels: brave, tender, perfect, and eternal.

Whenever she met Rupert he seemed in the process of winding himself up for some glorious exertion. She passed him racing down the stairs or came into the dining room as he was about to dash off to his friends (he was the first one awake in the mornings and the first to finish his meals). He always interrupted his dashes for her, though, to enquire how she was and to give smiling, polite answers to her questions about his activities. He played Rugby in the park across the street, fished in the river, cycled miles, listened to music with Phyllida, lavished attention on his snakes and on the dogs, Doc and Daisy, who followed him everywhere. He even practised the piano – without coercion.

On the afternoon of the first fine day Zelda was confined to bed with one of her colds. Louise sat on the chaise-longue, keeping her company and watching Rupert play harrowing Rugby in the park, his hair blown by the river breeze, and his thin legs covered with mud to the bottom of his shorts. With a shout, he threw himself exultantly on a boy twice his size. She turned to otiose Zelda and jerked her head in his direction.

'Boy wonder out there. How did you manage it?'

'He is rather splendid, isn't he.'

'I never knew till now why mothers go mad over their sons.'

'Wish you had one?'

'At the moment – and only if he could be like Rupert.'

'What's so marvellous about them is their combination of courage and sensitivity, the way they want to defend and help. They're like little knights.'

'Rupert's sensitive, then?'

'Oh extraordinarily.'

'And they're still like that here?'

'Some. Quite a tremendous lot, really.'

'Then what happens to them?'

'You mean why do they turn into brutes?' She shrugged. 'A few stay fine. Rupert will.'

'I'm sure. And what about Nicholas?'

'Nicholas. Nicholas needs so much love.' She paused. 'If anything should happen to me, Louise, you'll come and look after Rupert, won't you? You won't let him be turned into a bully by his father or a faggot by my mother.'

Louise laughed, flabbergasted. 'What do I know about being a mother?'

'Oh, he won't need a mother in the primal sense. You're his godmother, remember? It's your duty. Besides, he loves you.'

'He does? How do you know he loves me?'

'You're the nicest woman he's met – except me. And you're intelligent. *That's* what he'll need.'

'Oh come on, Zelda.' But the thought excited her.

'Anyway, promise me you will, there's a good girl. It will relieve my mind. The others, you know – they're such lunatics.'

'And I'm not?'

'You? You're solid and straight and true.'

'Solid, all right.' She looked down at her reclining body.

'But you must stop tormenting yourself. You're always engaged in some terrific inner struggle.'

'Easy to say, love. You don't have to – struggle, I mean. You're not compelled by some weird perversion to weigh and consider everything. You're your own truth. It's on you, in you, around you. The form fits the content. Excuse me, but you have no conflicts between inside and outside.'

'I have numberless conflicts!' Zelda's eyes opened wide from surprise that Louise could have failed to notice their profusion.

'Oh yes, but they're artistic conflicts. They're part of your style. You wear them as elegantly as your old dresses and silk scarves. My conflicts – huh! – aren't fit to be seen in. This beautiful mind I'm supposed to have – look at the wreck of an abode it's taken up, like some demented hermit crab.'

'But you're successful.'

'Bah! I should have been where I am now at twenty-eight. This damned deliberation over everything – should I, shouldn't I, with possibilities multiplying like measles. No wonder the beautiful mind cracked and collapsed.'

'Did it?'

'Not gloriously, of course. No divine madness, nothing that would place matters in the hands of the gods and relieve me, for a little minute, of responsibility. No, it was just doubt and nerves and unexpressed grief. Terribly mediocre, as you would say.'

'Perhaps you'll do better next time.' Zelda smiled.

'You mean right off the deep end?'

'Straight round the twist, my dearest old girl.' They laughed.

'Then what about godmothering Rupert?'

'He'll be most understanding, I assure you. It will be good for his emotional development.'

Nicholas came in simmering resentment.

'I say, are we having dinner tonight or what? If it's the kebab house again, I'll need money.'

'Oh darling,' Zelda blew her nose. 'How lovely to see you. Tell us what you've been doing all day.'

Bravely, Louise forced herself on him. 'Don't sweat it, Nicholas. Auntie Louise is taking everyone to Pontevecchio.'

'Loulee, you're too sweet.'

'You know, of course, that little brother will insist on bringing Phyllida. So that means Oliver too, unquestionably.'

'Well find a friend and bring her along. Don't want you to be bored.'

'Hmmmmmmm.' He pressed his lips together and walked out. He was nearly six feet now, his bones grown large to accommodate what would soon be real masculine bulk. There was moodiness in the hunch of his shoulders and aggression in his chin. He had passed that delicate point of balance on which Rupert still rested. He would be good-looking and treat people badly, especially people like Louise.

In the end, the loud and messy meal included Alice who was depressed because her living room was being redecorated. They arrived back in a rainstorm and everyone ran for the house. As they all rushed through the door at once, the telephone rang. Zelda went to pick it up, and as she did so, a young man with blond hair and a great many studs and zippers stepped out of the little room. He seemed about to cry.

'I've been waiting for hours, Zel. Where have you been?'

Zelda stopped short and put her hand to her mouth. Rupert ran upstairs with Phyllida, Nicholas answered the phone, and Louise stood where she was, trying to smile and absolutely riveted. Then Zelda flung herself on the young man.

'I forgot! I forgot! Oh kill me, I forgot. Ellic darling, I'm an idiot, a monstress. Can you forgive me?' He unstiffened as she held his face between her hands and covered it with kisses. 'You know I haven't a brain, darling. You know I can't remember – '

'Mum!' Nicholas shouted and held the receiver for her at arm's length. 'It's Dad!'

'Oh dear God!' She took it. 'And you say I haven't any conflicts, Louise.'

Louise stared at the person who had been stood up while he stared at Zelda, now herself nearly in tears.

'Rupert! Rupert!' she cried above the music coming from upstairs. 'Speak to your father. I can't bear it.' With a sob she disappeared into the little room, followed by Ellic, who slammed the door behind them. Nicholas sauntered off to the kitchen. Louise stood alone in the entrance hall. There was a click from the receiver as Rupert took the upstairs extension. Slowly, quietly, she walked to the telephone, caught the sound of Richard Lacey's voice, hesitated, then put the receiver back on the hook.

III

It was all out at breakfast.

'Rupert says he won't go.' Nicholas reached for his fifth sausage.

'I didn't say that.' Rupert was calm but serious. 'I said I'd rather not take the train.'

'Why not? It's better than the bus. Anyway, hard luck! You *have* to take the train, so it's no good whining.'

'I'm not whining. I'd prefer Mum to drive me, that's all. Will you drive me, Mum?'

'Oh darling, it's such a dreaful mix-up. If I drive you, how will I get Nicholas to Devon? I told your grandmother Lacey months ago . . . '

'Put him on the train and pay the fare, Zelda.'

'Nicholas, I am *not* going to pay Rupert's fare. I've paid for both of you the last three times, it's awfully unfair, your father never pays for anything, it's always me, it's intolerable, I absolutely refuse to pay, you know it's his turn, he's the one who's so wild to have Rupert up there, and in this dreadful weather, oh I suppose I'll have to pay.'

'Of course if I had a motorbike, these predicaments – '

'Why don't you drive me, Mum?'

'Quite honestly, darling, I don't know what to do.'

'Pay his fare.'

'Drive me. Please.'

'The depressing false economy of some people. The meanness . . . '

Zelda turned to Louise who was, as usual, audience of one. 'It's just like Richard to upset everything like this. He says I've broken my promise and he's writing to the lawyer. He swears we made all these arrangements about Rupert's holiday and I have no recollection . . . ' She sighed. 'And now Ellic's in the midst of a *crise*. He says he'll absolutely collapse if I don't spend this week with him.' She discussed everything in front of the boys. 'And the thing is, I do *understand* how he feels – it's so dreadfully difficult to be eighteen – and I can't disappoint him. But then if I appear in Argyllshire with Rupert *and* Ellic I shall be called an unfit mother and I don't know how I'll get Nicholas to Devon. If Nicholas were to take the train – '

'Absolutely not!'

' – but then there'd be no one to pick him up. His grand-mother lives miles away and can't drive any more. Maybe *Ellic* could drive Nicholas – no, no, he'd only complain and make a fuss. Oh bother!'

'All your men.'

'Yes. Aren't you sick to death of hearing about them? Poor Louise, I'm so sorry – goodbye, darlings, goodbye – I'm so sorry about this. We were having such a lovely time.'

Louise couldn't tell her how interesting it all was – torture and fun simultaneously. An alien country, lush and danger-ous, in which she was entirely alone.

After putting down the phone the evening before, she had gone upstairs to prepare for bed. (Louise went to bed early; she felt barely alive without eight hours' sleep.) She stood before the bathroom mirror, listening to the slamming of various doors. Front door: Nicholas, a secret fag in his mouth, out for a prowl; Zelda's door: she and Ellic, recon-ciled, going cosily to bed (no midnight chats and Horlicks in the kitchen, then); Rupert's door: Rupert – with Phyllida? – playing music and rough-housing with the dogs. She felt just a little sorry for herself.

The attractions of Zelda's domestic life plus her own deci-sion not to plan, or at least to try not to plan, had made her postpone calling Alex. Well, she would do it now. She was becoming extraneous anyway. She knew the signs. They took longer in manifesting here than in the few other places she visited, but eventually they appeared. Eventually she was in the way of someone's love or someone's trauma or some-one's breakfast. Her hosts would sense her watching them and all of a sudden want their privacy back. It never came to their asking, though; she would know, and she would simply leave.

She dialled Alex's eleven-digit number and waited for the voice she had not heard in five years.

'What do you want?' it snapped. 'It's eleven thirty, you know.'

'Ha! You're there. It's Louise.'

Silence, followed by an explosion. 'Loulee! My dear, where are – let me just get a glass of wine.'

She pictured him scuffling about his den, hair no doubt completely grey by now: felt slippers, Afghani wool hat keeping his ears safe from the draughts, stacks of books everywhere, battered piano. He was back.

'Tell me everything.'

Louise said she wanted to visit.

'My dear, it's too awful. Hubert [his lover] and I are going to Amsterdam to spend Easter with his family. It's so important – the initial confrontation, you know.'

'OK, OK,' she said to hurry over her annoyance. It had been five years, after all. He might have waited a day or two.

'But that's no problem.' He tried to generate excitement to cover his guilt. 'Come anyway. The house is yours, Loulee, and perhaps you'll still be here when we get back. It would be heaven to see you. Stay as long as you like, naturally.'

'That's very nice. How do I get in?'

'Oh, no one locks doors in Llanbuilthmawr, my dear. Just walk in. Do you remember how to get here?'

'I could find it, I suppose. Mountain road on right, heart-shaped lake, et cetera, et cetera. Anyway, it doesn't matter. I mainly wanted to see you, so I don't know what I'll do now. I might come, I might not.'

'My dear, I'm terribly sorry.'

He went on about his love life, his composing, his unending war with the Welsh.

'Well everyone told you not to buy the damn house.' She couldn't help the snarl.

'The house! Darling, it's not the house. I adore the house! It's Mr fucking Owen and Mr fucking Griffith – '

Louise watched Zelda pile marmalade on to a piece of toast, legs crossed, white Victorian nightdress pulled up over her knees. She had to get out, otherwise she would sit there for ever, watching and watching.

'I'll drive him,' she said.

Zelda stopped, mouth open, gooey toast in mid-air. 'You can't.'

'Why not?'

'Because you can't. I won't permit it. Louise, you're on

holiday. We've inflicted enough on you as it is. Oh I did so look forward to our being quiet and private together. It's just – '

'Your men. I'll drive him.'

'My men. Oh dear, are you sure it's all right? No, no, you can't, you're too good.'

'Then let me be good. Who else should I be good to?' she laughed. 'Come on, Zel. You want – need a few days alone with what's-his-name. I know you've been keeping him away because of me. Rupert has to go to Scotland one way or another. I'm his godmother. I'm on holiday, and I'd like to see Scotland. Besides, you said I should look after him.' There, she had done something spontaneous.

'I didn't mean quite so literally or quite so soon. But, well, yes, you darling, why don't you drive him. Of course, you're absolutely right, it solves everything. And I'll pay for the petrol. You'll have a marvellous time, I know. Oh, you are lucky, Loulee, to be able to alter your plans like that, to do just as you please with no one to hold you accountable.'

'You think so.' As if it were a privilege to be lonely and unloved.

Ellic came in, barely conscious and wrapped in Zelda's dressing gown. He sat on her lap and began feeding her spoonfuls of marmalade straight from the jar. Louise excused herself and spent the rest of the day at the British Museum.

They would leave on Friday. She bought maps and showed them to Rupert, asking him about routes and scenery. She thought it might please him to be consulted like this. On the other hand, she worried that it might appear as condescension and watched him for signs of resentment. But apparently he was right with her, offering enthusiastic suggestions and anticipating no boredom at the prospect of their spending two or three days alone together.

Zelda, in a flurry of enthusiasm, was washing all his woollies. Nicholas also became involved in their plans, as did Ellic, who had moved in. That afternoon, Louise almost dared to feel included. Sitting at the dining room table with maps spread in front of her, Rupert beside her, and faces peering over her shoulder, she began to see the landscape opening up. Already she was driving down those roads, she and Rupert,

moving forward into a green and hazy future. She was
excited, and had to stop herself putting her arm around her
godchild.

They would take the A6 via Derby and Matlock. (Louise
had never seen the Peak District.) That way they could visit
the Lakes and stop at Keswick. Then on to Carlisle and
straight up the A74 to Glasgow. After that, they would
abandon everything to whim and weather and meander down
the peninsula. But naturally, they agreed, they were leaving
themselves open to adventure. Anything could happen.
Everything could change.

'I'm a wonderful navigator, Louise,' said Rupert. 'You'll
see all the best places. Who knows, we might never stop –
Orkneys, Shetlands, top of the world!'

Zelda hugged him. 'You're a wonderful everything, aren't
you?'

There was, however, a block at the end of all these beautiful
roads, and that was Richard. Louise was uncertain what to do
and how to behave once they had arrived at Lochgilphead.
Zelda was pressing her to stay a few days.

'It's splendid, Louise. You'll love it, I promise you.'

'And what about Richard?'

'Oh you know how charming he is. He's only beastly to *me*.
He'll be delighted to have you. In fact he'll insist.'

Louise was not so sure. Richard was accomplished and
clever, she knew, and not really unkind. He had always been
polite to her, but only to keep himself from being accused of
ignoring her. He was dramatically male and did not like his
females upstaging him. She possessed too much information
for his taste, and she suspected that he found her in some way
gauche. She did not want to be tolerated, she did not want to
have to be charming to the girlfriend, and she did not relish
seeing Rupert under his father's influence – Richard organizing games, hikes, fishing trips for him, giving him jobs and
responsibilities, making him be a little man.

'Play us a tune, Rupert,' Louise abruptly said.

He hesitated; he was on his way out. Reluctance clouded his
face, but only for a moment.

'All right then, what shall I play? That Handel piece you're
so fond of, Mum?'

How gallant and obliging he was. She had never known a child to accede so beautifully, never known one to play so sensitively before going off to trounce his friends in the park. Perhaps it was the English system. The way these little masterpieces still were turned out was amazing. But how long, she wondered, before he became a Nicholas, a Richard, a more sophisticated version of her father and brother, or even, for that matter, an Alex?

IV

Louise was awake and at the car rental office by eight thirty. She could have gone the previous afternoon, but was reluctant to pay for an extra night. Why have the car sitting outside the house, doing nothing and costing her money? Petty luxuries irritated her. She was secretly sensible about finances, and others, to whom she was always generous, were unaware of the little ways in which she denied herself. Another of her quirks was evident as soon as she turned on to the Fulham Road: she was a very bad driver. She had the habit of braking too often and making abrupt stops and starts. Nervous and easily annoyed, she talked to herself, shouted at other drivers, and was addicted to the horn. Her bad eyesight (she would not wear her glasses) and the disorientation of driving on the left made the mile and a half back to Zelda's a nightmare. She parked the car and sat gripping the wheel, shaking, trying to collect herself, nearly in tears.

Indoors everything was chaos. A crucial attachment to the fishing rod was missing, and Rupert's woollies were still steaming away on the radiators. He and Nicholas were arguing about his bringing Daisy, the sheep-dog who had just committed an atrocity in the bathroom. It would be at least two hours before they went anywhere. Louise felt a twinge of anger at her old room-mate. Zelda had all the help and all the money she needed. Why couldn't she have managed this better? She settled herself with a copy of the

New Statesman to wait it out, looking up whenever the door opened in case it might be Rupert.

Zelda entered with twenty-pound notes fluttering from her bag, several of which she tried to press on Louise. But Louise feigned huffiness. As Rupert's godmother, she said, she must bear full financial responsibility. A bad martyr, Zelda sighed and left, trying to remember what she had been doing before it occurred to her to offer the money to Louise.

At a quarter past twelve they were ready, Rupert in gum boots and school scarf, trousers that were too short, and a jacket that wouldn't be warm enough; Louise in Alpine boots, a pair of Levi's which exposed the full breadth of her backside, and a goosedown jacket that made her look like a big blue marshmallow. The fishing-rod attachment was still missing.

'Never mind, darling. You can borrow one of your father's, I'm sure.' Zelda kissed him, then Louise, her brown eyes sending off warm glints of pleasure. It was so easy for her to delight in the happiness of others. Nothing ever seemed to threaten her ego. She stood at the gate between Nicholas and Ellic — both the same height — smiling and waving in the clear light of early April that made Louise feel exposed and out of place. Zelda blew kisses and brushed back a strand of hair from her forehead. 'God bless,' she called. It *was* easy for her. She was surrounded. She couldn't fall down; there were so many people to prevent her falling. For Zelda, the world opened up like a great big peony.

Louise started the car, eyes burning. If only she could feel that way, even for a moment.

Rupert settled himself in the front seat, the Roadfinder Atlas open on his knees and Daisy's chin resting on his shoulder. At the eleventh hour he had won his case and she had been allowed to come.

He looked surprised at Louise's first angry outburst. Then he laughed.

'Auntie Louise, it really is better if you put it in fourth.'

'Father been teaching you to drive?'

'Yup.'

By the time they reached the Finchley Road, she had had three near-collisions.

'Oh fucking hell!' She slammed the brakes again. The Friday traffic was awful.

'You never told me you were such a terrible driver.'

She turned on to the M1. Then they relaxed and played the tapes Zelda had bought them, Louise whistling along with the music and Rupert keeping up a one-sided, nose-rubbing conversation with Daisy who was wild to get into the front seat. By mid-afternoon, they were rolling over the smooth Northamptonshire countryside, discussing Defoe, Stevenson, French verbs, Gerald Durrell, the Russian Revolution, and the most likely geological components of the landscape.

'You ought to be my tutor, Louise. I'd sail through my O Levels. Whenever I ask Mum a question, she gets very excited and interested and says she's sure she used to know but oh dear she's forgotten.'

'That'd be fun. I'd certainly like it a good deal better than what I'm about to do for the rest of my life. But didn't you already come top of your class without my assistance?'

'Only in three subjects. Where are we sleeping tonight?'

She looked at her watch. 'Why don't we floor it as far as Derby, get off this motorway, and drive through the mountains, maybe have a walk if it's still light. Then we'll find an inn, eat a gigantic supper, and stay the night.'

'Super.' He consulted the map. 'Perhaps near Matlock. Then we can carry on through Manchester some time tomorrow.'

'No rush.'

'None at all. And Daisy would love a romp, wouldn't you old girl?'

Louise thought of the only dog she had ever owned – a nasty Yorkie that bit people in supermarkets.

They stopped for a late lunch at Rupert's favourite transport café. Afterwards, Louise waited in the car for him to complete his interactions with the pay scales, bell fruit machines, and fortune-telling apparatus, and Daisy her investigations of some withered cypresses. She glanced – always a bad idea – in the rear view mirror, which showed her a silly putty nose and hazel eyes. Nice lashes, really, but oh those eyebrows. When she was a child, they had caused her to be called serious; then, at school, had made her the subject of several crude lyrics. She

remembered the time at university when some boy, not
intentionally callous, but taking her good humour too much
for granted, had made a smart remark about them. How tired
it had made her feel, and then how quietly gunned down,
when she noticed among that array of ensuing grins, the
incalculably small but definitely present uplift at the corner of
Zelda's mouth, too. Forget it, she told herself. They're bushy,
so what? You could do something about them, but what's the
point? Would it make any difference when everything else is
so badly arranged?

Rupert returned to the back seat and promptly fell asleep, so
that she lost the way outside Derby and found herself, panic-
stricken, on the road to Uttoxeter.

'Rupert, for God's sake, wake up. We're lost.'

Without reproach, he navigated her back through the
dismal suburbs and safely north on to the A6.

'There. Now follow the signs for Belper. I'm going to carry
on with my lie-down.' He crawled into the back seat with an
ecstatic Daisy.

He *was* a darling. Her own brother would never have been
nice like that. Stupid, the way she wanted him to be, the way
she still tried to talk to that plaster-cast of his father, hoping
she might get something out of him besides business and
skiing and hypoglycaemia.

Clouds gathered. A few drops hit the windscreen. Then
came a clear patch. The prospect looked beautiful but
unsteady. Sunset, though, was wonderful. She and Rupert
watched it from the top of a high ridge, walked back to their
hotel, and ate the huge dinner she had promised.

That night, with Rupert asleep on the bed next to hers,
Louise stood and stared at herself in the mirror, still naked
from her bath. She had had a good, if rather too sturdy, figure
once. Great tits, legs always a bit like a Rugby player's. But
now, oh damn, now. Five years of sedentary existence had
turned the muscles to pie dough, and she was spreading in all
directions. Of course it might not be as bad as she thought.
But soon, very soon, she would be beyond repair. She glanced
at the puckers in her collapsing bottom, then back at Rupert.
She thought she was going to cry. But it was cold, and she
dried herself in a hurry. Wrapped in a Tartan dressing gown,

she sat and watched her sleeping godchild by the dim glow of the bedside lamp.

The weather next morning was terrible − gusting winds and rain slashing against the window. Rupert looked outside and hitched up his braces.

'Bad luck, old girl.'

'Never mind.' She gave the automatic English response, like a congregation of the faithful to the celebrant priest. ('*Ite missa est.*' '*Deo Gratias.*')

With Daisy dripping from her morning walk, they huddled in the car and consulted the map. Hiking was definitely out.

'Now somehow we've got to get through this Manchester mess. Let's see, where the hell are we?'

'Head for Buxton, I guess.'

Louise started the car. 'You're on.'

The rain and fog precluded any view of remaining mountains. They chatted about school, then Louise grew nervous of the traffic and the wet road, and they travelled tensely, in silence. Manchester was getting closer and the surroundings uglier.

'If this weather keeps up, we might as well drive all day.'

'Yes.'

'I can't stand it.' She hunched over the wheel.

'We'll be in Scotland all the sooner, though.' She wasn't sure, but she thought his eyes sparkled.

'You'll be glad to get there then.'

'Yup.'

'Miss your father?'

'In a way.'

Was she angry? Absurd. After all, why shouldn't a little boy love his father and want to see him? Still, she couldn't help feeling suddenly odd and cold towards Rupert, and wondered if he would be glad to be rid of her. Of course he was getting bored. How could she expect him not to be?

She wouldn't stay. She knew she was being touchy, but that settled it. She would leave him with Richard, drive the short way back alone − screw the scenery − return to London, and get straight on a plane to − Florence, maybe. Hell, why not? She might as well be looking at paintings as looking at people. These third-person relationships that enticed then depressed her — better to be away from them, far away.

The road became a blur. She had been forced to suppress more tears in the last few days than in the last year. She had supposed she was having a good time, not thinking and being loved. Of course it had been an illusion, unconsciously cooked up with the help of Zelda. She was still an alien. She had known it the night when she saw the children and the snakes, and she knew it now when Rupert mentioned his father with that excited, happy gleam. Louise considered her life facet by facet, inspecting it like some evil diamond. She had acquired the habit of self-torture early on and was aware of the way she worked on herself, for ever posing questions, computing her own pain. Well, if you were one of the unfortunates born with the masochistic penchant, best accept it. And yet, one couldn't live, one just *couldn't* live without somehow thinking well of oneself, even if there were no apparent justifications, even if father and brother and nearly every man you met reminded you in a hundred little ways that you were awkward and unattractive.

They stopped for lunch, then Rupert again crawled into the back seat.

'Louise,' he asked dreamily, as he snuggled up to Daisy, 'what are you going to do?'

Louise was shocked. She thought he meant ultimately.

'I mean your job. What's your job going to be like?'

'Oh,' she began in the off-hand, dismissive manner she always adopted when forced to talk about herself, 'a "Situation Vacant" as *The Times* would say, in my old college. Graduate professor of Social Sciences. Give me a chance to write — that's the plan anyway. Money's OK, considering how little I'll actually be doing.'

'Will you teach?'

'Oh I can't teach. I'll just be a human trying to explain human behaviour to other humans. What garbage.'

'Will you be rich?' He was drifting.

'Oh I'm rich enough. My father — ' She broke off at the thought of her cocksure father. Past sixty, and still with his succession of pretty, moronic, and genuinely sweet girl-friends, all of whom she ended by liking or feeling sorry for by the time he had dumped them for a new one. (He even, years ago, had tried to date Zelda. 'Darling', she said, 'I must tell you in all honesty that he's a complete creep.') But he made a lot of money. He knew his limitations and never doubted his capabilities. There was no defending him, he was a rank materialist. 'Loulee,' he would lecture her in his Delaware accent, stretched out in boxer shorts, listening to old Count Basie records, one hand tinkling a Jim Beam and soda, the other stroking his grey crew cut, 'you oughta fix yourself up.' All she could manage was the hair cut.

Yet she stayed. She stayed in her cell, talking to him on his way to or from meetings and airports, stealing self-consciously past as he watched quiz programmes and held hands with the adoring concubines. She stayed, knowing he would pay for analysis and schools and for the time to agonize over books and typewriter and interviews. She stayed, hoping one day to discover by some inadvertent word or gesture of his, that in fact he really loved her.

'Then you can leave home.'

'Leave what?' she checked the mirror. Rupert was asleep on wheezing Daisy. It was one of his magical attributes that he seemed always older or younger than he really was. Never thirteen. Right now he was a little child, relaxed and trusting, with parted lips. Oh he was special all right – high and lovely and special like his mother. Louise was not special. Some people, academics and colleagues, had implied that she was, but she never believed them. She knew. She was unbeautiful, and banned for ever from the realms of feeling. Obsessed as she was with the right decision, with sorting out the one choice among infinite possibilities, she could never just *be*. She queried everything, tore herself apart, made herself ugly. No wonder she went unloved and that delight eluded her. She *did* see the truth about herself. But the truth was such a killer. She wondered why she always tried so hard to arrive at it, knowing perfectly well that when, after endless and painful processes, she found it, it would kill her all over again. Why want/need to understand? For the deeply ungratifying reward of an explanation?

'Oh God!' She had nearly side-swiped a car and was being reprimanded by the blasts of multiple horns. She looked to see

if Rupert was still asleep and, as she did so, missed her turning.
It took a few moments for her to realize that she was no longer
on the M6. She had gone wrong at Horwich. Louise swore
quietly, trying to drive in the inching traffic and simultaneously read the map. From what she could make out, they
could get back on the motorway at some place called Walton-
le-Dale.

She went on, listening to the windscreen wipers, Daisy's
snores, and *Rigoletto*, which she kept barely audible so as not to
wake Rupert. She looked at him again in the rear view mirror.
This time it was Zelda's face that she saw. Dear, haphazard
Zelda, the best friend she ever had, especially that first year at
college, before her father was recalled to Britain with a heart
condition. When he died, Zelda had saved the family by
marrying Righteous Richard, as she called him in her letters.
Louise did not care to think of him. She would confront him
soon enough and be compelled to hand over to him the
precious offspring of her only kindred spirit.

She laughed at herself for the Anne of Green Gables style.
But it was true. That year with Zelda had provided her deepest
and liveliest human exchanges. As a child she had hidden in
books, then later buried herself in academia, safe from the
living. She counted the number of years she had been in
school: eight primary, four high school, four college, extra
year to complete double major of history and French (she
never had been able to choose between them), two of graduate
school where she found herself for a while in sociology,
transfer to Philadelphia, more research, then lingering in
tortured deliberation over that bloody thesis. That made, oh
Christ, thirty years altogether, and here she was coming up to
Walton-le-Dale.

'You fool, Louise!' she shouted at herself. She had taken the
wrong turn.

'Damn, damn, damn!' She pounded the wheel.

'What is it, Loulee?' Rupert was awake.

'Nothing's up Doc. Just me and the British. Sleep some
more.'

She couldn't tell him they were headed towards Liverpool.
He lay there, awake she saw, but quietly musing and not
seeing the road signs or the squalor of the industrial suburbs.

'We'll be in Lancaster soon.'

She didn't reply. She flew past one exit after another – Wigan, St Helen's, Warrington, feeling as grim and awful as what was out there on both sides of the road.

What was it with her that nothing in her life had ever been *graceful*? Was it some snapped strand of DNA, a bad planet, a severed heart line that made her directions all muddled and put her for ever on the wrong side, as though she were right and everything intriguing and delicious were left? She was coming fast at another chance to turn off. She could still reverse it all and confess her idiocy to Rupert. But she drove past, telling herself that they would stop at the next transport café and reorganize themselves. Meanwhile, her life was turning out a mockery and a waste. No love, no children. Only a thesis and a hateful job. Only credentials. She couldn't believe it, didn't know how it had happened, couldn't stop it. The template was fixed once and for all. She passed the café, knowing she must decide, and now. But she was wound up tight, unable to stop thinking or driving. She turned on to the A49.

Rupert was rough-housing with Daisy. Any moment he would sit up and ask her what on earth she thought she was doing, and she would have nothing to tell him, except all the things she was not doing. How absurd she was, thirty years in school, still living with her father. She thought of him, then her brother, her dead mother, then Zelda, Phyllida, Nicholas and finally Richard. She saw signs for the A51 and Chester, and all of a sudden realized that over to the west, beyond the factories and the junk yards and cooling towers and pylons and council estates was everything beautiful. She swung on to the verge, stopping at the junction of the A49 and the A556, and leaned over the steering wheel. Rupert jumped into the front seat.

'Where are we?'

'I'm not sure.'

'Where are we going?'

'To Alex's house.'

'Whose?'

'School friend of your mother's,' she mumbled into her goosedown sleeve. 'And mine. More mine, really, but it's been a long time.'

'What about Scotland?' She knew he was uneasy and couldn't look at him.

'We'll get there. Look, Baby, I'm tired and we've lots of time. I'd like to spend a day or two with my friend. Do you mind?'

'I don't if Daisy doesn't.'

She looked up. He was smiling at her, but with questions in his eyes. She had to hug him. He did not resist her, but they were separated by Daisy's efforts to climb into the front seat.

'It's a beautiful house. Overlooking the sea.' She was nearly crying with relief and joy. 'Valleys, forests, castle. Really enchanted. You'll love it.'

'It's all right, Loulee, if you went the wrong way. Can I fish?'

'In a perfect heart-shaped lake. Trout, boy, trout!'

They drove on, Rupert taking over again as navigator and Louise racking her brains to remember the route she had followed five years earlier.

'Bala Lake! Get us to Bala Lake, and I can find the way from there.'

They stopped for a grand tea in Chester, ate three cream buns apiece, and developed their new project.

'After all, we said everything could change.'

'Yes, and that we must take any opportunity for adventure.'

'Well, here's to adventure.' They clinked tea cups.

As they set off again, very gay this time, despite the continuing rain, Louise still was not aware that what she was doing amounted nearly to kidnapping. For once, something had decided for her, and to that something she surrendered all responsibility.

V

The sky cleared and the sun came out, opening up the west like a painted fan. Louise, not usually given to such things, interpreted the change in weather as an endorsement of their new plan.

'Let's make it to Bala and do the rest of the trip tomorrow morning. I can't possibly find my way up to Alex's in the dark.'

The road turned winding and narrow as they travelled into the hills, passing lonely moorland farms, glacial lakes, and valleys with a steepness and beauty almost Himalayan. As the night and the landscape closed around them Louise relaxed. She had him again. In a bed and breafast on the thin, prim main street of Bala, she slept her best sleep of the past five years.

Finding the house was not easy. The second wrong turn brought them to a village of surly and diminutive residents, one of whom, an old man, gave them directions in unintelligible English. Half-way up the mountain, his indicated road became a dirt track. Since there was no room to turn around – the road was squeezed between menacing six-foot hedges – Louise was forced to go down in reverse, and was a shattered wreck by the time they found themselves back in the same dull village.

'Why don't we try that first turn, Louise? The one after the bridge that you said couldn't possibly be right.'

This road, no more than a paved path, was so steep that Louise had a vision of them toppling over backwards and falling off the mountain.

'We can't make it.' She panicked.

'Yes we can. Put it in first.'

By a supreme effort the car jerked itself on to a level stretch where they found the piece of Welsh paradise they had been searching for.

'My dear, this is it! Heart-shaped lake, see? Forest on the right, Mr Owen's farm, and there's the Plas at the top of the hill. Rupert, we're in Llanbuilthmawr!'

They were very excited and speculated loudly, Louise with a flicker of remorse, as to what they would find when they arrived.

Near the top of the hill they turned off, bumping and lurching over Alex's utterly neglected driveway. With relief, Louise stopped the car, and they sat without speaking, staring at the decayed outbuildings, the skittish bantams, the nonchalant sheep, the stunted oaks, the flourishing rhododendrons, and the ancient, sprawling farmhouse with ravens on its slate roof and stones tinged green with moss.

'Sixteenth-century,' Louise said at last. 'Let's get out.'

She guided Rupert to the edge of a steep slope sprinkled with ewes and their new-born lambs, and turned his shoulders so that he faced west, full into the mellow-dramatic beauty of Merioneth.

'There. Didn't I tell you?'

'It's wonderful, Loulee. We're so high.'

'Very high. That piece of ocean is Tremadog Bay, and that's Lleyn peninsula. There's Portmeirion – Bertrand Russell used to have a house near by – and if you step over a bit to the left you can see the towers of Harlech Castle, nope, too hazy today. The little church at the top is locked 364 days of the year and Snowdon is over there.' She was postponing the house itself. 'Wait until you see the sun set into the sea. Really spectacular. Alex has been sitting on this wall every evening for the past eight years, drinking margeuritas and watching it.'

'Where is Alex?'

The lie could not be put off any longer. 'Probably shopping in Portmadoc. Want to go in?'

Her eyes took a moment to get used to the dark kitchen. The place was unkempt as ever. Alex loved accumulating objects, any objects, and loathed putting them away. The freezing stone floor probably had not been washed since the day he moved in, and the cobwebs and gangly geraniums, both of which he treasured, flourished and multiplied and collected more dust.

'He doesn't appear to be here.'

'Guess not.' Louise put her bag on the table and was quick enough to snatch up an envelope with her name on it before Rupert saw.

'Come on, I'll show you the house,' she said and pushed the note into her pocket.

There were twelve disordered rooms and a variety of beds, all unmade.

'It's like Goldilocks and the three bears.'

'Some perverse version of it, yes. By the way, there's a ghost.'

'Whose?'

'A miner.'

'Have you seen him, Louise?'

'I don't see such things. Supposedly he's been in the house for years. Quite harmless, though. I assume he's still here.'

'Golly, I hope we'll see him. Do you think we will?'

Downstairs was especially interesting: the entrance hall, its floor of rectangular stones laid out in concentric circles (the centre rumoured to have been the slaughter stone of some obscure Druidic sect); the living room, huge and messy with a plethora of disintegrating couches and a walk-in fireplace; and Alex's den, filled to capacity with books and a Bechstein, every surface branded by the magenta rings of wine glasses.

Ashtrays overflowed on to the cheap, unhoovered carpets. The storage heaters plainly were unequal to the Welsh climate, and all the rooms were damp and draughty. For those with eyes to see, though, the place still retained its rugged beauty. 'It could be made divine,' Alex had said, and rightly, 'if one had a fortune to squander.' But it was unmanageable; it was impossible. To save it for good would have required a stroke of will, finance and imagination on a scale quite beyond Alex. So it slowly crumbled around him, and he masked the noble, rough-hewn skeleton with his own eccentric veneer – things such as stuffed geese in fur pieces and cocked hats, chairs painted silver and skulls painted gold, faded Moroccan souvenirs, mauve perspex, popular art from Bengal and Quernavaca, altars of eggs, rubble and plastic angels, pornographic pictures, and the ubiquitous geraniums – all of it covered in the cobwebs he forbade anyone to disturb. He liked his madness.

As the sun set, Rupert said he supposed Alex must have stopped off somewhere after shopping. A wind blew down from the mountain, whistled round the chimneys and found its accustomed way through every crack. They shivered. For a moment prospects looked bleak. But Rupert donned another jumper and announced that he would make a fire. With Daisy at his heels, he found the coal and in thirty minutes had the Aga going. He lit a fire in Alex's study, emptied the redolent ashtrays, then sat down to investigate the music collection. Louise was relieved when she heard his attempts at the slow movement of a Mozart sonata. He must, she thought, still be content with their adventure.

Locked in the bathroom, she read Alex's note. He apologized again, but said that, barring any unpleasantness with

Hubert's parents, he would stay two weeks in Amsterdam. He offered her the run of the house and indicated the location of everything critical. She tore the letter to pieces and flushed it down the loo. Of course he had known when she spoke to him on the phone how long he would be away. Why hadn't he just said? Probably wanted to avoid her. Afraid the boyfriend would find her uncouth. On the other hand, his absence suited the 'adventure' beautifully.

Louise laid out on the creaking kitchen table the assortment of London goodies Zelda had sent as a peace offering to Richard. They dined by the light of a candle which had been rammed by Alex into a gigantic ox skull.

'What does Alex do?'

'I guess you'd say he's a third-rate musical genius and a bit of a devil.'

'That's what I thought.' Rupert yawned. 'I'm going to bed now, Louise. I've already found some linen and chosen my bedroom. It's the one above the kitchen.' He kissed her. 'Don't worry. I'm sure Alex will be back soon.'

Louise sat alone, listening to the gale and to the sound of Rupert's footsteps overhead. She calculated that she had one happy night and one happy day before the magic circle she had made around them would be broken by his restlessness and by the miracle of modern transport and communication.

In the middle of the night she awoke to the sound of the wind beating against the house like giant wings. She did not know at first where she was, then thought of the lambs in peril on the mountain and then, with a sinking in her stomach, of Rupert down the hall. She got up and took a torch from where she remembered seeing one in the bathroom. Shivering in the dark, she opened the door to his room and turned the weak spotlight on his bed. For a long time she stood and looked at the white face, the tousled hair, the band of freckles across the nose, the parted lips revealing the gap between his front teeth, the arm flung bravely out into the cold, as though something wonderful were nearly within his grasp. Her teeth were chattering, but she could not tear herself away. A loud gust made him turn over, and she quickly switched off the torch. He had not woken up, but she dared not move for another minute. Satisfied he was asleep, she tiptoed back to her room.

By morning the wind had dropped, but the ground was covered with snow. In the garden, daffodils bent under their white weight, and neat hoofprints punctured the yard. Louise stepped out into the sunshine. She watched a hawk take off from a post and soar over the valley. Except for the ravens, everything was quiet. But where was Rupert? She ran to the living room window and sighed with relief when she saw him on the steep rise behind the house. He was wearing the Bloomingdale's jumper she had given him for his birthday, and was attacking an oak tree with an imaginary sword, lunging and feinting, expending his boy energies in the snow.

'So Alex didn't come?' he asked at breakfast as he broke open one of the bantam eggs he had collected.

'Nope.'

'That a pity, Loulee. Are you very unhappy?'

'Not too. But let's wait one more day. Do you mind? He'll probably come back this evening. He's never away long.' Rupert said nothing. 'I thought we might take a walk before the snow melts, then drive to Portmadoc and buy some supplies for Alex – just to thank him, you know.'

'Of course.'

They put on extra sweaters, went down through the oak forest behind the house, and out across the valley, Rupert running ahead with Daisy, then back to tell Louise the names of the birds he saw, to point out interesting approaches to their destination – the wooded hill opposite – or to present her with one of the sheep skulls that littered the ground. He was her knight and she a princess – a plump, barbarous princess for such a refined little knight, a princess with bushy eyebrows, she knew; but she had been raised to exalted status by his devotion.

The snow had nearly gone, but the sun was dimmed by thin strands of cloud that looked to Louise and Rupert like vast, hovering spirits. This was not at all like English countryside. The bones, the lamb carcasses, the high-circling birds of prey, told them the place was wild and full of violent occurrences.

'Shall we go up, Loulee?' Ahead of her, Rupert was doing handstands at the edge of the forest.

'Ready when you are. Can Daisy make it?' But Daisy was already tearing through the trees.

They followed a rocky stream, energetically at first, full of the sweet, stinging air, then more slowly as the rocks became larger and the climbing more difficult. Louise asked for a rest. She sat on a flat stone and watched Rupert scampering about on the boulders above her, jumping from level to level and splashing in the shallow pools. Something cold and soft landed on her nose. It was snowing again. In a moment the air was full of whirling flakes, and a wind was rising.

'Let's go, Rupert.' She stood up.

'Oh Louise, we can't yet. You must see what's up ahead – the most marvellous, magic place, covered with ferns and plants and enormous trees, and there's a waterfall. It's fairyland, really it is. Do come and see.'

'Can't, Baby. Believe me, I've had it. Besides, look at this damned schizophrenic weather. We'd better go back before we're caught in a blizzard.'

'Rubbish, Louise!' He was silent. 'Oh, all right. Come on, Daisy.'

He landed beside her. 'You'll be sorry you missed it.'

'We'll come back.'

He looked at her quizzically. 'But there won't be time.'

When they reached Plas, the snow had stopped.

'I told you Louise. We should have gone on.'

The next morning they drove across the man-made peninsula that divides the bay, singing loudly and interrupting each other to point out some spectacular mountain view. In Portmadoc she bought him a fishing-rod attachment to replace the one he had lost. The return trip was made by the longer route, with the car full of provisions and Louise growing nervous. A confrontation was coming. She must stop this nonsense and let him go, let them both go up to Scotland, following regular routes and regular intentions. But when they returned, she went into the barn, ostensibly to chase away a sheep that was devouring the bantam feed, and, before Rupert could see her, lifted a bale of hay and slipped the car keys underneath it, telling herself as she did so that she must be crazy.

'OK,' she turned to him brightly, 'let's get all this stuff in the house.'

'It's rather a lot, don't you think? Looks as though you were expecting an army to lay siege to Plas.'

Louise imagined all of them storming up the hill, tinged pink with the late afternoon sun, angry and righteous: her father, her brother, Zelda, Richard, Alice, Phyllida, Nicholas, demanding she give him back. She set her teeth. Not yet, damn it.

She made him tea and did the washing up, watching him whenever she had the chance.

'Have you seen the car keys?' she asked as he began to collect his things.

They searched the ground floor.

'You're positive you brought them into the house?'

'Positive.'

She tried pockets, gloves, cuffs, drawers, bags, looking everywhere with a perverse zeal. By four o'clock it was snowing again. Louise looked with satisfaction at the grey-white valley.

'We can't leave,' she said.

There was disappointment in his face, the first he had shown her, and just for a moment the shell of his gallantry cracked. Obviously, he wanted to be in Scotland. He wanted to be with his father, doing boisterous things in his company, not bored here with her in this mouldering wreck of a house. She was furious with him, but kept silent as she held down and smothered her anger. She pretended to be kind, said consoling things, offered hope, made promises. Honest, straightforward Louise had never practised such successful hypocrisy.

'Dad was expecting us yesterday. We said we'd call.'

'Yes, my dear, but we also said everything could change. Now let's make a fire and maybe read for a while – didn't you bring *The Charterhouse of Parma*? – and then I'll make supper and tomorrow we'll be off. It's only one more day, you know.'

'What if we never find the keys.'

'Nonsense. We'll find them.'

'But can't we call?'

'Sure. After supper. It'll be cheaper then. It *is* Alex's phone.'

He sighed. 'I know.'

She cooked a huge meal, remarking constantly on how

lucky it was that they had bought all the food. They ate,
played records, and talked about school. He seemed happier.
When Louise asked him to fetch a cardigan for her, he jumped
up with his usual obligingness and took the fragile stairs two at
a time. She grabbed the pair of secateurs she had hidden behind
a geranium and went quickly to Alex's study. There, with
Daisy sniffing at her hands and heels, she lifted a corner of the
carpet, took up the telephone cord, and made a bad job,
nervous as she was, of cutting it in half. Keeping the pieces
together, she covered them again with the carpet.

When Rupert came in, she was sitting in Alex's big chair, an
address book open on her lap, dialling.

VI

Rupert had not cheered up. Louise found him the next
morning sitting on his bed and hugging Daisy. She sat beside
him and put her arms around him, but he moved away and
leaned his head on Daisy's fur. An old pain, one she thought
she had got used to years ago, rose up with a brand new
virulence and stung her hard. Calmly, she asked Rupert to
help her look for the keys. This time they would search
outside as well.

'Why do you suppose Alex had the phone cut off?'

'I doubt it was his choice. Probably couldn't pay the bill.'
She was edgy. She had not slept well and had been up twice in
the night to look at Rupert. Covering the torch with a shirt,
she daringly had knelt by his bed, so close, this time, that she
could feel his breath on her face.

'Louise, what *could* you have done with the keys?'

'Baby, if I knew that we'd be in Argyllshire by now.'

After their fruitless search, she made him sandwiches and
sat down to watch him eat them. But he fed half of them to
Daisy. He was very unhappy. She babied him, encouraging
him to eat and saying how his lack of appetite distressed her,
telling him not to worry, that they would find the keys, that
Alex would be back soon, that they could go fishing. It was

strange, this new role of consoler. Well, she was his god-mother, and she was looking after him.

Another day passed. They caught trout in the heart-shaped lake, Louise cooked them, and Rupert's spirits improved. For a while he seemed to have forgotten everything, but, after supper, he announced that in the morning he intended walking into the village to telephone. Time was running out for Scotland. Everyone would be worried.

Louise smiled and forced herself to exclaim what a good idea and how enterprising. But when he started for bed, she grabbed his hand and pulled him to her, implying with an ardour she could not control that she wanted her good-night kiss. Cool, though not uncivil, Rupert drew his hand away.

'Good-night, Louise,' he said without a smile. Louise remained seated at the kitchen table.

At least he hadn't refused outright. He might, after all, have rejected her totally, might have fled, might have . . . Instead he'd been, well, not unkind. And it amazed her that he had stayed so long with so little complaint at what was becoming a real predicament. He hadn't rebelled, so he must still trust her. Perhaps, when it was all over, he even might not hate her too much. But she was mad. What was she thinking? Forgetting again that he was only a little boy.

Louise continued to sit and call herself names. What had she let happen? She who planned everything, who sorted and sifted possibilities like a panhandler after gold, had done so many spontaneous and irrational things lately that it made her head spin. She never had been inventive in a devious way. And now here she was, practically a criminal. She couldn't hide from the word, it gave her almost a dreadful satisfaction. But this couldn't go on. She couldn't keep him prisoner like this (there was another word from which she no longer flinched). It would come to an end, and then what? How many days had gone by she did not know. A week? More? She thought of Zelda; she saw her friend's puzzled reproach. The vision made her run upstairs, get the torch, and go to Rupert's room. She must see him sleeping one last time. She crept closer to him than she had ever dared.

There he was, peaceful, exquisite, and no more hers than he had ever been. But she loved him; she could not let him go.

After all, if one had captured a fairy or an angel, would one be so anxious to turn it loose right away, to send for a priest or the police or donate it to the Smithsonian Institute? Wouldn't one simply *look* a while in beautiful, private astonishment, and relish the deep pleasure of looking? She closed his door, and, as she did so, turned the key in the lock and took it with her.

She intended to be awake and dressed long before Rupert, but fell into a heavy pre-dawn sleep in which she dreamt that she wandered through a vast Baroque supermarket, everyone speaking French, and her Yorkie biting the thick ankles of matrons. A repeated sound made her drag herself back to consciousness. Somewhere a dog was barking. In an instant she was dressed, already knowing what had happened. She flew to Rupert's door. It was still locked, but inside she found only a hysterical Daisy. Through the open window she could see Rupert setting off in the direction of the village, keeping up a determined, downhill stride, but unable to resist scattering congregations of sheep whenever he passed them. The classic means of escape in the form of two tied-together sheets flapped against the side of the house. It was silly. It was awful. She had to catch him.

He could outrun her easily, so she began shouting after him the only words which had any hope of slowing his pace once he realized she was following him.

'Rupert, I've found the keys!'

He did not hear her, so she was forced to run and shout at the same time. Her voice cracked, and, even though she ran downhill, her chest ached and her knees buckled. She tripped and fell, got to her feet, tried to call him once more, slipped on the wet grass, and fell again, rolling over twice before she could stop herself. When she looked up, Rupert was coming towards her, reluctantly, she could tell. He stopped beside her. He made no effort to help her stand.

'I found the keys.'

'I heard you.' He had shut down like a portcullis, and all access was closed to her.

'We can leave.' She managed to get up. 'I didn't want you to walk all the way to the village for nothing.'

'My door was locked.'

'Really? Well, it's an old lock. You must have turned the

handle too hard when you went to bed. I remember the last time I was here, someone locked themself in that room. You should have called me.'

'I didn't want to wake you.' He was being sarcastic, or he was lying. Something irreparable had happened between them, but she went on trying to deny the catastrophe.

'Why don't we have one last walk?'

'I don't want to walk.'

'Well you were just about to walk all the way to the damn village,' she flared, then caught herself. 'Please, Rupert, come with me. Just a little walk. I love this place and I'll probably never see it again. Besides, I need to relax after all that exertion.'

'By walking?'

'You know I do odd things.'

'I should say!'

He had relented. He *was* kind. Like his mother, he could not help being compassionate. Louise felt a surge of love for him, for both of them. They set off in an edgy peace.

'My god, what's that?' She grabbed his arm. A lamb ran past them, looking as though it was shedding its skin and dragging half the fleece on the ground.

Rupert came near to laughing. 'Oh that! That's a trick. I've seen it in Scotland. Some ewe has lost her baby, and the shepherd has skinned it and tied the fleece on to that orphan, hoping she'll take it and feed it.'

'Be its foster mother?'

'Yes.'

'And it's all a trick?'

'Yes. You Americans don't know much about real things, do you?' He walked rapidly to keep in front of her.

'Rupert,' she called, 'show me some birds again. I mean, tell me their names.'

He turned and faced her, obviously annoyed. 'I can't just *show* you birds, Louise.'

'Oh,' she said flatly. 'OK.'

They climbed the banks of the same stream, going much further than they had the first time, and Louise had to work hard to keep pace with agile Rupert.

'Come on, Louise. We're nearly there.' He was a little boy, and could still forget everything in the moment.

'Nearly where?'

'The special place.'

'Oh yes, I remember.' She tried to sound gay. It took her several minutes to be where he already was.

'Isn't it splendid?'

Exhausted, Louise sat on a rock, looked around, then up, slowly taking in the drama of the spot. They were at the foot of a waterfall. On either side of the pool by which she sat boulders rose to a height of thirty feet. Water dripped from between every crevice, and overhead, beech trees arched their bare reddish branches. It *was* an enchanted place. The banks were covered with giant ferns, red and green moss, and another plant which Louise did not recognize. She saw Rupert chewing a bit of it.

'What's this stuff?' she called to him. He gave her that look of contempt which she had not seen until she asked about the lamb.

'Wild garlic, of course. Why don't you eat some?'

'I never knew garlic grew like this, just wild in the woods. Of course, now I recognize the smell. Incredible, it's everywhere. Do I just eat the leaf?'

He looked down at her like an elf and said nothing.

Louise pulled a plant from among the thousands moving gently in the wind, their sheen changing with the changing forest light. She put the moist tip to her nose and sniffed.

'Oh!' she jumped back at the combination of hot and damp, fire and mud. She bit off a piece and chewed it, listening to the birds, the water, and the creaking branches. The leaf was soft, the flavour sharp and hot. Garlic, dispeller of evil; purge and protection.

'Do you wish Phyllida was here?'

'No.'

'It would be nice for you both. You'd have fun.'

He shrugged.

She wondered about the time and was glad she had left her watch on the bedside table. It was beautiful here. It was the end of the world. She couldn't bring herself, even now, to suggest that they leave, and thought how wonderful it would be to die in this place.

Rupert stood beside her. They had not spoken for several minutes, and his appearance startled her.

'Better go,' he said.

'Go?' She pulled up another piece of garlic. 'There's no rush. It's not even tea time, and I'm so tired.' Louise leaned back and looked at the beech trees.

'You're hoping it will be too late – '

'No.'

' – to leave.'

'I didn't mean – '

He looked away and kicked his foot in some water, making a high arch of sparkling drops.

'I saw the ghost.'

'Really? What was he like?'

'A miner.'

'Did he speak to you?'

Rupert turned on her a furious little face. 'He told me you're a liar, Louise. He told me to run like anything to get away from you.'

They looked at each other. It was all bare between them now. Catastrophe unveiled.

'I'm going.'

Louise jumped up, explanations rushing to the verge of speech. She saw him scramble over a rock and start to descend.

'Rupert!' she screamed and grabbed his arm, trying in her panic to drag him back to the top of the rock. He pulled away from her, lost his balance, and fell.

By a supreme effort she reached him. 'Are you all right?'

He was rubbing his knee where the blood came through his trousers. She threw her arms around him and held him hard, hugged him and kissed him, muttering apologies and endearments, using all of her strength to keep him from tearing himself away from her. But the claustrophobic embraces only increased his rage, and he kicked her as hard as he could in the shin. She let him go and stumbled backwards against a boulder. She thought he would run away, but he came straight at her.

'You bitch, Louise!' he screamed and swung at her with all his might. As she turned away to protect her face, he landed his fist against her breast.

'You cunt! You dirty slag! You hairy old sow! I hate you, I
hate you, you cow!'

He threw himself on her, pounding her with his fists,
pouring over her a torrent of abuse which rang out above the
waterfall, the birds, and the wind. She never imagined he had
learned such viciousness.

'Toad! Disgusting liar! You make me ill, you spy, you
pervert, you peeping tom. My father will kill you, he'll have
you sent to gaol, he'll have you put in the loony bin where you
belong, you nasty old bag. Why don't you just die, Louise.
Everyone hates you. You're nothing but a fat-assed fool. So
die with a needle in your liver and a red-hot poker up your
bum. Die, die!'

She could not fight back. She did not feel the slightest
impulse to defend herself. She only turned towards the rock
and held her arms tight against her body. As she did so, Rupert
delivered a swift, hard kick to her backside.

'I'm not a liar,' she whimpered. 'It was just this once. I've
always told the truth, all my life, always.' She looked up, but
he was gone.

No one had ever struck her before. Her lovers had not been
that sort. Her father, though he seldom kissed her, had never
administered corporal punishment to either her brother or
herself. Her mother, as far as she knew, had been a pacifist,
and gone neurotic but non-violent to her grave. Louise
crawled on all fours to a soft bank and lay down among the
garlic and the ferns.

'I knew it,' she whispered. 'You never liked me. You never
meant to be nice for good.' She lay there in hate, accusing him
as she wanted to accuse everyone.

The place, like all beautiful places, seemed to exaggerate her
own ugliness. Everything else grew lush and lovely. But not
Louise, not left-out Louise whom loveliness eluded. She felt
herself a female Caliban, savage in her bodily confinement, a
deformed thing amidst all these 'sounds and sweet airs', a
deformed thing housing a brain, which in turn housed only a
gnawing, plaguing hunger for explanations. She wanted to
rage and roar at the trick that had been played on her. She tore
out the garlic, flung it in every direction and smeared the
muddy roots over her face and arms. She stuffed fistfuls of the

plant into her mouth, spitting it out again, accidentally swallowing some, then gasping, coughing, nearly choking on it until she was worn out with her sick exertions. She lay flat, pounding the wet ground. At last she cried, long and loud. At last.

Was there nothing she could take from this place, a little bit of its enchantment to make the bleakness more bearable, something that would allow her to feel, even for a moment, dear God, like *Zelda*? Oh damn, guess not. All wishes and prayers go for ever unanswered.

Her objectivity was returning, and with it the old stoicism. All this panic fury suddenly struck her as ignominious.

'Better go back, Louise, and swallow your pill. Go back and admit you're all wrong and take your punishment.' She stood up, her clothes covered with mud, her body a big dull ache, and stood for a while watching snow fall on to the wrecked place where she had been lying.

VII

She started down the mountain, sore and freezing, stopping frequently to rest, and remembering, when she did so, the other time when she followed the same path with Rupert. She had no idea what he would do now or whether he would still be at Plas when she returned. Being in no hurry to find out, she stayed away until dusk, wandering in the upland meadows. She no longer felt the cold, and she didn't care that it was snowing. She wanted only to walk until she dropped down dead.

Eventually, she found herself back in the yard. She knelt in the snow to pick some of the daffodils which had been planted nearly a hundred years ago and now grew in giant clusters. Previously, she had had no inclination to pick any, but it occurred to her that she might as well enjoy them for the little time she had left. She opened the kitchen door, her arms full of flowers and was astonished to see Rupert standing at the Aga.

'I'm afraid Daisy made rather a mess in the bathroom,' he said. 'I cleaned it up, though. Want a fried egg?'

She put the flowers on the table and stared at him.

'Well, yes or no?'

'What?'

'*Do you want a fried egg?*'

'Love one.'

When Rupert had finished eating he pushed his plate away and said, 'I was going to telephone, but I thought we'd better sort out our story first. I'm not a talebearer, but – well you'll be in trouble, you know.'

Louise put her face between her hands and spoke to him through the spaces between her fingers.

'Yes.'

'Dad will be very angry. We were meant to be in Scotland a week ago.'

She looked to see if he were gloating, sympathetic, or still, underneath, really angry. She didn't understand how they could be sitting and talking this way, reasonably and simply.

'I'll have to tell them something.'

'God, I know,' she whispered. There seemed no venom in him now, and she was too exhausted not to be direct.

Rupert began to clear the plates away. The candle in the ox skull flickered and went out. It was night.

'I'll get another candle,' he said. Of course, he knew the irrational location of everything. Louise made no move. Had she been alone, she would have sat in darkness until morning.

'How can we talk like this?'

'Like what?' He struck a match.

'I mean, we said terrible things a while ago. We hit each other.'

'No. *I* said terrible things and *I* hit you. I suppose I'm sorry now, but you were very provoking.'

'I won't be any more.'

'You won't try to keep me prisoner, then?'

'Oh no. Don't worry.'

'I'm not worried, because if you did try, I should simply escape you.'

'Like Fabrizio from the Farnese tower? Like this morning?'

She almost smiled.

'I was rather good, wasn't I?' He stood by her and laid a warm, beautiful, dirty hand on her shoulder. 'You must return me, OK? I suppose I could go alone, but I'd rather you drove me.'

'Naturally. It's the least I can do. But how can you be so – '

'Grown up? I'm hardly a baby, you know. I fight with Nicholas and forget it. I've seen Richard hit Zelda then cry and kiss her five minutes later. And sometimes Phyllida is – well, it's puberty and . . . ' He pulled back his shoulders a little. 'I do know about these things. I do *understand*!'

'That's amazing.'

'Why? Did you think I were some little upper-class twit?'

He took away the knives and forks and did the washing up. They did not speak again until bed time.

'You won't lock me in.'

'Oh no.'

'And we'll leave tomorrow.'

'Yes. Wait, tell me something. Does Richard really cry?'

'Of course he cries.'

She was silent as Rupert stood waiting.

'Was that all you wanted to know?'

'You mean he cries about Zelda. He loves Zelda.'

'Think so. Says he does.'

'Ah, how interesting. And you love Phyllida?'

He blushed a little. 'In a way.'

'I see.'

'Is that – '

'All? Yes, that's all. Go to bed and leave me to my mortification.'

He smiled. 'You'll survive, I expect.'

They were away by seven thirty.

'The very first phone box, then?'

'Yes,' Louise answered, thinking of the forty pounds she had left on the music stand to compensate Alex for the cut cord.

'What will you say?' She had to know.

'That you lost the keys and went a bit funny, that there was no phone, that I'll explain later, that we're on our way home.'

He was turning her in, but not completely.

At Dolgellau, Rupert made his call while Louise waited in

the car. She was surprised at her lack of emotion. She had
expected something more definite to have come out of the
catharsis on the mountain. She wasn't sure what, but certainly not this steady-state numbness. Perhaps she was suffering a delayed reaction and would thaw, blow up, or dissolve
later.

Rupert bounced into the front seat.

'Dad's in London!'

'What! Why?'

'Why do you think? They thought we were lost, dead,
maybe. The police have been looking for us.'

'My God. And are they furious?'

'Right now they're just glad. They'll probably be furious
later. At least Dad will.'

'I'm sure. So what do we do, old chap, go back to London?'

'Yup. Daisy'll be happy. She misses Doc.'

'You mean Daisy loves Doc.'

He nuzzled the furry face. 'In a way.'

'Well I'll be damned.'

They went on in silence, driving through the same scenery
they had passed more than a week ago. Already it was greener,
with the fire of rhododendrons here and there on the hillsides.
Louise was sad. She knew she would never see it again.

Just outside Birmingham she treated Rupert to lunch. Then
they joined the M1.

'Shall I explain?' she asked suddenly.

'You mean your horrid, silly behaviour? Do you want to?'

'Well, what's the point of being verbal creatures if not to
indulge in the luxury of explaining ourselves?'

'You mean explain human behaviour to humans.'

'In a way. What I really had in mind was something more
like one would write in one's diary or tell one's psychiatrist.'

'Then *I'll* be your psychiatrist,' he said grandly.

'But you can't be. You're my – no, guess you're not any
more. All right, be my shrink. Forget you're you, and I'll tell
non-Rupert about my relationship to Rupert-Rupert.'

'Tell me, then; I mean, tell him.'

'It's something like, well, Shinto, if that doesn't seem too
silly.' (Explanations, indeed! Where was *this* one coming
from?)

'That's a Japanese religion.'

'Yes. And one of its, to me, very sensible tenets is that gods are travellers, gypsies moving from one place to another, taking up residence here and there but never staying long. Like lightning, you don't know where one will strike next, and nothing is unworthy to be the house of a god — a stone, a plant, a tree, a Coca-Cola bottle — ' she hesitated — 'you. That's why the devotees make shrines everywhere: to commemorate a little god's visit.'

'You're teaching, not telling, Miss Dent.'

'I'm coming to the telling. Believe me, I can only do it this way. So the phenomenon took place. Before my eyes. A little god came into you, I mean into Rupert, and took up residence for a while in him and shone out of him, so brightly, that I was dazzled by him, and I worshipped him, and, as gods do, he made me mad.'

'And has the little god gone?'

'Yes, he's gone.'

'And it's so simple then. That's all there is.'

'No. It's not so simple. There's much more. I'm only explaining about me and Rupert. The other part, the part about me alone, we'll have to save for the next session. Now, what do you say to that, little shrink?'

'I say it's time you pulled your socks up, Miss Dent. That will be three thousand pounds, please.'

'Will you take a cheque?'

'Sorry. I can't accept cheques from loonies. Cash on the line, as you Americans say.'

They were in Neasden before Rupert broke the intervening silence.

'There's something I've thought of. Maybe it will come to live in you.'

'What?'

'The god. Why not, you said anything or anyone can receive it. We all seem to have a turn. Perhaps you just haven't had your turn yet.'

'You're too clever by half, little shrink.'

'Oh me! I'm wonderful. My mother says so.'

Louise saw now what he would become, what he was already becoming. She needn't worry about his being ruined,

parents and godparents notwithstanding. But at the same time
– and it was a bit sad – he was no longer what he used to be.
The little god had gone.

She nearly ran down a pedestrian at a zebra crossing on the
Finchley Road.

'Your driving's not improved.'

'Not likely to either.' She smiled.

'What will you do?'

'Such questions you put. I was going to drop you at Baker
Street tube and disappear for ever, but I've changed my mind.
I don't think I'm such a coward. Having bad nerves doesn't
necessarily mean one lacks fortitude. So – I'm taking you
back.'

'Hurrah! Then you're going to be wonderful too.'

'Not *too* wonderful. I'll be as wonderful as they deserve.
Ten minutes' worth of wonderful should suffice. I'll tell them
exactly what happened, so you don't have to worry about
blowing my cover. They, too, have a right, I guess, to an
explanation.' She chuckled. 'Besides, I want to see his reaction, only to a point of course. I have to catch a plane for
Florence.'

'You're leaving?'

'How can I stay? Oh Zelda will forgive me and everything.
She knows all about lapses. It's just – well, let's say that at the
moment I'd rather look at paintings. I'm as wonderful at
looking as at explaining.' She glanced at him playfully.

They turned into Rupert's street. Nicholas was standing on
the pavement next to a motorbike, a dazzling vision of black
and chrome. He and the machine loomed larger and larger
until the car came to a stop outside the gate.

'Mum!' he shouted. 'Mum!'

The front door opened and Zelda flew down the path to
embrace Rupert who already had leapt from the car. She
kissed and caressed him as though she would never stop, while
Doc and Daisy jumped on them and each other, barking
hysterically. Alice stood in the background, dabbing her eyes.

Nicholas had a word with his brother, then started back
towards Louise as, with a deep breath, she too, got out of the
car. He stood in front of her and said something, but she didn't
hear him. Her eyes were fixed on Zelda's, and she read there all

the anticipated expressions of bewilderment, happiness, and pain. Behind Zelda, standing in the entrance hall, wearing a dark sweater and jeans, black hair, black eyes, taller than all of them and taking up the whole doorway, silent, judging, not moving, just waiting, was Rupert's father. Louise looked again at Zelda clutching Rupert (they were so pretty amid the buds and sunshine), then back to Nicholas.

'What did you say?'

'I said,' he repeated, resting one arm on the motorbike, 'so glad you could make it.'

Louise laughed. It wasn't funny, but she laughed anyway.

A View of Manhattan

'A very great man – Goethe, I think – once said that he enjoyed only a few weeks of his life. The rest was boredom and horror.' Amaryllis announced as Sheldon removed the combs from her hair, letting the coils collapse over her naked back.

'Guess what,' she said, 'I had a dream about your doing, that, Shel. The very same way, with all your inimitable tenderness. It just this moment came back to me when you . . . One of those dreams I had in the loony bin – you know.' She smiled.

Sheldon stood behind her chair which was pulled up close to the mirror. His reflection smiled back at hers – the old smile from years ago, fixed and full of assurance. She seized his hand and kissed the olive-skinned fingers with their nails bitten down to the quick.

'Beautiful Shel.'

He wound the pale blonde hair around his hand and used it to pull her head so far back that she gasped. He bit her neck gently, then harder, then released her. Their eyes met in the mirror.

'Time for the news,' he winked.

'Must we?'

She watched his reflection walk out of the bedroom, his back straight, his whole body constantly, naturally upright. Adonis at forty-one.

'Darling, darling Shel.' Amaryllis's lips formed the words he did not hear. A jet passed over. Lights went on in the Chrysler Building. She brushed her hair as he reclined before the twenty-eight-inch television, his feet on the glass coffee table, absorbed in Roger Mudd. In the mirror, she could see his toes twitching in black silk socks and undulations of smoke staining the bare atmosphere. Occasionally his arm reached into frame and flicked a cigarette at the ten-pound malachite ashtray.

The television was too loud. It made her want to grind her teeth. They were discussing the Situation again and saying those terrible words in that terrible tone: invasion, retaliation, armaments, deterrents, hot line. Why did he listen when he knew how it spoilt the magic? Oh, it was nasty and upsetting, and if it went on like this she would have to take her medication before six. (No, no. Mustn't think about it, Amaryllis. Repress, repress. Even Dr Lutisowski ended by saying it was better to do that.) Roger Mudd persisted: the Turks, the Chinese, the Iranians. She could make nothing of it. Shel could. They all could. They watched it all night and talked about it all day. It was a game to them − a noisy adventure serial of male games; an international football match; a vicious Sam Peckinpah fantasy; Big Boy Ian Fleming stuff to titillate their vicarious blood-lust. Couldn't they see how they were all in collusion, all of them, sitting there watching it, being entertained by it, believing in it, *making it exist*?

She would be ill if she didn't think about dinner, her hair, the evening ahead and all the pleasure she was suddenly able to bear, pleasure more poignant because it would end so soon. Quite right, Goethe, or whoever you were, only a few weeks', a few hours' gladness in a lifetime.

'Now . . . ' She took three deep breaths and arranged her make-up on the dressing table. Porcelain beige, plum blush, pistachio mousse, silverfrost pale blue. She wouldn't need the pills.

Without her make-up Amaryllis was a faded blonde, and this she knew. A bit old-fashioned, she wore full-length slips with beige lace at the bust, liked champagne cocktails, Russian novels and expensive, if a little fruity, perfume. Her hair was bleached, almost tastefully, her flamingo-pink nails lacquered every other day but somehow always broken and botched, her eyelashes dyed, too dark, and her body maintained in a semblance of its original sweetness by three sessions a week at the Lotte Berk Studio. She wore stockings not tights, French knickers, no bikinis, and in a house in Hampstead, London, England, in a table next to her single bed, was a drawer full of lyric verse as pastel as her concocted little face.

Sheldon Lasky adored her, had since university, always would. He loved her whiteness (still, as on that first morning nineteen years ago, startling against his darkness), the gap between her capped front teeth, the confused pathos of her eyes, and the fact that she was married to someone else. (Was it Exxon that jerk worked for? He guessed so, he couldn't bring himself to ask.) He loved her also because of the many years without her, during which she had maintained, all unaware, a subliminal grip on his emotions, and because she had been, from what he could make out, crazy. Her allusions to the hospital were vague. She talked a great deal about it without really telling him anything. She had been locked up for nearly a year, then alone in her bedroom, for months afterwards, still with the door locked. And he could tell that even now she didn't realize what had happened to the world in the interim. She got in and out of cars, answered the telephone, had even flown the Atlantic twice to make love with him in his hideaway thirteen storeys above First Avenue. But she was out of touch. Real things distressed her and, he knew by her expression, were distressing her now as she came towards him, dressed to the teeth.

'God you look great.' He held out his arms.

She knelt down before him shaking her head like a child.

'Oh Shel, no more now please.'

'Turn it off then, Honey.'

She incandesced immediately she flicked the remote control button and, as she stroked him under his shirt and talked nonsense, he forgot about the Situation.

'I know I'm silly, Shel. I have to be silly for a while. It's compensatory. You're compensatory. New York is compensatory.'

She hugged him. He was terribly responsive, she thought, for a corporate lawyer, and in a moment they were lying side-by-side on the leather couch she so disliked.

'Do you think I'm a noodle, a goose, one of those vacant little snippets in Turgenev?'

'I think you're an Orange Sovereign,' he said, referring to a variety of the thirty-eight of her namesake flowers with which he had filled the otherwise ascetic bedroom.

He smiled into the close-up of her face and, for the dozenth time since her arrival, lifted the skirt of one of those crepe dresses that must have cost the Exxon executive $500 a shot. She was more or less the same. Some of the elasticity had gone, but the giggle, the wiggle, and the near-miss intellect were still intact. When he was with her, everything he cared about, which was minimal but compelling, shrank to zero, though he tried not to let her see this. He kept a good deal from her (he kept a good deal from everyone), for instance that he was glad she couldn't live with him. She was in London with the jerk and Dahlia, and it was better that way. But he was *for* her, God he was all for her. She could – what was it they used to say? – *unman* him. Not physically, of course, quite the reverse, but feeling-wise. Oh Christ, like that time two years ago in the lobby of the Clermont. He had been saying good night to a client, no, to a woman he had thought about sleeping with but had changed his mind at the last minute – not unusual – and left her standing at the door to her room, politely disappointed in fox fur and a frozen yoghurt smile. He was heading for the bar, already sick on bad martinis and worse cocaine, hating London, the English, the creamy Victorian decor, hating having to spend all day being distinguished in the American way, suffused with melancholia, having run out of nails to bite, and wanting only to get the hell back to New York the next day. He had not thought about Amaryllis Potter – now, by some high marital fluke, Amaryllis Gardner – for five years. Then he saw her near the entrance, not looking at him, nor at anyone, but up into space at some flower, some star, some mythic creature hovering in that absurd pink and green rotunda and visible only to herself.

He approached her. (What was it she had been? A Russian major or something ridiculous like that. He had been sleeping with her as well as a few other girls then, one of them her best friend, but had been on the verge of confining himself to her for a while when what do you know, she had married a mediocrity from Harvard Business School and never finished her education, the dizzy broad.) He was about to speak to her,

pretending he wasn't sure she was who she was, when
suddenly he went to his knees. Impossible, but he, Sheldon
Lasky, exact and not expressive, fell at the feet of a woman he
had not seen for nineteen years and cried.

'Amaryllis, come and lie down with me.'

'Not now Shel darling, I'm with − ' She must have made
some indication towards her husband, but Shel was clutching
her skirt in both hands, had wrapped as much of it as he could
around his head, and saw, thought, felt nothing but her
thighs. He had never been more out of his mind.

She was perfectly understanding and in no hurry to end the
scene which was attracting quite a little audience. Instead, and
preventing her husband's interference, she stroked Shel's
smooth black hair and patted his heaving shoulders, appearing
not to mind the tears and snot all over her dress.

'Dearest Shel, always were most darling Shel, best of
Shellys,' she cooed in her acquired English accent. 'It's been a
dreadful year for us all, hasn't it. I know, I know. But you see,
we so seldom − almost never come here − this place − so
unusual − providential, I'd say. What do you think? A
miracle. Dearest darling Shel − there, there − fated, wouldn't
you say?'

Darling Shel did not go back to New York the next day. He
went to tea. At her claustrophobic little house, all pictures and
cushions, with hyperactive Dahlia crawling between his legs
(he disliked children) spilling the tea things, tearing up the
ten-dollar bill he had given her, and interrupting her mother's
already self-interrupted sentences.

'Is it true − someone told me this and now you've been one
for a while − that corporate lawyers, unlike accountants, hide
a Great Fantasy inside themselves and − Dahlia, please don't
do that − are still capable of Passion?' Was she serious?
Upstairs, the new one, ugly, unfortunate, three-month-old
Hyacinth, screamed in the agony of a missing or malfunctioning organ. Her life would be short and miserable, the
tasteless sport of a sadistic god, and would make her mother a
mad woman for nearly two years.

This was why Amaryllis had not come to New York, even
though she had promised that afternoon as they lay on Dahlia's
fluffy, crowded bed. She hadn't meant to make love with him,

not right away like that, and certainly not there in the company of three prickly Muppet monsters with Dahlia wrecking
the bathroom and Hyacinth shrieking down the hall. But she
had anyway. 'Sex makes everyone selfish,' she said.

She had been expected on the fifteenth. But no Amaryllis,
no telegram, nothing. She was locked up and drugged and
Hyacinth was dead. Months later, her brain cleared and she
tried to reach him. It had been difficult: office, partner,
secretary, old apartment, new apartment, ex-wife, several
faux pas, and finally her voice trembling at the London end of a
transatlantic call. Her aunt was ill in Providence, perhaps
dying, and would he like to see her. Yes, he would, said
pleasantly, with no trace of feeling, almost brightly formal.
That was how he always was on the telephone, but it made her
nervous.

'Hyacinth died.'

'I'm sorry, Honey.'

'They said it was probably because I was too old. Can I
bring you anything?'

'Just yourself.'

'Thank you for not – implying that it was a blessing.'

'That's all right.'

They resumed their love affair after an interruption of
eighteen years. It had been a success. Now she was back again,
glowing and amorous as some Elinor Glynn heroine,
ostensibly to spend Thanksgiving with the Providence aunt,
who in fact had died six months ago.

'No reason why he should ever find out. He takes no
interest – it's amazing, really – couldn't be less concerned –
you know he never makes the slightest – not a single enquiry
about my family. So I never told him. She died and I just never
told him, and I go on visiting. It's perfect. The only thing I've
ever successfully arranged.'

The thought of the deception made her enthusiastic. It made
Shel enthusiastic too, and he wrapped her in an all-round
embrace. Any expression of happiness on his part was always
mute.

'Let's never talk about things we don't like,' she said.

'Let's never talk.'

He stubbed out his cigarette, then made straightforward

love to her. Towards the end, he twice slapped her harder than
he had intended and, when they finished, she sat up, tenta-
tively examining the bright red patches on her thigh. He was
very apologetic and looked so earnest in nothing but his socks,
that she laughed and threw her arms around his neck. He
responded with an immediate renewal of caresses.

Shel's spontaneous affection always amazed Amaryllis. He
was constantly touching her, drawn to her as though she were
a soft magnet. She guessed it was because he was a Cancer, but
she had not known a tenderness like this in any other man.

She felt happy in a way that meant she was about to gurgle.
Ordinarily she would have tried to restrain herself, but Shel
was so tolerant.

'So,' she sighed, 'there is romance in our lives. And though
we exist in pain and greyness and a fifth-rate world, we can
come together and be each other's reward for all the desolation. And we'll never fight, there won't be time; only time
for compensatory love and pleasure. Darling Shel, forgive me
if I talk too much. It's the hospital and the medication and all
those months locked up in myself with no you. You have such
pretty brown eyes.' The kisses she gave their lids were like
two warm raindrops.

She would have to prepare all over again for dinner. She got
up, laughing at the state of herself, and went off to the
bedroom with her stockings falling around her ankles and the
pins dropping from her hair with little clinks on to the parquet
floor. Shel watched her with his knees pulled up against his
chest, holding himself in one of his noiseless inner chuckles
that never, as far as she knew, erupted into anything more
fierce. In a moment she returned and stood looking at him,
stark naked, all blue-eyed frankness.

'I thought it was gone, Shel, gone for ever, but you've
brought it back.'

'What's that?'

'My capacity to endure pleasure. For a while I thought that
if I ever had any again I'd be crushed by it. But now I can bear a
great deal, an inhuman amount, in fact.'

'You're such a good girl.'

Everyone was talking about the Situation. Its strident particulars invaded even the restaurant, normally so dark and quiet, the only place Amaryllis knew where there was no discernible contrast between red and green. She could hear the discussions at other tables. The waiters muttered over their chafing dishes and carving knives, using words such as retaliatory action and bandying about religious and aristocratic Middle Eastern titles which were by now familiar, despite her efforts to exclude them from consciousness, but which she could never have allocated to their proper spheres of influence. She took her pills in a hurry and, against doctor's orders, drank three champagne cocktails.

'I'll have the salmon with sorrel sauce, Dumples.' The waiter looked askance at the giggling blonde who leaned against amused Sheldon.

'Now tell me about your Lithuanian grandmother – or did you say Georgian? I adore all things Russian, especially – '

He kissed her hand. 'Zat, my dahlink, is rapidly becoming an inappropriate subject for enzusiasm.'

'Then *I'll* tell *you* about – Have you noticed how much more articulate I am when I'm drunk?'

Voices rose at the next table.

'Oh Shel, make them be quiet. Don't New Yorkers talk about baseball any more or having the streets repaired or conceptual art or adultery? Is civil rights a dead issue?'

'Darling, everything now is a dead issue – except the Big One.' He tried to summarize for her the intricacies of the Situation.

'But surely it's in their minds, Shelly darling, don't you think? Really a symptom of their derangement, a figment of diseased imaginations – just like the black holes. I realized that when I was in the loony bin. (I realized so many things in there, more than I could ever tell you.) *The black holes are in their minds,*' she whispered melodramatically, as though passing top secret information. 'The missiles are in their minds, the neutron bomb is in their minds. And they are projecting these twisted fantasies on to *you* and *me*, determined to spoil everything as usual. They hate beauty and happiness and want to kill them. No one can bear pleasure, or almost no one. What creatures they are. Loathsome, abominable. One

shrinks from one's own kind. But we're talking about things I
don't like and not being anywhere near compensatory
enough. What's on at the Modern?'

'You *are* more articulate when you're drunk.'

In the taxi he once more introduced the topic of Global
Crisis. Since the age of nine Sheldon has followed world
affairs with the same avidity as football. He was very well-
informed. But Amaryllis shrank from his statistics. No use, he
knew it was cruel to press them on her and dropped the
subject.

'Kiss me, Shel, a long, long wet one like only you can
deliver.' He obliged.

Amaryllis stood with her coffee cup rattling in its saucer,
looking out at the cold light of First Avenue. Any minute now
the pills would start to work. Last night she had loved the
city's evil glitter. This morning it seemed stripped, like a room
made ready for re-papering. United Nations Plaza was
humming. Several limousines had just arrived with police
escorts. Sirens whined, and a flotilla of white motorcycles
hovered near the sidewalk. 'Within that concrete monolith,'
she briefly realized, 'half-baked diplomats are deciding the fate
of us all.'

Some of the buildings on First flew American flags, and
street-level shops were adorned with political placards and
slogans. 'A resurgence of patriotism,' said the commentator
on the news programme Shel had insisted on watching before
going to bed. She shuddered. They were all mad.

She moved on to the bedroom with its spectacular view of
the Chrysler Building. 'It should have ended there,' she
murmured to that paragon of capitalist grace.

She watched Shel and listened to his regular breathing.
After spending an hour with her in the bath (the whole
apartment was redolent of the peach kernel bath gelée, amber
oil and goat's milk soap which she had dumped indiscrimi-
nately into their hedonist tub) he had gone back to bed and was
now lying perfectly composed on his back, arms folded across
his noble chest and head elevated on three pillows, the better to
take in a midday quiz programme which continued to flicker
away noiselessly against a bank of amaryllises.

'Big handsome Shel. It would be ridiculous, it would verge on the pathetic, if anyone else looked as good as you do.' He never snored, he never smelled, he never bristled. The fur lay smooth and soft as a Burmese cat's. He never tore up her face by neglecting to shave. Where she often wondered, did all the unpleasantness go, the repellent aspects of other men which he appeared not to possess. Into his melancholia, she supposed. Into his sad materialism.

The apartment, despite its enviable view of Manhattan, for which he had paid she could not imagine how much, but certainly more than he could afford, was a testament to his bare, moneyed existence. It seemed all empty spaces. The furniture, scrupulously impersonal, was placed at regular distances, no one piece having much telepathy with the others, but existing solidly, expensively alone. He had bought the place for her, he said (surroundings didn't interest him; he would have slept on a couch at the office), to be private with her, to be able to lie to his associates whenever he needed and say he had gone to the Keys for a week; and also, to make himself unavailable to his estranged wife, some smart, chilly woman from Philadelphia who had been no fun at all.

The refrigerator started up and she jumped, spilling coffee down the front of her velour dressing gown. All of America seemed to throb with the sound of refrigerators or to ache with the void left when they rested from their labours. This model was huge, antiseptic and vacant, except for Shel's jar of Coffee-mate, the marijuana in the freezer and the pineapple she had insisted on buying. She refilled her cup from the percolator, which looked like some mortal booby trap in a James Bond film. It was flanked by the most expensive blender and the most expensive juicer on the market, neither of which had ever been used.

Back in the bedroom, she sat down among the flowers with their big voluptuous petal mouths. Such a contradiction to their environment: Warhol print in *de rigueur* metal frame, walls otherwise bare, secondary television with video attachment, stark dresser, headless and footless queen-size bed, sci-fi reading lamp for Shel's sci-fi paperbacks and de luxe editions of erotic art. Her personal clutter seemed just as much a contradiction: odd female things strewn like flotsam across a desolate beach: shoes with four-inch heels and polka-dot bows, stockings, clutch bags, novels, make-up, perfume, pills – endless pills – and the boxes of marzipan from the shop on 89th Street, purchased for Shel, but consumed by her.

The bedside table stayed rigidly his: digital clock, pocket calculator, one of three phones in a three-room apartment, and an assortment of nasal sprays, any of which items might well be more vital to his existence than she. But that was a petulant thought and unworthy of a nearly forty-year-old woman who had learned at last to bear pleasure. Yet she resented the way the clock swallowed up the seconds, showed them to her in all their fleeting possibilities then consumed them before she had grasped even one. The minutes lingered on a little, but they too rolled back into the machine like eyes in the head of a doll.

On top of a chair that never had been sat in, cast-off clothes of the past three days alternated in layers – Amaryllis, Sheldon, Amaryllis, Sheldon, Sheldon, Amaryllis. The lowest stratum was the full skirt of pastel plaid she had worn on the plane. She had bought it because she wanted something big and accessible for their first encounter, something to be torn back without trouble for their immediate happiness. The question, she recalled, was whether he should meet her, not meet her. She changed her mind three times. She would arrive alone and, in the back of a taxi, think about coming closer to him all the way from the airport. Delicious for her, but the plan rather left him out. No, he must meet her, but only if he hired a limo so they could drink champagne and neck in the big back seat. No, they should come together joyously crash (he was getting tired of this); no dirty adolescent preliminaries, she would come alone to the apartment, yes, she was absolutely sure, yes, she would absolutely come. She booked the flight.

After her three-quarters of an hour in the lavatory, irritated passengers were banging on the door. Didn't she know they were landing in fifteen minutes? She tossed them her bravest lightest Shan't be a moment! and finished with the lip liner. Oh the airplane lights were savage. They showed her creases, pits, and hairs of which she had been unaware for months. And the static – it was impossible to give any structure to her hair (swept up with several combs, all different, curls on top

falling on to her forehead, she had seen it in a film; a bit
absurd, even she had to admit, but rather endearing). More
knocks. Oh God, and she hadn't even peed yet. Delicately she
placed strips of toilet paper on the seat and pulled down her
French knickers. The Fasten Seat Belt sign lit up and brought
an urgent stewardess. Would she please return to her seat *right
now*. Amaryllis stood up and began sweeping the cosmetics
and pills into an expensive leather satchel in which she carried
all her necessities and without which she couldn't go anywhere. Then she stopped, pulled off the knickers and put
them in the satchel. She took her two o'clock pills, wiped out
the sink as the sign politely but firmly suggested she should,
and returned to her seat, blushing at the indignant stares of
the passengers who, because of her, had missed their turn and
would be very uncomfortable for the next half hour.

Shel was sweeping the kitchen floor when she arrived,
stopping to sip tequila and bite his nails. He was very
nervous, she knew, but oh so glad to see her, though trying
not to show how much. He hadn't the advantage of her
superb and sexualizing anti-depressants.

'Darling Shel, I see you require one or two more tequilas,
don't you. But what if I were to put my hands *there* like
that?' She turned away coquettishly.

He grabbed her from behind, distorting her breasts with
his enfolding arms.

'I love you, I love you, I love you, Amaryllis, I want you,
I want you, I love you, love you, love you.' That was better.

'I know. I believe you, Shelly.'

She lay down before him on the bed and threw back the
plaid skirt. He acted not in the least surprised, almost as if he
expected her to be naked underneath, and tore her stockings
as usual. Then instead of doing the expected, he put his face
between her legs and kissed her and licked her, protesting he
could for ever, despite her sweetest persuasions that he be
inside her. But no, not until she had come three times (he
had a way of pulling at her with his oh so personal lips and
the pills made her tremendously relaxed) did he finally let
her taste herself on him and climb inside in the old-fashioned
way as though Eden had only just been lost and this were the
first of all. And she cried, and by the time he had done

everything he could think of to her with cock, fingers and tongue all at once, it was eleven thirty and too late for dinner.

She was about to move on to the next layer and relive the scene with Jean Muir dress when Sheldon raised his arm in a half-conscious gesture.

'Amaryllis,' he said with his squat Long Island A, 'weren't we supposed to be going somewhere?'

'The Weidenfeld Collection, but it's on until the 2nd.'

He kissed her palm. 'Get me a cup of coffee, darling, and the paper, then I'm prepared to go and love culture with you, even if the Oilers are playing the Steelers today.'

She dropped Sunday's *New York Times* with its three-inch headlines on his chest. 'There you are: disaster, bloodshed, massacre, trans-global conspiracies, mutilated children, nefarious politicians. How can you read it?' He started to say something. 'All right, Shel, I won't complain so long as you don't *discuss* it with me. Better your old loves, even.'

'There are no old loves, love.' He laughed his noiseless inner laugh that seemed to roll back on itself and consume itself like the digital clock consumed the minutes and seconds. He asked her to turn up the television which was now proffering the collegiate eurhythmics of June Allyson and Peter Lawford. She straightened the pillows for him, and he read grimly for an hour with his thick black-rimmed glasses sliding down on his adorable nose, drinking cups of black coffee, and smoking prepared-in-advance joints of Columbian marijuana.

As a result of not being able to avoid glancing at the leaders, all of which screamed of nothing but the Situation, Amaryllis had to take her medicine too soon, and so forgot most of what she read in the Book Review.

'Sweetheart,' she leaned over and rapped gently at the financial section with the longest of her pink fingernails. Shel smiled at her, reassuringly, over the top of page 131. 'We should go.'

He put the paper aside. 'I love you, Amaryllis.'

'Really? Even though the world is falling apart?'

'Even more now.'

She saw the sheet below his tummy jump gently as though he were playing a game with a cat.

'Shel, it *is* a Romance, isn't it?'

'Yes it is.'

'That's everything, you know.' She crawled inside and lay on top of him. 'It's so tangible, I mean, I can go to bed and lie down alone with it in the dead of night with screaming storms and darkness outside, and hold it and press it to me and the mad world dies and there you are inside me, deeper than deep, Shel, for ever rooted.'

He, then She, then a twilight zone of haphazard, half-conscious kisses.

'Backgammon?'

'Scrabble.'

They never made it to the Weidenfeld Collection.

An hour later, Houston was leading Pittsburgh thirteen to seven, but no one, particularly, was winning the Scrabble game. They forgot to keep score and took ten minutes over their three-letter words. Half reclining in a tangle of bed linen, they ate the marzipan and hardly spoke but smiled at each other a good deal.

'You were best,' she said.

His brown eyes dropped to where the velour dressing gown fell open, showing his skin that still reminded him of nectarines. 'No, you.' The crowd roared.

Slickly he slipped her backwards, scattering the plastic letters everywhere. 'Will we ever be able to stop . . . where did you learn these things, my love . . . My love, my love . . . I'm glad you're best.'

They slept. Houston won. It began to snow and lights went on in the Chrysler Building. The telephone rang nine times.

'Your wife?' Amaryllis groaned when it finally stopped.

'Did we fuck?'

'Don't you remember?'

'No,' he teased.

'Then I'll just have to give you an instant replay.'

'Amaryllis, are you – '

'Sore? I'm not, I mean I am, but all the better.'

'God, Amaryllis, what if I kill you?'

'Pretend you're – ' he came – 'going to.'

'Oh Honey.'

Thursday would be Thanksgiving. On Wednesday night she

remembered and insisted she cook him a turkey. He protested
lazily, would have preferred her not to. Food bored him nearly
as much as surroundings. But he gave in, she was in such a flap
about it. Anything she wanted, anything.

Of course the cupboard was bare, except for the pineapple
and the marijuana, so the meal would have to be bought and
cooked from scratch, and it was now eight thirty, Thanksgiving evening. They took a taxi downtown to Balducci's,
Amaryllis insisting that it was the only place sure to have what
she needed. Together they pushed the shopping cart, she
exclaiming at everything, he with his arm around her and
fondling her at every stop, wholly unembarrassed by public
demonstrations of affection. Glorious things she bought,
luscious, extravagant things, and even managed to infect jaded
Shel with her enthusiasm.

The turkeys were enormous, so they settled for a brace of
pheasants. She knew the most wonderful sauce to go with
them. He'd see, he'd be amazed at what an inspired cook she
was – and so organized – the consequence of those evening
classes that were supposed to help her regain her stability.
Cordon Bleu, Korean, Persian, Creole. You name it, she
could cook it. The whole thing would be rather like Sabrina
and Linus Larabee, wouldn't it.

'Didn't she make the soufflé out of crackers?'

'She *said* she could make a soufflé out of crackers.' His
memory, like his tenderness, was always surprising her.

On the way home they passed the UN, but she stopped him
with a kiss before he could say anything about councils or
situations.

Amaryllis had promised to call her husband on Thanksgiving. Since this would require a good many lies, she had
shut herself in the bedroom and was repeating planned false-
hoods in a low voice, leaving Shel to hover over the birds
which were spluttering vigorously in an oven big enough to
roast Hansel and Gretel.

Before telephoning she had hesitated at the bedroom door
and turned to him.

'Isn't it strange that the only way to have you all the time is
not to have you most of the time?' She said this with the trace
of a smile. Then she made him promise not to listen. But even

though he had been party, without remorse, to the installation of a few small recording devices in offices and, once, in a private residence, his character was such that he would not have dreamed of straining to catch any of her conversation. He was partially noble, and he was generous enough and sensible enough not to make her uncomfortable about her other life. It was so distasteful to him that he had no desire to learn any more of it than he already knew. Still, another in his place might have taken perverse pleasure in stirring up the mud.

Should he rescue her he wondered. Should he steal her away and keep her close for ever by installing her on the thirteenth floor? Should he overcome her fixation about paying for their lust with months of stoic drudgery, convince her that it was mad that they, at their age, should be martyrs to love? He thought about it, he was tempted. But he knew. In no time she'd want pet rabbits and plant stands and it would drive him nuts. She'd spend a fortune on shrinks and at Bendel's and want him to talk about Solzhenitsyn with her. Then there'd be the operas: *Traviata* all night when he wanted to watch a fight or go round the corner to a movie. She'd constantly be offering him pieces of information like *whose* exhibition it was that Mussorgsky had been to, reconstructing that damp afternoon in St Petersburg, or was it Moscow, and all when he had to keep his brain straight and make money. But he loved her, he could not resist her. She was an oasis of affection in a desert of dry sex, and when she left in two days it would break his heart.

Meanwhile, Amaryllis, behind the bedroom door, having her programmed conversation with the Exxon executive, was thinking not that she hated her husband or that he bored her so much, but that he was payment pure and simple. She felt almost grateful to him for being as bad as he was, for making the payment *so* painful, *so* repellent. That, of course, being part of the Trick.

Oh the Trick, the Trick; where would she be without the Trick?

She had begun to understand the Trick in hospital. Gradually, during those muddled, empty hours, she realized how she would have to conduct herself in the terrifying life-game in order to come out of it, not winning, surely, but with a little something, with anything at all. A bargain would have to be struck, a balance of payments worked out with an anonymous fate that didn't like anyone arranging their own terms. It would be difficult, but she would have to try. Otherwise the past would paralyse her. She would mope about Hyacinth, neglect Dahlia, loathe her husband, and be dull and empty for ever.

The deal took months to negotiate. Unable to reason, she was flooded by memories and dreams. But the memories were her indicators, her guides, her hold on life itself. For instance: a freezing afternoon in Boston, at a time of her life when her nails were the same colour as most people's and she was still carelessly beautiful. She was nineteen, Shel twenty-one. They had just met, had slept together once or twice, but were shy with each other and had paid a visit to some noisy acquaintances in order not to be too much alone until bed time. (Much more fun having their eyes meet every once in a while, making invisible bridges across the drunken chatter.) She was cold; she huddled into her chair and shivered. Shel caught the movement and, without hesitation, jumped up, removed from the wall a Navaho blanket, said to be worth a good deal and held in high esteem by its owner, and wrapped it round her, solemnly tucking in the corners. Someone gave a nervous laugh, embarrassed by the spontaneous magic of the gesture. But no one asked him to replace the blanket.

After Dr Lutisowski discharged her from the loony bin, she spent many weeks in her room, feeling as though she had been erased, like a drawing or a page of writing. Only a few indications were left on the paper, so faint one would have to hold them up to the light to see them. But the memories kept coming, most of them with Shel at the centre. They made her stronger, and she turned them over and over in her mind, fastening furiously on the scene in the lobby of the Clermont. 'Now that,' she would say to herself, 'was fate, Amaryllis, you fatuous, ruined, once intelligent woman. For God's sake recognize it and respond.' But she couldn't quite – not yet.

She went out into the world again. All she saw there were a great many people pretending to be grown up, and all she knew was that her best energies seemed to have ebbed away in

banks, restaurants, department stores, and school rooms
without her knowing it, until she found herself, too late, a
faded blonde. And those places were still there waiting for her,
ready to suck out her vital forces in the name of restored
stability. Wouldn't it be better to save what was left of those
precious forces and squander them on Shel? Belatedly she kept
her promise and called him.

Now as she said goodbye to the Exxon executive she felt full
of conviction, as though the whole aggregate of DNA inside
her had intended her, saved itself through her for this one
compensatory romance. And she didn't want companionship
or cosy stability or cultural compatibility or equality or
reasonable discussions ending in empty, literate com-
promises. She wanted high pleasure with impossible restrictions in between. Without the restrictions the pleasure could
not flourish; they made it grow up strong. *That* ladies and
gentlemen, was the Trick! And Shel — old handsome, tacit,
sexual fatalist — Shel was the perfect accomplice. He required
no explanations, no titles or offices. Like her, he could keep his
eye on the single thing that was important and not spoil it with
greed and vulgarity, like the crazy people who couldn't
control their appetites, and proved all their lives that they
hated beauty and pleasure. It was as though Shel had been born
knowing the Trick.

She put the phone down and thought of the pheasants.

'Shel, my Snookums, are you basting the peasants?'

He was sitting on the edge of the couch watching News at
Noon and biting his nails.

'God, Amaryllis, they've invaded Turkey.'

'And well-timed. They appear, whoever they are, to have at
least a sense of humour. But the pheasies, my sweetest
Sheldon,' she kissed the top of his head, 'they must be basted —
constantly.'

He followed her to the kitchen where she crouched by the
oven, fussing over the birds with a bulb baster, her hair
dropping into her face and the dressing gown sliding off her
bare thigh (she didn't bother with clothes any more). Shel's
normally pristine kitchen was awash with dirty pots, sticky
utensils, and exotic sauces. She had gone all out.

'Shel, what does it mean?'

'What, Honey?' He knelt down and slid his hands under the dressing gown.

'The invasion.'

'You wouldn't like knowing. Come and lie down with me.'

'Oh, darling,' she half turned towards him, 'I can't leave them. It's the critical stage. They must be basted every five minutes.'

'OK sweetheart, whatever you say,' he said putting his finger inside her and finding her still gooey from an hour before. Gently he tipped her forwards on to her hands and knees, lifted the dressing gown over her bottom, then pulled her backwards a little, fitting herself on to himself. She made a small sound. The bulb baster rolled across the tiled floor and collided with the refrigerator.

'Don't forget the – '

'Oh yes – ' Holding him inside her, squeezing him a little to keep him amused (it was a good trick of hers; only one girl in a million, he said, could do it), she opened the oven door and checked the dinner. The birds could wait another five minutes, she guessed. He flattened her stomach against the cold floor and pushed into her until she was too breathless to ask him to stop, then rolled her over and kissed her, his tongue straining towards her tonsils. In a moment of wonderful panic, she realized he was completely out of control. Suddenly she was upright again, then reversed, her wrists breaking and the skin being rubbed off her knees as he clamped his fingers so tightly into her hips that she thought he must puncture the flesh.

'Should you look at them?' he gasped.

She stepped over collapsed Sheldon to retrieve the bulb baster. The pheasants were safe.

'Amaryllis, get me my cigarettes?' He smoked one where he lay.

'I think he's getting wise. I can feel it. I know he suspects something. Whatever you do, don't answer the phone. What do you think? What if my uncle were to develop – what disease besides cancer makes you take a long time to die?'

He held her hand across the remains of Thanksgiving dinner.

'You're running out of relatives, darling.'

'Then what about old school friends – no, I guess that's considered very out of fashion now. Come to think of it, *you're* an old school friend. But it's no good unless I lie – have to lie. Being out of commission for so long, I don't know what excuses people are using. What's the fashionable excuse this year? For all I know the truth could be fashionable. Am I being fatuous? You just let me run on, Shel, you really should put a stop to my delirium sometimes. No – no, don't. You're such a darling to be tolerant of crazy me. That's why you know so much more of me than I do of you. I tell all. I babble all. Look, I can't control it!' She made a helpless funny gesture with her hands. 'I should have been smooth, accomplished, but I'm not. I'm blowzy and I know it, but still I can't shut up. You, you're so mysterious, like an Egyptian statue. You stand for so much and say so little. You tell nothing, it makes me mad with desire. You'll be bored with me if I don't shut up . . . do you know what I did when Hyacinth died? I locked myself in my room and masturbated for an hour. I don't know, maybe it wasn't an hour. It was a long time though. It wasn't until a week later that I took all the seconals.'

She broke off with a wistful look, not sure what he would think, not sure what she herself thought of what she just had told him. He read hesitation, sadness in her eyes, but not embarrassment. He gave her a big, reassuring smile and pressed her hand in both of his.

'Sex and death?' he said cheerfully.

'Yes,' she smiled back at him.

'Leave the dishes, love, the cleaning lady comes tomorrow.' He took a bottle of tequila from the rack and motioned her towards the bedroom. 'Game starts in five minutes.'

'Another afternoon of fucking and football. You'd think we were still in high school.'

She looked out of the window at grey Manhattan and at the United Nations where activity appeared to have died down.

'No Situation today?'

Shel had switched on the television and was already asleep, his head nearly upright on a mountain of pillows.

Late that afternoon he found her in the midst of one of her extended bathing rituals. And he could not resist, sleepy though he was, letting her play with him as she sat in the bath, lap, caress, and stroke him until his knees buckled and he grabbed at the hot towel rail, which was how he got blisters on his left hand. Then she lay back in the bubbles and he reciprocated with his second and third fingers, meanwhile squeezing her slippery nipple and watching ripples of pleasure make mild contortions of her face.

'How is it,' she asked him afterwards, as he sat on the toilet and she on his lap, with streams of water running from her wet hair over her back, 'how is it that I can do more dirty things with you than I've ever done with anyone, yet love you like I loved the baby Jesus when I was six?'

'I guess because it's fate, and I'm a fatalist.'

'Funny answer.' But it was true. He simply followed his nature like a cat stalking a bird.

'Funny question.'

The next morning – their last – he found her in the kitchen. She was standing at the counter and wearing no make-up.

'What are you doing?'

'Making crackers.'

'Out of what?'

'A soufflé.' She burst into tears.

Shel switched off the news and frowned slightly as he helped her with her bags. The Situation was bad that day.

'Don't forget the black holes,' she tried to be light. 'They're the same as the missiles. Don't believe in them and they don't exist. If you have to think, think of four months from now. Think of me.'

'Get the window seat next to the wing,' he advised, fumbling with the buckle of the suitcase on which Amaryllis was sitting, drawing blue rings round her eyes. 'It's the safest.'

'And it's a clear night. I'll have a wonderful view of Manhattan.'

Time to leave. She felt sick and had to take a good many pills before she could get into the elevator. On the way down he sheltered her in his arms. She expected him to be stoical about this, but could feel his heart pounding against her ear.

'I won't attempt to tell you how I feel at this moment.' The doorman was putting her too many suitcases into a taxi. 'But

I'd like you to say once more that you love me.' He said it. He always obliged her.

She stepped into the back seat. Shel placed himself between her and the door and caught her hand. 'Amaryllis,' he said, then stopped. This was difficult for him. 'Your little finger is worth more than – more than the whole damn Chrysler Building.' He kissed the pink nail and closed the door. When he looked up at her through the open window, tears were streaming down his face.

By the time the taxi reached the lights at 41st Street, she was blubbering uncontrollably, and had to shout at the driver through the glass partition to ask him for a cigarette, her first in two years.

He caught her eye in the rear view mirror. 'Luvahs nevah say good-boi,' he grinned.

She fumbled with the leather satchel and the cigarette, so absorbed in a packet of Kleenex that she nearly forgot to turn around when they emerged from the Mid-Town Tunnel (that initiatory tunnel, where one steeled oneself first to endure Manhattan and then to endure being without it) and admire her favourite of all views. To leave New York was so dramatic. To leave New York was to leave herself; but herself, like New York, was better to visit than to live in. New York, lived in, became London or Stuttgart or Akron, and one shouldn't marry one's mistress. So, time's up, Amaryllis; time's up Sheldon. Such a little time, but worth the approaching weariness, oh very worth it.

From the rear window, the city gleamed and winked and altered its aspectual relationship to her whenever the taxi changed lanes. At this distance, far from its seamy streets, it was almost holy. She wanted to compose a hymn to the high city to express her awe and her gratitude. They left it behind. They were well into Queens now with signs for the airport rising up and disappearing before them. She cried some more, putting her face inside her fur coat to smell Shel on her, or rather the mixture of his smell and hers. What would he do tonight, she wondered – drink tequila and smoke grass until he passed out, get naked into bed and watch a boxing match, ring up a tart? *Was* he able to go twenty-fours hours without someone in bed with him? She must ask him next time.

When they arrived at JFK she had to beg another cigarette from the driver, whom she over-tipped, as was her habit. The reflection in the automatic doors showed her looking frightful, so after checking in her luggage and over-tipping the Red Cap, she spent nearly an hour in the Ladies repairing herself. She did not succumb to the desperate urge to take her ten o'clock pills at eight, and tried to keep her mind from wandering to the thirteenth floor and what naughty Shel might be doing there. Her face was satisfactory. Amaryllis was one of those women who look their best when a little distraught, and she was not unaware of the men who eyed her in the bar. She took a tuinol with two champagne cocktails to steel herself for the take-off and kept her nose in the air. Not one of those men could compare with Shel.

She had her window seat. She fastened the belt and opened a novel for appearance's sake, to keep at bay the middle-aged Irish lady beside her who, she could sense, was burning for a chat. She held tight through the take-off, blinking back tears as best she could (the Irish lady would certainly try to mother her), then raised her eyes long enough to catch the stewardess's attention and order two splits of an indifferent champagne, all Pan Am had to offer. She began drinking, the satchel just under her feet in case she should need the nausea pills. The plane circled the city in a wide arc. She turned in her seat and pressed her nose against the window, straining to see the Chrysler Building. There it was, its silver spire gleaming below her, and beautiful Shel only five blocks away.

The spectacle faded as the plane turned north towards Boston, but was still visible through a haze of tears and beginning-to-work-at-last-tuinol. There was nothing for it, she must borrow a Kleenex from the Irish lady. Wiping her eyes, she turned once more towards the window for a last look, and was just in time to catch an enormous incandescence in the sky, so brief she was not sure she had really seen it, and so brilliant that she thought for a moment it had blinded her. Then eruption inconceivable. The plane shook with its reverberations. Passengers rushed to her side of the cabin to watch a colossal pillar of flame fly up to heaven.

The Situation had resolved itself. New York was burning.

The Chrysler Building had split in two, and its halves were melting like fantastic ice-cream cones, while five blocks away, the pitiful fragments of Sheldon Lasky's body were hurtling towards the inferno of First Avenue in a cascade of poison brimstone.

Amaryllis stopped crying. For a moment she stared straight before her, not noticing that the Irish lady had fainted and hearing neither the shouts and sobs of the other passengers nor the garbled announcements of the captain trying to make known to them in broken tones that the plane would, if possible, hold to its original course. Naturally they would be kept informed of any new developments. They were not to panic, please, please. There was static on the intercom, then something about Gander.

Amaryllis poured the remains of her champagne, leaning her arm against the plastic tray to steady her hand. Holding the cup in one hand, she reached for the satchel with the other and pulled it on to her lap. Slowly she took out the bottles containing her medication – there must have been a dozen of them – and lined them up on the tray.

'Time's up, Amaryllis. Time's up, Sheldon. Time's up, New York.'

People still clustered at windows and pointed behind at the flaming horizon. Ignored announcements were repeated on the intercom. Stewardesses tried in vain to assist hysterical passengers. The pandemonium was such that no one noticed Amaryllis, safe in her window seat, unscrew each of the safety caps with difficulty, but not cursing or breaking a nail as she ordinarily would, take the pills of various colours, one by one from their containers, and, along with little sips of champagne, slowly and systematically consume them.

White Places

Celeste was first cousin to Cissy and Killer. Peachey was Celeste's Best, meaning her best friend. They always said 'Bests' to keep their true relationship a secret, and to be able to talk about the secret without hurting anyone else's feelings. That was the important thing, Celeste said, that no one know and that no one get their feelings hurt. Of course Cissy and Killer knew, but that was all right because they were first cousins to Celeste and so practically first cousins to Peachey.

The four of them had a club. The name and nature of this club was changed every three or four weeks, depending on what Celeste was reading. Celeste talked like a book and was fond of titles. She liked being President, Secretary, Madam Chairman and Grand Duchess Genevra Samantha Roberta della Rocca of Upper Vernocopium, a place even more important than Oz. The others let her be. But everyone knew it was Cissy who ruled.

Killer was the youngest and the fattest. Her shoes were always wet and untied with her socks sliding down into the heels. She had cold sores and was only in fourth grade. Her name was not really Killer. It was Charlotte Mundy Fletcher Doyle (mixed marriage: Roman Catholic and Presbyterian). Like just about every awful thing, the nickname was an invention of Cissy's. It came from one of their earliest games in which she and Celeste, starlets sharing an apartment in Beverly Hills, were stalked by a dangerous maniac known simply as The Killer. Their pretend boyfriends, a producer and his brother, the world's most daring stunt man, came over and over again to their rescue. Over and over they carried off

Killer, bound and gagged, to a lunatic asylum. That was how it began – a crude game by later standards, but the name stuck. Cissy's and Celeste's parents tried, without success, to stop the children calling her by it.

'Chaaaaarrrrrrrrlotte,' Cissy would sneer across the dinner table, 'pass the potatoes, Chaaaaarrrrrrrrlotte.' Cissy wasn't afraid of anything. Eventually though, when she behaved like this, she would be sent off to bed where she would lie awake, waiting to pinch her sister's fingers with the nutcracker as soon as she fell asleep, which was usually within three minutes.

Mrs Doyle insisted the others be nice to Killer, share with her. Once she even had cried when her youngest daughter came home wet, though uncomplaining, from the swamp. They had been on a Royal Expedition up the Nile, led by Robert Redford and Cissy in a sedan chair. Killer had been thrown to the crocodiles after attempting to kidnap the baby Moses. Later, Killer had listened with her ear to the door as her mother reprimanded Cissy.

'Cissy, why are you so mean to Killer – ' She stopped impatiently. 'Oh for heaven's sake, you know I mean *Charlotte*.' It was too late. Mummy had said it and that made it true for ever.

Killer was six then, and Cissy was eight. By now the Pretends were much more complicated, and included a wide range of malice and glamour. (Cissy was maddeningly inventive.) But they were still variants on a single theme, and always ended with the Finding Out, the unmasking, at which everyone ran shrieking from Killer. Why the others liked pretending to be weak and frightened and in danger when really they were so strong, stronger than she would ever be, Killer could not understand.

A tried and true Pretend, used when all else had ended in boredom or hair-pulling, was The Crazy Doctor. Killer, in disguise, would come to the grown-ups' bedroom – it had to begin in there – to prescribe for one of the three, who were always orphaned sisters. Eventually, they would guess her wicked intentions and race, screaming and laughing, to the attic, down again, through the upstairs rooms and out on to the lawn, pursued by Killer who was well-versed in the terrifying snorts and snarls she was required to make. Once outside, she would be caught, rolled up in a blanket, tied and taken off to be burnt at the stake, then released and made to play her part all over again until parents put a stop to the game.

They spent school vacations at each other's houses. Easter at the Doyles' and Christmas at Celeste's. This time, Peachey would be with them. Peachey was too small for her age, but very energetic. She was called Peachey because she once had been taught by her father to respond, at the top of her chipmunk voice to all enquiries after her condition with the answer 'Peachey Keeno!'

Celeste's father and mother were very indulgent. Even when the girls kept them awake until four in the morning, they did not complain very much. Killer always fell asleep first. The others ate crackers in bed and pushed the crumbs on to her side. They made raids to the kitchen for peanut butter sandwiches at two a.m. They came back and covered Killer's face with toothpaste. By the beam of a flashlight, they held a club meeting and read comic books under the covers. Peachey wrapped all their apple cores in paper and put the bundle down the toilet. The next morning the plumbing was blocked, and Killer stood, serious-eyed (she had been banished by the girls until three), watching Auntie Lillian mop up the bathroom on her hands and knees. She was given a jelly doughnut and allowed to watch Tom and Jerry until called to come and be a werewolf.

There was a blizzard. Killer was frightened by the silence and by the way the snow climbed the window panes. When she pressed her face against them, she imagined that she had gone blind, but that her blindness was white instead of black. It seemed hard to breathe, and she wondered if everyone were going to be buried alive. She thought she might like to go home. It would be nice to be tucked in by her mother and to watch her baby brother kicking his feet like a small fat bug or dribbling breakfast down his pyjamas. But she was too scared to tell Aunty Lillian any of these things. Besides, she had to stay here and be a Body Snatcher.

Celeste said that they should make puppets and a theatre and put on a puppet show. They thought of nothing else for the three days the blizzard lasted. Cissy and Celeste wrote a play and made posters to advertise the event, while Peachy and Killer worked happily and messily with balloons, cardboard tubes and papier mâché. Aunt Lillian was very patient. She and Uncle Raymond, along with all of Celeste's and Peachey's dolls, were forced to attend three performances, and to applaud, exclaim and congratulate on each occasion.

They experimented with the left-over flour and water paste, and invented, by the addition of sugar, milk, vanilla, corn syrup and a dash of laundry starch, a drink which they called Plush and which they forced Killer to taste after the addition of each new ingredient. That evening Killer threw up her supper. Cissy said that she thought it was disgusting, and that Killer was not mature enough to have been allowed to come.

When the storm ended, they put up signs and tried to sell Plush from a snow fort which they built at the end of the driveway. The snow was very high there, nearly six feet, because the blizzard had been such a long one and the snow-plough had had to come around so many times. No one bought the drink but Uncle Raymond who tasted it, tried to smile, and said he would finish the rest in the house, if that was all right with 'you girls'. They lost interest in Plush. It turned sour, stank and Auntie Lillian carefully asked permission to throw it out.

They decided to enlarge the snow fort. They built half a dozen each winter and knew everything about their construction. This was to be the biggest they had ever made. To celebrate its completion, Cissy said, they must make up a brand new Pretend. Celeste agreed. Then Peachey and Killer agreed. They worked even harder on the snow fort than they had on the puppet show, talking and planning every minute for the Important Celebration Pretend. They were very excited, Killer could tell. She saw how much it thrilled them to make believe. To her, inside, it seemed almost frightening, the way they were always at it, never never getting tired of it. Why did they want to be something they weren't, to change everything into what it wasn't? Killer liked everything as it was — just plain with no Pretend, no titles, no talking like books, no ruling, no dressing up, no punishments, no Madam Chairman or Grand Duchesses or Cleopatras. But that was her secret. She knew that somehow it was wrong to like everything as it was, just plain. So she didn't dare tell them what she really liked.

What she liked was what they were doing now: sitting on top of their snow fort, watching people go by on the street – slipping and sliding, it was so funny – smelling the snow and sucking silently on the long icicles that hung from the maple trees and that tasted so sweet. Killer sat and sucked and felt happy to be with the others, happy about not having to do fractions, happy about the graham crackers and marshmallow they would be eating at four when Pretend was over.

Peachey, in a burst of Peachey energy, put snow down the back of her neck. Killer was soaked through anyway. They all were. But they hardly noticed, they were so warm with activity.

'Now this is the game,' Cissy announced, 'and you have to remember it. We've decided, so no changing the rules. Me and Celeste and Peachey are sisters and we're of noble birth. Our *real* mother dies and our father the Duke marries this woman Elvira, who pretends to be nice but who isn't – who's evil really. That's you Killer. You have to *seem* nice at first, remember that otherwise you'll spoil everything. Then we find out that Elvira has killed our *real* mother and is plotting to kill our father and steal our inheritance and make us homeless orphans. Then – this is Celeste's part, she invented it, she says I have to say so – a prince saves us! He catches Elvira making a cowardly escape. Then he marries Celeste and introduces me and Peachey to his two brothers who are Paul Newman and Steve McQueen. Elvira goes to prison. Do you hear that, Killer? Are you listening? You're going to be shut up in the snow fort – don't interrupt me, you *have* to be. Do you want to spoil the game for everyone else? That *would* be something you'd do. Anyway, my word is law, so you're going to prison. We'll come back for you after we've been to the palace to recover our gold and attend the banquet.'

'But – what about my graham crackers?' Killer knew she mustn't cry.

'You can have them later – if you do everything you're supposed to.'

'OK.'

Now they were carrying out the dolls to be the Duke's

courtiers. Dolls and dolls − Celeste's dolls. Peachey's dolls, vacationing at Celeste's to visit their friends and relations. Killer didn't really like dolls, not even Dorothy, the most beautiful, with her long brown hair and bridal gown. She played with them, but they were not her friends. She preferred real things like babies and kittens and beach balls and toads and desserts.

Under Cissy's direction the Pretend went off perfectly. The arrival of the prince and his brothers was very exciting. With their invisible help, Elvira was tied and gagged and dragged off to prison. To make sure she would never again be free to plot against them, the three sisters and the three brothers placed pieces of cardboard (they had not told Killer this part) over the front and back entrances of the snow fort. These they covered with packed snow over which they dribbled a little boiling water. It froze almost immediately, making a nice smooth surface. Then they went off to the palace.

Of course they were not going to the palace. They were going to eat graham crackers with marshmallow and watch cartoons. They were going to tell Auntie Lil that Killer had run off to play with some children and didn't want her snack. They would be warm and giggling and eating her graham crackers. Afterwards they might take their sleds to McLin's field and have a snowball fight with the Dewhurst boys or go with them to the housing project and tip over the garbage cans.

Killer was cold and lonely. Her wet snow suit was no longer made warm by the heat of her body. They had tied her so tightly that she could not move. She looked round at her small prison of white. She could see, feel, hear the white, the whiteness of crazy nothing that scared her so much. She longed for Celeste and Cissy and Peachey. She wanted them to come and get her. She would play any game they liked, be any terrible person, she was so lonely here in the white.

They had walled her up with her accomplices in the plot − the three least loved of Celeste's dolls. They were no help. They had bad characters and did not care what became of her. Buster was a villain like she was − always trying to wreck plans, to spoil balls and ceremonies, to kidnap Dorothy. And June. June would do anything to attract men's attention. She was spiteful with short hair and told lies. She was also stupid and got the lowest marks at school. No one would ever marry June. Jackie, the dirty yellow and white rabbit, had been good at first when he arrived four years ago as an Easter Bunny. But he had allowed himself to be corrupted by Buster. Celeste said Jackie was a failure. His many crimes had made him unhappy, but it was too late for him to change his ways. Killer knew that she and Jackie and June and Buster were what Peachey's mother called Lost Souls.

Killer rubbed her tongue over her cold sore. It tasted like metal and tomatoes. She could never let it alone. Tomatoes made her think of last summer: picnics at Lake Acushnet, then fights in the car, after which she would cringe under the glare of Cissy's green eyes; Cissy and Peachey throwing jelly doughnuts at her and her throwing them back – the only time she had ever defended herself; Celeste covering her face with Ipana toothpaste in the middle of the night; Cissy and Celeste frightening her with ghost stories and tales of torture so that she lay quaking in the dark as she was quaking now in the white; Quaker Meetings on the lawn ('Quaker Meeting has begun, no more laughing, no more fun, if you show your teeth or tongue, you will have to pay a forfeit'); the Mermaid game on the beach and Cissy whipping her with one of those long flat strips of seaweed. 'Peachey, you may take one giant step. Killer, you may take one baby step.' Oh the games, the endless games she could not resist. She must always play, never say no, never complain, please them by letting them hate her and be afraid of her. It was such a funny thing. Why was it like that? She couldn't really understand Pretend. And Pretend was so important. Pretend was everything, because without it you were only yourself.

How come Cissy and Celeste could make things up? They could think so fast. If she could think fast too, she almost realized before her thoughts slid back into simply people and things and events, she might not have to be always The Crazy Doctor. Not only could Cissy and Peachey and Celeste think faster and eat faster and run faster; they seemed to need less sleep, less food, less love than she did. They seemed, with the exception of jelly doughnuts, not even to *want* any of those things. Killer longed for them. She longed for them now. But if she tried to get out of the snow fort before supper, they'd be sure to call her a spoilsport and to torment her all night long.

Better stay here a little longer and freeze. They would have to come back for her, because sooner or later they would need her for the games. They would not be able to have any of the good ones without her. She tried to feel very certain that they would come, but her heart was tightening, tightening and sinking. Her crime had been so terrible this time. No one could forgive her. Perhaps not even God could forgive her. She had broken the third commandment. She had killed the Duchess and tried to steal the inheritance. No, there was no chance of God forgiving her. He was going to let her freeze to death with Jackie and June and Buster, the Lost Souls. He would make the others forget her. He would make Auntie Lil and Uncle Raymond forget her, even her own mother and father probably. He *could* make everyone forget her. That kind of thing was easy for him. They probably had forgotten already. Or maybe it wasn't God at all. Maybe *they* wanted her to die, to freeze to death with Buster and June and Jackie. Get rid of the trouble-makers, the wicked ones, all at once. What about Mummy? She was always so kind, but that might be a Pretend too. She might really have been plotting with Cissy and the rest of them all along to wall up her little girl in a snow fort. Killer couldn't help it, she cried.

She cried until she had no more strength to cry. She began to give up, to fall asleep, to float away to a place where there was no more cold, where nothing was white, but all nice greens and reds and blues. Something was carrying her up to the sky, like Ragged Robin in the orange tree – up and up, away from the white. It was Uncle Raymond. He was pulling her out of the snow fort, he was untying her, he was picking her up in his arms, taking her to the house, muttering over her.

'Oh my God, poor Killer.' She could not open her eyes, she was so tired. 'My God, poor little Killer.' She liked Uncle Raymond. He was a nice man.

The hospital where Killer spent the next two weeks was very white. When she first awoke, she was frightened and thought that the snow fort had grown larger and cleaner and more occupied. It was warm in the hospital (she saw quite quickly that it *was* a hospital) and there were lots of people, mainly kind, who leaned over her, gave her things, asked her questions in quiet tones, took things away, moved her about – sometimes hurting her, though not meaning to – and gazed at her for long stretches of time through her plastic tent. Their expressions were of worry, sorrow or silly cheerfulness, if grown-ups, and of questioning uncomfortableness, if children.

Killer hardly spoke. She *could* speak, she knew that, but she did not want to. She looked back through her plastic tent at all those queer expressions. Sometimes she smiled at them a little. Mostly she slept. Slept and dreamt. She dreamed they played the Mermaid game, and that she chased Cissy and Celeste and Peachey for ever along an empty beach.

When she was very much better, they took the plastic tent away and let the children come near her. Cissy's green eyes were still defiant, but she spoke nicely to her sister and called her Charlotte. Killer understood that Cissy and Celeste had had some kind of punishment, but that now everyone was pretending that nothing had ever really happened.

Peachey held her hand and leaned over her. 'Bests,' Peachey whispered. Killer blinked at her. Did she mean it, was she making believe? Killer didn't understand, but smiled to let Peachey know that she was pretending she did.

Celeste even offered her Dorothy to keep for ever and be her very own. Dorothy with her bridal gown and long brown hair.

Killer hesitated. Then she spoke for the first time since the day in the snow fort.

'Can I have June instead?' she asked.

Simple Pleasures

I wonder, was Antonia a wicked woman after all. For a while I referred to her débâcle as a very good joke. I called it 'a supreme irony', and described it with triter phrases. But the truth is that I was pretending. The truth is that I miss her terribly, for ours was a singular love. No, no, Antonia was innocent, I'm sure of it, and wholly good. After all, who knew her better than I?

She converted me. She taught me the simple pleasures. Before her I looked for them loud and big, strong and scarlet. Silly of me.

The third time I met her, I remember thinking I'd boast to her, shock her, she was so absurdly green. I told her about amphetamine sulphate and five in a bed. She looked at me blankly, then kindly. I felt a fool, and I was a fool. We dropped the subject and went into the garden where she showed me some pale green, lemon-scented irises and mentioned a man she had been in love with for a long time. She was mad for irises.

'Think how magnificent they must have been growing wild on the plains of Afghanistan and the mountains of Persia. Simply oceans of them, I've read. So obliging to have let themselves be tamed like this.'

I had met her two years before. A lover of mine, someone much younger than I, who worked for her husband, took me to their big house in Richmond. We did not expect anyone to be at home. We expected to be alone, to steal the Armagnac and use the water bed. But she was there when we opened the door, come back suddenly from a holiday gone wrong, standing in the middle of the kitchen, smiling, with tears in her eyes. I thought I had never seen anyone so still. She made no gestures. She spoke, blinked and occasionally smiled. Her name was Antonia Terrant.

We liked each other straight away. That did not prevent me, however, from having an affair with her husband. Not much ever could prevent me having affairs, although I have given them up now because they are so time-consuming, and I must work to perfect my art.

The romance itself was insignificant, except that it provided an occasion for my meeting Antonia again. She claimed she was not upset by it. She despised Eric, and I was just one of his many amours. He was never important to me. I liked his erratic dominance, his brain, I suppose, and his unpredictability. But in the end, it was the idea of an affair with him — he was a little bit famous — that I really liked. I never loved him, certainly not. When he stopped calling I was unhappy for two, maybe three, days. Then I was invited to Paris and forgot all about him.

Antonia surprised us once by returning to the Richmond house, a few weeks after their separation, to ask him to do her a favour. She and the children had moved out by then, and Eric and I were in the midst of an intimate supper. I could not turn around, but sat stiffly in my chair as she stood behind me, talking to him, without emotion, over the top of my head.

'I have to insure the Renault. Would you mind filling in the forms for me?' She showed no agitation. Her pain, if it existed, was driven inwards while her exterior maintained its eternal quiet.

'You'll have to learn to do these things yourself now. Yes, all right, give them to me.'

His usual intimidation ensued, pitched at a low key, but none the less minatory. Eric was wielding a prime weapon from his very complete arsenal: Antonia was an innocent, unfit for life in the real world. Her helplessness exposed her to constant danger and duplicity; she was selfishly putting their children at risk. He was fraught with anxiety at his family's perilous position. Obviously, she could not cope without him. Here she was again, having to rely upon him for the simplest things. What if anything catastrophic should occur, and she and the children so vulnerable in that big house in the wilds of Fulham. Either she ought to be properly protected or come back to him. Had she seen the man from Banham's yet? No, of course not. Well, QED.

What hypocritical crud, I thought. But she made no attempt to defend herself.

As she was leaving, she touched me on the shoulder.

'You must come and see me, Daisy. I've bought a house on Ellerby Street.'

Still unable to look at her, I mumbled that I would when I could.

A year later, I went to see her. She was having her flute lesson, but asked me to wait until her tutor, a student from the RCM, had left.

'Didn't you tell me once that you played the piano?' She poured the tea and put the pot, in its cosy, back among the assortment of jams. I've never known her eat much besides nursery food.

'Ages ago.'

'Why don't you begin again? We could play duets.'

'I'm afraid my piano is in storage, and Pickford's are charging me thirty pounds a month.'

I had lived in four different places that year. It was one of my transient phases. Just then I was renting a second-floor room in the house of a pretentious and mediocre girl in Chelsea. I had never got round to decorating the place, and my belongings were stacked and strewn everywhere. I did have linen, though, and managed to keep in good order the bed I almost never slept in.

'But you can use mine. Come and practise here until yours can be liberated. Please do. It would be so good for you, and for me. And now I must go.'

She stood up and rested her fingertips on the table. She had a way of lengthening out the corners of her mouth as if she were about to smile, but the smile only hovered, and was seldom completed. Though five years older than I, she was pretty in a wistful childish way. I said I thought she must be fond of Mozart.

'Oh yes, but I like Pergolesi best, probably. I *must* go – my pottery class, you know.' She hesitated. 'Come and look at the garden.' It was then she showed me the irises and mentioned Fleming.

'Why don't you stay? The children won't be back for a while, and you can have a go at the piano with no one to make you feel self-conscious. The music's in the bench.'

I stayed and stumbled through a Chopin Mazurka, and though frustrated at the way my playing had deteriorated, I felt buoyant in a little girl way. I remembered the sensation of flying when I played Debussy, and how secure and stable the world seemed when I attempted Bach.

Antonia's children returned and made me too uncomfortable to go on. I was unused to children. They had never been part of my life. I loved love and friendship and the thorny joys of a free existence, and scorned family ties. How mediocre of her, I thought, to have wasted her best energies on physical immortality. (She had given birth to three of them by the age of twenty-two. I, careless with sex as with everything else, had had three abortions.) Such middle-class cosiness seemed to me a life without challenge, and I still think, in a way, that it is, although her influence has modified my opinions.

I came back. Gradually I grew used to the children and began to require the consolation of her presence. Let me explain. I had been lucky in a superficial and ultimately destructive way: small windfalls, doting relatives, temporary jobs with wealthy people who were attracted to me until they discovered how unreliable I was. I had been too well brought up not to be interested in dissipation, and for several years had pursued it back and forth across the continent, doing frivolous things with frivolous people. This tame, clean person who went to pottery classes and did Tai Chi was unlike anyone I had known since primary school. I was intrigued by the way she strove to better herself when she already seemed too good to be true. Tea times with her were restful after the tumult of my nights before. Besides, I had very little money (there had been no windfalls that year) and at Antonia's house dinner was on the table promptly at eight o'clock.

She didn't smoke. She had taken neither drugs nor a job, and lived simply but graciously in the old fashioned way: on family money. That, for an American like myself, was also intriguing. Sometimes she would sip a sherry or a little

champagne at the weddings or christenings where her presence was required by rich and jolly relations. That was the
closest she came to what might be considered indulgence.

At six o'clock on a Tuesday she was sipping one of those
rare sherries, looking at me and my neat vodka over the rim of
her glass, her eyes blinking at what seemed half the rate of
other people's. Like a calf or a beautiful fish. But I mustn't
lapse. This is, after all, outwardly directed.

Begin again. My playing had improved to the point where
we felt confident enough to attempt the Poulenc sonata.
(Beyond us, of course, but one must have a challenge.) This
was at my insistence, since her timid taste was committed
almost entirely to the Baroque, and she was frightened by
modern clash and abstraction. We sat at the Bechstein in her
large comfortable living room, the white French doors open
to the garden, all yellow-green light, mixed water and air.
London can be so beautiful.

'Let's try it again from bar thirty-two.' I always pushed her.
'Not quite so bloody allegro this time. And you're *still* playing
that semi-quaver as E natural.'

'Not now, I'm tired.' Antonia put down her sherry.
'Fleming came at two this morning and we talked until five.
It's left me feeling all confused. You know what I'm like if I'm
not in bed by eleven. Pathetic, isn't it?'

'Come on then. We'll play it out.'

'No Daisy, really. I'm sorry. Today I'm dark and tangled
inside.'

It was useless. She had gone limp. 'He's the one you told me
about, isn't he – or is he? Who *is* Fleming, anyway?'

'The godfather of my child, the husband of my best friend,'
she sighed, 'my only love.'

'Oh.'

This was the first time she had wanted to confess. I kept
silent and let her continue.

'Not that Rowan is my best friend any more.' (My little
spasm of jealousy was calmed.) 'She's been horrid, really, to
him and to me, and I find it hard to forgive her.'

'Was she the dark bony one we met at Peter Jones last
month?'

'Yes.'

'She's a cunt.'

'I know. That's what Fleming likes. Someone impossible. He's frightened of nice women.'

'Is he nasty too?'

'He's the most charming man I've ever met. He's intelligent and boyish and quite fair. Most people consider him entertaining.'

'And you adore him.' I found it hard to understand why all this hadn't been aired before.

'We've been lovers for years – off and on.'

'You mean when he was with that gargoyle and you were married to Eric?'

'Oh for ages. It started just after Carrie was born.' She paused. 'I can't tell you how terrifying it is.'

'Why?'

'What we feel is so strong. It scares us both to death.' She gave me one of her uncompleted smiles. 'So he runs away.'

'*He* runs away.'

'Well where would *I* go?'

'True enough, my dear. Except anywhere you wanted.'

'I want to be with him.'

'Then *qu'est que c'est, le problème?*'

'That we're scared to death.'

I threw up my hands. 'It's too silly, Antonia. Go grab him and force him to behave.'

'You make everything sound so dashing and simple, Daisy. You're rather, well, sweeping, wouldn't you say?'

'You mean I scare you to death too?'

'Sometimes.'

'What a blossom! You are wonderful.'

I really was very free then. A messy blonde, I lived in a shambles and cared for nothing but fun and art and travel. I did what I wanted and took the consequences, and thought anyone who didn't follow their own true will (I had read rather too much Crowley) was a fool. That's how I was – a simple, brazen girl.

I suddenly realize I have been describing myself too much. This is Antonia's story, after all. I promise not to describe myself any more.

By the following week we were playing with enough

confidence to go on to the second movement. At least I kept saying we were, and she believed me. One afternoon, she caught my enthusiasm and made an announcement.

'You know I sing.'

'Really? Are you feeling brave, then?'

'Quite brave.' She actually laughed.

'Well, well ... ' I stood up and opened the music bench where there was a tattered book of Italian songs.

'The Pergolesi,' she said. 'I think it's number eighteen.'

She composed herself as I flipped through the pages.

'I shall probably squeak. It's been a while.'

She stood next to me, her fingers intertwined. On top of the shiny black Bechstein, a bowl of blue irises vibrated slightly with the music.

'*Si tu m'ami* ... ' She sang a frail soprano, high and thin like those wispy clouds that accompany fair weather.

'That was sweet,' I exclaimed. 'That was lovely. Shall we try it again?'

'No. Yes. You're quite right to bully me. All right, once more for luck.'

Antonia quavered, faltered, giggled and somehow got through to the end. It is impossible to describe the special rapport that grows out of such mutual exertions.

'You're in good spirits today.'

'Fleming loves me.'

'How could he not?'

'It's settled now.' She moved to the table where the tea things were waiting for us. We sat down for our break. 'Or at least I've settled it in my mind.'

'And?'

'It's simply a matter of waiting.'

'For what?'

'For the children to grow up or go off to school, for our responsibilities to be over, for us not to have to be in London.'

'He has his children with him?'

'Two of them. There are four, you know. He has to look after them and keep his job. And Rowan spends so much money. So, in about four years, I think, we can be together.'

'And you intend to be true?' I was flabbergasted.

'More patient than true.'

I thought her mad. *I* waited for no one and nothing. But something in her resignation made me feel alternately like laughing and crying.

'Then we'll have a cottage in Devon and the children can come and visit us. We'll have a simple, beautiful life. Oh, here are the books you lent me.' She handed me Djuna Barnes and a biography of Shelley. 'I found *Nightwood* a little depressing.'

A few days later came one of my windfalls: an invitation to a week in Rome. There, in the company of an art historian friend, who had been given an inordinate sum of money by an American museum to write a book which he had so far spun out into three years of research, I consumed a quantity of indifferent cocaine, attended a party with 250 homosexuals, and squandered my small allowance in the Piazza Navona. I thought of Antonia only once. Her relationship with the mythical Fleming was beginning to bore me. But after a week with the art historian, I felt dried up and was happy to return to the oasis of her personality. I gave a detailed account of my experiences and offered her the remains of my smuggled cocaine, which she politely refused.

'You have such peculiar friends, Daisy.'

'And you', I almost said, 'have such dull ones.'

We took up our afternoon musicals again. If either of us were feeling blue, we would encourage the other to 'play it out'. Mainly I goaded her, demanding she continue when she had convinced herself that she was too muddled to go on.

'E natural! E natural!' I would hammer the note.

'It's the three against four. I get muddled.'

'Then I'll count it for you. Anyway counting doesn't help. You have to *feel* it.'

'Oh dear, I don't think I can. We'd better stop.'

'Rubbish! You can, you can. Don't you dare put down that flute. There! That's it, see?'

The sessions usually ended in hysteria. Carried along by a single momentum, we would be running a high parallel course through Corelli, Haydn or Handel, when suddenly I would scream or she would choke. After some brilliant passage which seemed far too proficient to have been played by us, we would stop, amazed by our accomplishment. Breathless, our fingers in a paralytic tangle, we would collapse in a fit of giggles. Then came tea, or a walk in the park, and more of our intimate chatter. (Too precious, too rarified. Completely unreal. That's what anyone would think, I know. But I swear that's how it was.)

'I thought we were rather good today.'

'Good! My dear, we were superb. Where's the brandy?'

'Are you glad we started playing together?'

'It's the only stabilizing factor in my existence. It's so sweet, so mellow.' I poured myself a drink. 'Jane Austen, somehow?'

'"You've delighted us long enough, my dear,"' we quoted in unison and laughed at our simultaneous recollection of Mr Bennet.

'Well, at least we don't inflict it on anyone else,' I said. 'All those chirping and tinkling young ladies putting their fathers and swains to sleep. Reading about them used to amuse me, but now I've come to understand the addiction.'

'It's a part of female friendship that's been lost,' Antonia observed. 'And it's sad. No one knows how to entertain themselves any more. They watch bloodshed on the telly, go to Sensurround films. They seem to need such enormous, but always vicarious, thrills. Why do you think it is?' She actually put questions like that. She was for ever asking things I would have been too proud to ask.

'It's called decadence,' I answered glibly, 'and it has its charms. But you're right. People have become big jaded babies.'

'It took me so long to discover the simple pleasures. My mother's friends were all performers or composers. She entertained the great, I suppose. We would go to the theatre or the opera or the concert hall and watch them do their magnificent thing. None of us would have dreamed of attempting a poor little performance of our own under such intimidating circumstances. Oh, we were taught to play or sing or dance or whatever, but also to keep our place, especially children like me who showed no particular talent. It's wonderful to be free of all that, to be, well, middle class, I suppose, and pursue music or anything else for its own sake, with no ambition and no reward.'

'And no criticism.'

'Because it's not professional. Like growing irises, shaping clay, reading, going for walks. One does it to keep one steady and good. As a civilizing influence. To make life beautiful.'

'But life is also upset and corruption.'

'Not here.'

'I've brought a bit of it into your comfy living room.'

'Oh that's different. That's yours.'

'Then you don't mind *my* corruption.'

She half-smiled and patted my hand. 'You'll get over it. Here, I found that volume of Rilke you wanted.'

I was extremely poor that winter, and she offered me £500.

'Antonia, darling, what can I say?'

'Say yes.' She held out the cheque. 'Now I must rush off to meet Fleming. We've just half an hour to have tea before he collects his children and I go to my Tai Chi class.'

She put on her mac and went out into the foul night. I watched telly with Carrie, finished the leftovers in the fridge and hurried to keep an assignation with an actor who, I felt certain, was about to become my new lover. Of course I squandered the £500 and was forced to sell one of my bracelets. All the same, things weren't too desperate, as I was carefully maintaining a Platonic relationship with a drug dealer.

Antonia finally introduced me to Fleming. Oh, he was charming all right, both ingratiating and detached, but a four-year wait? He worked for a literary agency, was tall, fair, and very, very, slippery. She could never hold him. He talked to me about art and to her about Tai Chi and the children. After an hour, he brushed her forehead with a kiss and dashed off, saying he would return at ten.

The next day I found her limp and red-eyed, unable to take up her flute.

'He wants to be a monk,' she said, staring straight in front of her.

'Rubbish.' I went looking for the vodka.

'No, really. He says he loves me too much to live with me and feels he must go to a monastery in Nepal.'

'In his Cerutti suit?' Fleming feigned a careless elegance.

'But I understand,' she pleaded his case. 'You see there are two distinct and warring elements in his nature – '

'Oh he's just an old fart in a fit of phoniness. Why don't you forget it and come dancing with me?'

I forced some vodka on her, lent her a pair of red high heels that she could not quite manage, and took her to Dingwall's, where she sniffed her first cocaine in the Ladies. I must give her credit, she tried. She downed two more vodkas and did not resist when a young lout seized her by the arm and pushed her on to the dance floor, his pelvis locked into hers like two freight cars.

'It was wonderful,' she gasped as, three hours later, I helped her up the stairs to her bathroom and held her head while she vomited into the loo.

Bravely, she sampled Tai grass as we listened to *Tristan* and ate peanut butter sandwich after peanut butter sandwich. Each day we played it out, but I could not dispel her melancholy. I resorted to sex and slyly introduced her to an East End friend of mine who was rather terrifically good-looking and took her briskly to bed. Poor Antonia. As I said, it wasn't as though she didn't try.

At the end of March I moved in with her. I took the upstairs room which overlooked the garden, shifting to it my books, records and clothes, most of which had remained unpacked for the last six months. The room on Rumbelow Road where I scarcely had lived anyway, was vacated, and I took up life with Antonia in earnest. Our friendship moved that much closer to perfection.

Fleming passed through his Buddhist phase (a transit, I discovered, which he made regularly like some asteroid), and began to join us once in a while for dinner, occasionally even spending the night. Antonia bloomed, dreaming, I suppose, of the house in Devon and their South Coast Nirvana, which was now a little less than three years and five months away. We played duets every afternoon, or I played and she sang. I paid no rent and kept up my anarchistic life-style.

When did we have that conversation? (Time has become so blurred lately, I often have trouble − but, of course, that is what happens when one lives only to perfect one's art.) That conversation with Fleming seemed to summarize all our characters so well. I thought so, even at the time. Africa, right. We were drinking brandy and talking about Africa as seen through the eyes of Jung, van der Post, Isak Dinesen, etc. Fleming was drinking as much as I, though not with quite the same Dionysiac gusto. We began to plan an imaginary journey.

'Living in the bush.'

Antonia's eyes grew like big brown moons as we jokingly and inconsistently developed the fantasy.

'Huge jungle flowers,' she breathed.

'Trekking across the veld behind a seven-foot Zulu.'

'Nights under the stars, campfires, terrifying noises.'

'Inscrutably wise native guides.'

'Danger.'

'A tree house,' Fleming put in.

'Oh what a good idea,' we exclaimed together.

'The solution to all our problems.'

'Safe from the beasts but still near them.'

'How wonderful!'

'But how would you build it?'

Fleming gave an elaborate and highly detailed account of its proposed construction. He was very imaginative.

'Then what would you do?' Antonia asked. 'When it was finished, I mean.'

He didn't hesitate. 'I'd have brought in by bearers the complete works of Enid Blyton, get them up to the tree house by an ingenious arrangement of ropes and pulleys, by which contraption I should also assure myself a continuous supply of cassis sorbet and Coca-Cola, and read straight through them in perfect contentment.'

'Oh Fleming,' Antonia was truly shocked. 'But what about Africa?'

'Yes,' I joined in. 'What about going naked?'

'Stalking game?'

'Eating raw flesh – well, nearly raw?'

'Fucking. What about *fucking*?'

It was my turn to be a little shocked. I had never heard her use the word.

Fleming chuckled and crossed his legs, leaning his blond head on the back of the most comfortable chair in the room. 'I'll leave all that to you primal ladies. I was going purely for the well-earned rest.'

He was teasing, but disappointment was plain in Antonia's face. Was this the man whose passion scared her to death?

Two weeks later he went back to his wife.

'But she's a horrid bitch,' I exclaimed. And she was.

Antonia replied with one of her half smiles. 'Perhaps he just needs some punishment,' she said and explained to me the gruesome particulars of his maternal relationship. There seemed so many good reasons to forgive him. He soon left Rowan, as Antonia had predicted he would, but did no more than call to announce that he was back in his own flat and that they might resume their furtive tea times once a week. Plainly, she was becoming frustrated to the point of acute neurosis. So I was not surprised when she announced between the fourth and fifth variations of *La Follia*, 'I'd like to meet some black people. I don't mean I want to take them home with me or go to bed with them or anything like that. I'd just like to, well, dance with them, if you know what I mean. Don't you think that would be lovely?'

(Remember? I said she made statements like that.)

'You told me once, Daisy, about a certain discotheque – '

Naturally I took her. The mammoth Formica dive was not really my style, but anything, I thought, anything to aid the liberation. If she felt bumping bottoms with West Indians would help . . .

At the entrance, though, she balked. The noise, the lighting, the smell of sweat and spilt beer were too much for her.

'Trouble?' I took her arm.

'Oh dear,' she was trembling slightly. 'Silly of me. Pathetic. But I think I need a little fortification.' She turned on me that calf gaze and I burst out laughing.

'Well, well,' I said and steered her towards the Ladies. The room was full of the laughter and smoke of black girls, all in satin trousers, cinch belts, lurex tube tops and rolled-down day-glo socks. I pushed Antonia into a cubicle and passed her a packet of cocaine and a fiver under the partition. Next door I could hear her ladylike sniffs and snivels, interrupted by suppressed coughs and choking sounds. She could never learn to do it properly, and I was irked at the thought of the little white clouds I was sure were being wasted all over the walls, floor, and loo. She passed the packet back to me, and I hoovered up the remains. When we met outside, I impatiently brushed away the two pale half moons still clinging to the down beneath her nostrils.

'Darling,' I chided her under my breath, 'don't you realize that if you walk about with that on your upper lip, *everybody* will want some? It will be an awful nuisance. Now come along.'

Again, I must say that her efforts at decadence were admirable, noble even. Methodically, she sampled each of the various ways in which she might abandon herself. We bebopped with a few builders and delivery boys, and even struck up an acquaintance with some black lesbians who eyed continually Antonia's childish and pretty person. But nothing seemed to work as well as Vivaldi, and we came home that night exhausted, edgy, and unfulfilled.

'They're lovely,' she sighed and slumped into an armchair, 'so lovely. But I simply can't keep up with them. You look tired, Daisy. Shall I make some Horlicks?'

Soon Fleming was back in her life, declaring that, though she scared him to death, he did, after all, probably adore her and almost eternally would. He spent two or three nights a week with her and, just once, an entire weekend. She seemed as happy as she deserved to be.

Musically we were reaching a kind of apogee, both of us seeming to feel and to give all that was best in ourselves. Yes, yes, I know it sounds corny. All so precious and *raffiné*. But it is true.

I have heard it said that playing music together is like sex, but that is a crude generalization. The players do not strive for each other nor for their own pleasure merely. They strive for the music itself, for the thing within which they are united, while remaining simultaneously distant from it and each other. The music is their goal, and it both enfolds them and leads them on. Nothing can quite equal the therapeutic effect of this activity. Whenever we finished a session, I felt blossom-light, clarified, the world in perspective, washed clean, its colours no longer muddy, but translucent and true as those in the back garden with its irises and watery light. Then I would soil myself, mix myself up with dinner parties, discos, and drugs. It was all so silly. But it was a way of life I took for granted and could not let go of.

My health had deteriorated. What attractions I possessed as

a messy blonde had been smeared somehow, covered with a film, their piquancy drained off by people I didn't like and night after night of – but I promised not to describe myself. Let me just say that I was saved, as was my wont, by the generosity of a friend, a good-natured homosexual, worn out by his recent lover and with money to spare, who invited me on a three-week tour of French châteaux. Of course I said yes, but was surprised at how sad I was to say goodbye to Antonia. Like the wrench a mother must feel when forced to separate, however briefly, from her child. But what do I know?

My friend and I had a wonderful holiday, dining in four-star restaurants and drinking Loire wines, free, happy and not encumbered by love. I sent Antonia postcards of Chambon and Chenonceaux and bought her wine and truffles with my friend's money. But I heard nothing from her. We were moving too fast, and she was a painfully slow writer. For her, all self-expression, save music, came only with difficulty.

Sated with scenery and cloyed with cream sauces, I arrived back in London at the end of August. It was after two a.m. on a warm, damp night when I turned the key in the lock and tiptoed into the dark hall.

'Fleming?' I heard Antonia's voice, frail and uncertain, as on one of her bad days with Pergolesi.

'No, it's me, Daisy,' I called, not too loudly, since I didn't know whether the children were at home or on holiday.

She stood at the top of the stairs, the lamp from her bedroom shining out into the hall and providing a mild backlighting that lit up her rumpled hair like a halo.

'Oh gosh I'm pleased to see you,' she hugged me harder than she had ever done. 'I've missed our playing so much.'

I could see that there were tears in her eyes and, sensing immediately what the trouble was, I suppressed an urge to gush out the hedonistic particulars of my holiday.

'Fleming?'

She sank on to the bed. 'He's definitely entering a monastery.'

'Oh balls!' I threw down my bags and began a compensatory annihilation of his character, a service one woman is always obliged to render another who feels devalued by the loss of her man.

'He's a spineless creep, and don't try to blame it on his mother.'

'But he's the only man I've ever loved,' she moaned.

I was a little exasperated. 'You should have been nastier. You should have been cuntier. All this subservience, this waiting, this sacrifice – four years, my ass!'

'Three years and four months.'

'No less horrible. Your being so goddam nice has only encouraged him to do his worst. As though he had to be naughty for both of you.' I was pleased with that. It seemed to me a real piece of insight. Thus encouraged, I'm afraid I got rather carried away. 'Give them what they want, I always say. Guaranteed to make them regret everything. And remember what Scott Fitzgerald said: the only sure way a woman can hold a man is to bring out the worst in him.' I knew that wasn't quite consistent. But it sounded wonderful, at least to me.

Antonia dissolved. 'Oh Daisy, I wish I could be as cynical as you are.'

Cynical? But I was a Romantic.

Her resignation defeated me. So I tried the only thing I knew to save her: simple pleasures. We played every afternoon, sometimes mornings as well (the Third Fitzwilliam sonata), walked in the park, weeded the garden, drank endless cups of tea. The roses were in their second bloom, and we sat outside in wicker chairs and read and sniffed the delicate fragrance and soaked in the warm September light. I devoted myself entirely to the restoration of her confidence. As a result, I was becoming a homebody. But the alteration in my life-style was gradual, and I was aware of the change only later, when left alone with no dinner parties and no unlovable but distracting people.

September passed quietly and, for the most part, prudently. At the end of the month, however, I received an invitation from an old acquaintance, someone from the amphetamine sulphate days, now fast becoming history. She was an heiress, impatient to squander another lump of her fortune on an extravagant party. Hundreds of people would be there.

'Should be a screech,' I perused the invitation over breakfast. (I got up early now and actually ate in the morning.) 'Why don't you come with me?'

She hesitated, looking momentarily frightened. 'All right.' She half smiled and blinked.

I forced her to tart herself up. She alternately giggled and protested, but on the whole, seemed to enjoy the masquerade. We were going somewhere – and we were getting somewhere.

Our hostess had outdone herself. A pink and white striped marquee occupied half of the huge Kensington garden. The place was lit by lanterns, and waiters carried about trays of champagne, reefers and immaculately laid out lines of cocaine. It was quite magnificent and generous in a way that English parties seldom are. In the old days, not certain as to the arrival or location of my next meal, I would have made straight for the sumptuous buffet and stuffed myself. Now, with Antonia paying the grocery bills, I could turn up my nose at the goodies and concentrate on my friends, nearly all of whom were present. I was pleased to see them, but could feel myself being pulled once more towards the downward spiral of their lax existence.

Antonia was quiet, smiling, having a good time, I assumed, though not drifting far from my side. She looked whimsical and lovely, was much stared at but seldom approached. I realized she was talking to someone, but paid little attention, taken up as I was by the fatuous conversation and feeling quite elated from the champagne and coke. She spoke in her normal, quiet voice and so, above the din, I could hear little of what she was saying. When I turned round at last, I saw her standing next to a slender man with blond hair and a quizzical expression – Fleming! And on his right arm the tallest black woman I have ever seen.

'Oh Daisy, this is Lorraine,' Antonia smiled, still to the point of paralysis. 'Fleming, of course, you know.'

I shook hands with the statuesque creature. She was easily six feet tall, and wore a red sequinned dress. I later found out that she was a member of the chorus line in *Ipi Tombi*.

'Lorraine used to work for Fleming before she went to the West End.'

(Oh Antonia, will you never remove that sweet half smile? Has it been frozen to your face for ever? You don't move, you don't flinch. How can you bear this?)

Mercifully, they were leaving. As they walked towards the exit, I watched the slow swinging movements of Lorraine's big body. She was a good inch taller than Fleming and, I was willing to bet, twice as fit.

'Charming couple,' I said, but Antonia did not respond to irony of either a high or low grade. She looked somewhat shaken, but nothing like what I knew she must feel. I wanted to kill him.

'Shall we go? We can you know. I don't mind.' I had never been so solicitous towards anyone in my life.

'Oh no, it's all right. Really, Daisy.' She paused. 'She's lovely, isn't she?'

I could neither believe nor endure the composure.

'For Christ's sake have a drink at least,' I pushed a glass of champagne into her hand. I knew she already had formulated a dozen excuses for Fleming's betrayal, and might even be forcing herself to feel glad at his acquisition of such an exotic paramour. Better Lorraine than the saffron robe – that was the way her mind was working, I felt sure.

We left early. In the taxi I encouraged her to let out her emotions, but she refused to do other than assure me that really everything was all right, she had quite come to terms with the whole episode, et cetera. So I let it go, hoping against hope that the encounter might produce a positive effect and end this sick relationship once and for all.

The topic of Lorraine and Fleming sank. I left Antonia alone for two or three nights, my social life having undergone a renaissance as a result of the party. In the afternoons we worked on a Vivaldi sonata. She appeared cheerful enough, certainly not pining. Or so I supposed.

I found her at breakfast one morning, engrossed in a Kelway's catalogue which had just arrived in the post. She was selecting varieties of hybrid irises, circling names with a felt-tipped pen.

'What do you think, Daisy? Blue Smoke or Lothario? I'm definitely having the new plicata. I thought perhaps Magic Hills, this year, to go alongside my Topolino. Let me show you the new dwarf. Oh, by the way, I'll be going off earlier than usual this afternoon.'

'Tai Chi class?'

'No. Tea with Fleming. We're meeting at his office and rushing out. We'll only have about twenty minutes.'

I was thunderstruck. 'Good God, Antonia!'

She put a finger to my lips. 'There, there, Daisy. You didn't think we'd stop being friends, did you? The relationship is much too deep to – but let's not discuss it. I'm sure you're bored to death with the whole thing by now.'

'But what about the house in Devon? What about three years and three months to go?'

She shrugged – the first remotely cynical gesture I had seen her make.

'Do you think you could wait here until I return so the children won't come home to an empty house? I won't be much later than seven. Oh, and perhaps you could post this order form to Kelway's. I won't have time to get to the Post Office today.'

I moodily replied that I would be glad to do both.

She smiled and kissed me. 'You're a good girl, aren't you, Daisy?'

I heard the particulars of the shooting from Fleming's secretary. When the phone rang at nine that evening and I was told what had happened, I left the children with the next-door neighbour and took a taxi to Marylebone police station. *Where*, I kept asking myself, *did she get the gun*?

They would not let me see her. She was locked in a cell with her ex-husband, her lawyer, and a couple of doctors. It would be some time. So I sat and waited with the middle-aged woman who was being detained as a witness. She had seen it all and, though still suffering from the after-effects of hysteria, was more than willing to discuss the shocking incident with whoever was at hand.

She said she had recognized Antonia from her previous visits to the office, and was delighted, as usual, to see that sweet face again. ('She always looked so frail, don't you know, as if the least little gust of wind might blow her away.') I could imagine her walking into the office without a trace of agitation. 'Yes, that was how she was,' the secretary affirmed, 'still, really still, just as you say.' The woman had been seated only a few feet away from Fleming's cubicle, and so, Antonia not having bothered to close the door, had overheard most of the brief conversation. She could see, through the ribbed glass of the partition, Antonia's blurred form, her hands in the pockets of her coat, standing before Fleming who was still at his desk. It was all very subdued. No voices were raised. Some of what they said she could not now recall, but the end bit, yes, that remained in her mind 'clear as a bell', and would do, she had no doubt, until the day she died.

'What would you say if I told you I was going to kill you?' Antonia had asked.

'I'd say please don't be silly, Tony. Think what an incon-venience it would be and how embarrassed you'd feel by all the fuss afterwards. You'd loathe the attention and only be guilt-ridden for putting everyone to so much trouble. I'd tell you it was absurd because you're just too good.'

'If I hadn't been *good* I could have had you.' There may have been a catch in her voice.

'Oh,' he kept up his light tone, 'but your goodness is terrible.'

'So it is.'

Antonia took the gun from the large pocket of her coat and shot him. She fired all six bullets, three of them lodging in the pale green wall behind his chair, one hitting him in the lung, another grazing his skull, and the last tearing open a hole in his throat slightly to the left of his Adam's apple. She must, I thought, have been aiming for the head. No poetic gestures like putting one straight through the heart of stone, or, as it would have to be in his case, papier mâché.

The secretary was unclear as to what followed, except that, in the midst of the pandemonium, Antonia simply stood there, the gun still in her hand, offering no excuses or protest-ations, showing no emotion, attempting no escape. She simply stood there, passive as usual, not a bit of trouble to anyone. When the police arrived, she quietly let them lead her away, begging the pardon of the horrified secretary as she was forced to squeeze past her in the crowd.

Rowan was at the hospital with Fleming. His chances of survival were slim. He never regained consciousness, and at five twenty-five that morning he died.

About the gun. It had been in the house all the time, since she had first moved in. I had never known. Who would have thought Antonia would keep such a thing? The source, naturally, was Eric's fanatic paternalism. He had always kept one and insisted she do likewise, in case of burglars, for the good of their children, all his usual rubbish. She was never strong or energetic enough to argue with him, and, I suppose, like the good girl she was, she did as she was told, allowing him to stuff it away in some drawer and then forgetting about it – I am convinced of this – until the morning when she decided to put it to use at last.

I deliberately have avoided describing my own responses to this affair. It is, after all, Antonia's story and is meant to be outwardly directed. I will not coat it with speculations nor mar its classic beauty with subjective considerations. I shall finish it quickly, appending only a note on my current circumstances, for the sake of veracity and so that all may know the effects on me of her exquisite influence.

She remains in hospital, bulwarked by husband, children, relatives and doctors, a great furore having been made about her arraignment, or possible arraignment, and trial. To this date, there have been so many postponements and legal complications that it seems unlikely she will ever stand before a court of law. Nor that she will ever be released from the hospital. She remains quiet. She reads. She makes no resistance. I do not think they are giving her many drugs. But she daily runs a gauntlet of psychiatrists and, I am told, will continue to do so for some time. Believe it or not, Rowan has seen her, and on several occasions. (The woman always struck me as having an appetite for this sort of thing.) I have not seen her. Eric, now completely in charge, has prevented any meeting, and I have heard that he considers me an evil influence.

He has taken the children back to Richmond but, strangely enough, has allowed me to stay on in the house, probably as watchdog, until arrangements about its sale have been completed. But, like Antonia's arraignment, the proceedings have met with constant delays and complications.

So I have remained. I try to keep up the garden, especially the irises, and to tend it as she would have done. And I practise. Oh, how I practise – six, sometimes seven hours a day, alone now in the big living room with Antonia's flute still on top of the piano, and that is sad. Of course, I shall never be great, never do anything important, never give a concert, or appear in public. But all that, as she taught me, is an illusion. What I do, I do for its own sake, to make life beautiful, and as a civilizing influence on this terrible world. I have a part-time job, which helps to pay for my lessons and for my simple needs. I do not drink or take cocaine. I have attended no dinner parties, made no trips to the continent. No one calls me. I have discouraged familiarities of any sort. Oh yes, I attend evening classes. You see that I am working in every way to improve myself. But for this I need quiet and freedom from distraction. Soon the house will be sold, and I must face the possibility of a harsher existence. My own piano will have to be got out of storage. How I shall pay the bill, I do not know. Until then, I intend to continue on this day to day basis, improving myself, perfecting my art, hoping that Eric will let me see Antonia. Perhaps one day I shall have a lover again or even find someone to play duets with. Of course that may not be for a long time. No matter. I can wait.

Death in Sussex

The monthly meeting of the Grindley Garden Club had adjourned, and the President, Secretary and Treasurer were sipping their usual sherries.

'Why is it we never take as much care of our death as we do our life?' The Secretary's *non sequitur* brought conversation to a stop.

'It's always puzzled me,' Harriet continued bravely. 'I mean, you wouldn't dream, would you Jean, of not sending the children to a good school. You wouldn't ever serve your family TV dinners, and you *certainly* wouldn't not tend the garden. You wouldn't dream of not having your hair done once a week or not doing yoga to keep your breasts from sagging. You'd never go without novels or *The Times* or day returns to London, would you?'

Why didn't they reply? Probably sensed she was getting on to something unpleasant. What *had* she been doing for the past five years with these cows?

'Of course not,' Harriet answered for them, determined to go on. 'You make life nice and protect it from every horror and deformity. But what have you done for your death? Nothing, I'll wager – just left the whole thing to some grotesque natural cause.'

Fiona and Jean stared at the dried floral arrangement that crowned the television. This was not an idea they felt comfortable with.

For Harriet, looking after one's death was more than an idea. It was the truth, blatantly obvious and universally ignored; brutal reality, all there was in life.

'I'll drive you home, my love,' Fiona made the customary offer.

Silently Harriet watched the downs, the flats, the sheep, Alfriston church, the Long Man rising up on the right. She had watched them for years, until she almost no longer saw them; watched them on the way to Sunday outings at the Seven Sisters, on the way to be married, to Garden Club meetings, Polegate Station and The Sussex Ox; on the way to her mother-in-law's, the hospital, the doctor. She watched them for what was probably the last time.

She knew that her silence distressed Fiona. The living or rather the lively, are always nervous in the company of such determinedly introverted musing. Especially if the musing concerns death.

Like most people, Harriet often had reflected upon the various methods by which one might leave the world gracefully. 'And how would you like to die, Harriet, given the opportunity of directing your own death?' In a field (preferably a Constable field with cattle, steeple and willows); gazing at a broad expanse of sea; in the midst of apoplectic love-making; or in a deck chair to the accompaniment of Mahler's Third or Fauré's Requiem. When she despaired of love, David, or her ability to effect anything whatever, it might, with less grace, be Beachy Head or the rails of the Bakerloo Line. But these were fantasies, temporarily and perversely comforting which, before last week, she had not planned on acting out.

Now that she did have the opportunity of directing her own death, she realized that the scenario and production involved certain practical problems. She was not averse to a few unavoidable indignities, but death must not be botched. Death must be done well, and she was determined to succeed, to succeed at least in death. So she began to plan, really to plan it, to exclude messy chance and to set her own scene. As she sat beside Fiona, watching the landscape she did not see, Harriet was calm. She had made up her mind, or rather what she had been informed was left of it.

No question of hospital. (The final prognosis, blandly delivered to her and David, had made her certain of that. She simply had thanked Dr Berkowitz, walked out and not gone back.) They were not going to get at her, the ghouls, to crack her skull and drain her veins and tear out her organs before her soul had gone to the realm of the faithful departed. It was not going to be that. It was not going to be one of those rooms with tubes, drips, dials, sterility and claustrophobia where, near the end, they quietly hung a cloth over the mirror, did it, of course, while you were asleep, out of consideration and sensitivity, naturally, so that when you woke up you would not see how you looked. You would never see again how you looked. And Harriet liked very much to see how she looked. Besides, David was one of those men who were afraid of hospitals. It would be difficult for him, so she would tell him he needn't come every day. He would be relieved, then guilty, and so almost never come. Hugo might come. Hugo seemed afraid of nothing. But then her son was so noisy.

She never had been brave, and did not hope suddenly to discover unsuspected inner resources. And she was still at heart, if not in practice, a Catholic. As such, she looked for mercy, not justice, and so would have to arrange her small death-drama accordingly.

Fiona dropped her at the gate, unaware of what Harriet had planned for June 16th. Oh, her mind might be rotting, but it was a mind made up.

Harriet seldom made up her mind, and her accomplishments in arrangement were confined chiefly to the herbaceous borders. There was one next to the beech hedge and another beside the ten-foot brick wall, built to exclude dogs, rabbits, children, neighbours and other undesirable life forms. There was also the rockery, the woodland garden, the lily pond, the island bed with its exotic shrubs and naturally, the rose garden where thirty-eight varieties reigned supreme. Harriet adored her flowers. Every day, mindless and happy, in all weathers, and just lately with the help of Mr Tripp – David insisted she have help now – she dug, manured, mulched, sprayed, pruned, watered, propagated, top-dressed, divided, transplanted, sung, talked, and prayed them into a fabulous fertility.

The borders were her favourites. How resplendent they were, especially now at six in the morning on June 16th, every little chloroplast and stomata, every drop of oestrogen giving its all. Were they not wholly good, she thought, as she always thought. She watched them from the bedroom window. She had known herself to stand transfixed like this for an hour, staring and staring at them, with no thought except that a rabbit with a watch and a waistcoat might come bustling along the path, that he might beckon her, and that she would surely follow. She tore herself away. There were procedures to be got through.

Procedures had begun two weeks ago, just after the last Garden Club meeting. She had tried very hard not to get mixed up or to forget anything vital. First, the means, the medicine. She got the palfium, enough of it, that is, by lying. (Harriet seldom told lies, there were so few occasions which required them. She never lied even to David. She loved him and he did not love her, so she could leave the lying to him.) The bottle was hidden in the greenhouse. Once she had buried it in the No. Two Potting Compost, she immediately felt safer. She was taking pains with her death. She was looking after it.

Second, the day. Quite simple, really. Couldn't have worked out better. Of course she wouldn't have *done it* before Chelsea, no matter what. But Hugo's A-levels finished on the 16th, so he would not have to worry about missing classes afterwards. The holiday in Greece might have to be cancelled, but that wasn't planned until the end of July. She doubted they'd put it off, although the subject of putting it off might come up. Oh, in the end she guessed they'd go, all right. The 16th was also a Wednesday, and Wednesday was David's golf day. So. The 16th it was. She had hoped for sun and had checked the weather reports, but they were ambivalent as usual.

Third, the location. Well, she had known that from the beginning. She hadn't really taken seriously the Constable landscape or the Bakerloo Line. The place would be where her soul was, where she had expended it, squandered it even, because there was nowhere else for it to go. She could see her soul from the bedroom window. There it was among the hardy perennials.

It was the 16th. It was seven thirty and David was up and shaving. Harriet looked at herself in the mirror, carefully and

critically. She had had her hair done in a new style, quite
becoming, with a fringe to cover the ineradicable creases in her
forehead. It was good, she thought. Had worked wonders,
really. And the streaking – well, a bit expensive, but worth it.
At Valentino's they did virtually every other strand, and used
aluminium foil and not those nasty rubber caps. Yes, it was
very natural, very tasteful. Where was it she had read that
'anyone who cares about the way they look can never be a
good gardener?' She had proved them wrong, whoever they
were.

As for the lines around her eyes, she guessed she had grown
used to them over the past few years. She covered them with
her favourite fluid base. It was quite effective, especially for
the first hour or so, provided one always looked *up*. Then she
applied a blusher and the particular shade of brown-black
mascara that went so well with her grey eyes.

She inspected herself again, leaning over the dressing table
with its array of bottles, tubes, phials, sprays, sponges,
pencils, brushes and cases, all carefully chosen and thought
out. She didn't realize that they were wasted because no one
looked at her any more. It had been months since she had
caught out some man in the midst of a double-take. But she
liked her make-up. She had vowed long ago that she would
keep on with it to the end. Well, she was.

> Quarens me sedisti lassus
> Redemisti crucem lassus
> Tantus labor non sit cassus.

Grace, redemption, clothes. Harriet selected what she
would wear. She wanted everything to be special today, and
clothes were a major problem. She had been losing weight for
some time, slowly at first, then alarmingly, now shockingly.
She hid her emaciation with floral shirts of linen and silk, tied
at the waist, or with big belts, and two sizes too large. She
took great pains to make them into a style and nearly succeeded. Her well-cut trousers conveyed the illusion that she
still possessed hips and a bottom. Over the shirts and trousers
she sported huge jumpers, fat knit cardigans or vast fringed
shawls – all to conceal the fact that her flesh was meagre in the

extreme, and that soon none of it would be left. Where was it
going, she wondered. Was it being turned to air, water, dust,
dreams? But she must not think of that. Such questions, she
supposed, would be answered soon enough. Right now she
must make Hugo's packed lunch and see David off. She
splashed herself with L'Air du Temps, applied her lip gloss
and went downstairs.

Hugo was running late. In eight minutes the minibus would
be waiting at the end of the drive to take him to St Wilfred's. He
was complaining about his sandwiches and about the muesli
bars Harriet persisted in slipping into his lunch box, and which
she suspected he daily exchanged for a Mars or a Mint Aero.
She tried to force a yoghurt on him, but he made a face.

'I'll put strawberry jam in it if you like.'

'Yuk!'

David sat down opposite him and they discussed Saturday's
match over their cornflakes. Hugo recently had won £65 on
the Pools. Harriet guessed he would be lucky in life and not in
need of much instruction from his mother. He had a kind of
blind wit which never failed to recognize opportunities. She
could not imagine how he had got to be a son of hers.

His father warned him of the time. Tie askew, Hugo
grabbed his lunch box and raced for the door. Harriet made a
desperate move to catch him by the arm intending to kiss him
whether he liked it or not, but he was already half-way to the
gate.

'Goodbye, Darling,' she waved from the doorway at his
disappearing back.

When she returned to the kitchen, David had left by the
back door. She chased him down the hall – why was it all
going so fast? – and caught up with him by the Pieris.

'You're going to Chichester today, aren't you, Darling?'
She smiled at him breathlessly.

'Mmmmmmmm.' He was rifling his briefcase which sat on
the bonnet of the car. He frowned a little. Perhaps he had
forgotten something.

'And then . . . and then it's your golf date with Dudley, isn't
it?' She was trying desperately not to pant. Her heart was
beating so, she was sure he could hear it.

'Right.' His face cleared. He hadn't forgotten whatever it

was after all. 'I won't be back until after eight, so don't wait supper for me, darling.' (They had rehearsed this fifty times already. He simply took it for granted that his wife would forget everything.) 'Oh, and I'll collect Hugo on the way home. So you can listen to "Gardener's Question Time" in peace. That'll be nice, won't it?'

Daringly, Harriet took his face between her hands. At her touch the old alarmed expression flashed in his eyes.

'I hope the weather stays fine,' she said. 'It's such a lovely view from the Seaford Course.' She kissed him on the mouth.

'Yes,' he replied as she held him still. 'Yes it is.'

She had not tried to seduce him the night before. She had thought she might, but there would have been no point in it. She laid for a while, though, with her arm across him and he had let her, and not rolled over *too* quickly. But this morning she wanted to do something. He would see her for the last time wearing her best colours, green and mauve. So few women could wear mauve, really.

She kissed him again, longer and harder this time as he stiffened under her hands. She must let him go now, she really must.

He backed off, relief all over him. She saw that she had left a red smear on the corner of his mouth and impulsively wiped it off with the tail of her silk shirt. David frowned at the scarlet stain.

'That was a bit silly. It'll cost a fortune to have that dry-cleaned.'

Harriet shrugged and smiled. 'I'll take it to Jeeves in Belgravia. Hugo can pay for it with his next Pools winnings. It'll save him buying me a birthday present.'

'If that's a hint,' he replied with feigned cheeriness, 'I do remember that it's the Third.' He was trying, he had been trying for weeks, so hard not to run. She had to forgive him everything for not running. He started the car, backed it down the drive.

'Goodbye, Darling,' she called so loudly that he turned and gave her what he must have thought was a jaunty wave.

The Rover disappeared behind the cypress hedge. Harriet stood holding herself, determined to listen until the last rumble of the engine died away. But David had stopped and was letting it idle.

'Lovely day,' she heard him say. He had met Mr Tripp in the drive.

'Yeah, well it do look fine, but mind you it'll be bloody hot this afternoon, and just you wait, there'll be thunder and hail and that'll be the end of the hay. Same thing happened two years ago, very same. Ruined the harvest. But it don't do no good to moan. Nyaw, don't do no good. You can't win, nyaw. If it weren't the heat, it a been the bloody damp and the hay'd a rotted.' (He spoke as if the devastation were a *fait accompli*.) 'Nyaw, you can't win. I say Mr M, you heered about that chappie axe-murdering his wife and dogs over by Chiddingly?'

Harriet heard David's condescending chuckle, the one he reserved for Mr Tripp, the cats, and herself. She imagined his hand raised in a parting victory sign as he pulled away from the loquacious gardener. The gravel crunched under the back tyres. The car accelerated. He was gone. Harriet put her fingers in her mouth. David. For ever gone.

She must get down to it now, she really must, the way she had planned, the way she had worked out so carefully to the last detail, in case her mind should go fuzzy, or a headache overcome her and she should forget or misplace something. She was frightened that David's departure might bring on one of her mental lapses, so frequent since this Thing had begun boring away at her brain like the worm in the heart of the rose. She went immediately to the greenhouse where she had left herself a letter.

'Harriet Dear,' it said, 'you will find the medicine in the No. Two Potting Compost. Get it and place it before you on the work table so that you will not lose sight of your goal. Instructions for D and Mr T are behind the tomato plants, along with two drawing pins for attaching them to the door. The Marian Missal is on the bench next to the gloxinias. Set the computer for watering. Make sure Salammbo is not asleep in the potted palm. You have left a glass on the bench. Fill it from the watering can and take your medicine like a good girl, saving a bit for later. Don't worry, you *did* hide the razor and the vodka in the hedge. I saw you do it. They are waiting for you should the medicine prove insufficient. Don't forget the Missal. Good luck, Darling. God will forgive you. Now open the windows and close the door.'

She had toyed with the idea of a suicide note, just to lend a little formality to the occasion, and had wondered for days, afraid to ask, if it was still considered *de rigueur* for this kind of death. In the end, she guessed that notes were an outmoded custom and that people didn't leave them any more. Besides, no one had been interested in her sentiments or explanations when she was alive. Why should they suddenly want them just because she was dead? A simple Goodbye, Darling would do. Moreover, this was not, strictly speaking, a suicide. It was a rite – and a right. She felt quite sure of this despite what she had been taught at St Catherine's. God, she kept telling herself, would forgive her, would forgive even her unspeakable act, provided she went freely, believingly forwards with it, loving her flowers. To love them was to love Nature, and to love Nature was to love God. They *would* save her, they and a few of the old right words.

Harriet was intelligent enough to know that nothing she had ever been told could prepare her for the final jumping off. One couldn't rehearse Death. Educated guesses notwithstanding, it came eternally as a surprise. But the valedictory, the ambience . . . surely one should make something of them and surely one needed something to give form to the preliminaries, to prevent the End turning out a terrible mess. One needed something to ease one into death, to get one safely started and make the process aesthetic. As a brain-damaged person without verbal or symbolic capacities, she felt inadequate to supply this something. She was also conservative and in a bit of a hurry. (This remission was not going to last for ever.) So she fastened on what was familiar. She decided to use the Mass for the Dead.

It had taken a while to unearth the Marian Missal which, at sixteen, she had won as the biology prize. She found it in a box along with an old uniform, some pressed flowers, a few birthday cards and her diploma from St Catherine's. Thankfully, the missal was an early edition and not the vulgar friendly item which has since replaced it. The old words were still beautiful, strong like pillars of marble that one might cling to. It occurred to her how long she had gone about as an outsider, a Londoner and a Catholic among these Anglo-Saxon Sussex Protestants. She had even married one, and in her desperation discovered gardening.

Harriet set the timer on the computerized watering device. (David, clever man, had installed it himself and saved them a small fortune.) It would operate automatically each evening at six, and see everyone through what she assumed would be a certain amount of excitement after her death. She looked at the plants in their boxes and pots, dozens of them, all beautifully laid out. Some of her happiest hours had been spent here in the greenhouse, alone on rainy spring afternoons with the portable radio and cups of tea that went cold. Lightly, she kissed a few of the plants.

'Goodbye, Darlings.' Tears rose but did not fall. She caught herself slipping away, nearly losing hold of the procedure. She must not linger in sentiment, otherwise there would not be time to devote the whole day to her death.

She posted the notices to David and Mr Tripp on the greenhouse door. They contained instructions for the care of all indoor plants, as clear and specific as she could make them. *They* would be her farewell note. She hadn't anything more to say to humans – except a postscript regarding cremation. Hallowed ground might now be out of the question, but her body was not to be consigned to the flames. Let the good worms bore it to their hearts' content.

Quickly she took a few of the palfium. She made certain that neither Salammbo nor Clover nor Petrouschka was asleep in their favourite places, put the remaining medicine in her pocket, tore up her note to herself, took the missal and went outside, glad to be away from the already oppressive heat of the greenhouse. The day was fine with fat June clouds. Harriet went into the garden. Everything had been done that needed doing. She supposed she could start to die now.

The nearest end of the herbaceous border was bright with Hemerocallis Burning Daylight and Geranium Russell Prichard. Harriet loved the way their colours alternated with the sharp morning shadows. What a paradise she had made, what a Looking Glass Garden! There had been some terrible talk of its being open to the public one Sunday afternoon next year under the National Gardens Scheme. Harriet shuddered at the thought of all those strangers with their unruly children, expecting toast and jam on the grass. Over her dead body would they trample her potentilla and lythospermum.

It was Harriet's intention to spend her last day in this earthly paradise, safe from the distressing world. Slowly she would make her way through the border — reading the Mass and consuming more palfium as she went — to the far corner of the front garden where the beech hedge met the ten-foot wall. There, presumably, the medicine would take its final effect. If not, she would have recourse to other means. But she trusted this would not be necessary, everything having been arranged so well. Meanwhile, she would commune with her flowers, solicitously enquiring after their well-being, as she did each morning on her tour of inspection. And they would answer her. They would say goodbye. Goodbye Darling Harriet. Goodbye with love.

She went on her knees before a burgeoning flaviforum, encircling it with her arms and rubbing her cheek against a long smooth bud. An episode returned to her from *Through the Looking Glass.*

('Oh tiger-lily!' said Alice, addressing herself to one that was waving gracefully about in the wind. 'I *wish* you could talk!'

'We *can* talk,' said the tiger-lily, 'when there's anybody worth talking to.')

Dear, beautiful lilies, containing more deoxyribonucleic acid than any other creature, including man. They *had* to be miraculous, to have, inside them, the whole secret of life. She remembered ordering them from Blom's catalogue. 'Sweetly Scented Lilies Throughout the Summer,' it had said on the cover of the spring issue. How she pored over those catalogues, reading them hungrily as a novel. There had been times when she had been unable not to have a Blom's by her. She slept with it under her pillow, carried it in her handbag, lay a copy on the desk or the kitchen table where she would be sure to see it. Nothing Too Bad, she felt, could happen to her as long as a Blom's was nearby. Nothing too bad, like the pains of hell or the deep pit. Harriet opened the missal.

'Libera eas de ore leonis, ne absorbeat eas tartarus, ne cadant in obscurum.'

A cloud passed before the sun. Against the backdrop of a colourless horizon, she watched two doves disappear into the green-black branches of an ilex tree. Harriet listened to their yearning cries. There was something lyrical in them, a note she could hardly bear, it reminded her so much of what she would have liked. Love and the rest of it.

All had been impossible. Gradually, each longed-for thing had been abandoned because it seemed to tell her so pointedly that she could never possess it. Once she had thought of working. But she really didn't see anything virtuous or heroic in earning one's own living, and all the exciting professions were closed to her, she knew, because she wasn't wonderful enough. She didn't want to be a secretary or a social worker or a dental assistant. She wanted to *make* something lovely, to *be* something lovely. Of course there was Hugo. But mother-love was strange to her. How could one mother something like Hugo? And David had slipped past her, outdistanced her long ago. Pathetically she had gone on trying to catch up, to get his attention, waving and shouting and gesturing to him from way, way off. He just never noticed.

Then there were the Interests: she would paint in oils, learn the guitar, invest in stocks. But she knew, even before she tried, that she would let each one go. She had let everything go. Even acquaintances, even friends. Slowly her life had shrunken away; it had dwindled to the dimensions of the garden, then to the dimensions of her own dwindling flesh.

She greeted an aquilegia, pushing her nose into the pollen of its delicate trumpet. Oh it was good. It was all goodness and grace and redemption. The sun came out again, burning her back through the silk blouse. She turned to face it and felt the first rush of dizziness, followed by a softly spreading nausea. She crawled to the hedge and vomited quietly. Panting, she dragged herself back to where the agapanthus leaves were already enormous and read from the missal.

Let them, oh Lord, pass from death to life, that life which thou didst promise to old Abraham and his seed.

She heard singing. Someone was coming up the path. Harriet could not raise herself, but saw through the foliage of a peony

Sarah Bernhardt, a pair of patched green gumboots standing beside a hoe.

'Mornin', Mrs M. Doing a bit o' weeding are you? Well, say one for me while you're down there.' It was Mr Tripp again. What *was* he doing here on a Wednesday? 'I will get to that patch down the bottom, but the growth is so bleedin' dense this year, and since you went and put in that island bed, Mrs M ... wyall, I always say, you know, *you don't want too much garden.* I mean now, look at you Mrs M, with all due respect, out here on your hands and knees, working like a black in this 'ere heat. Nyaw, you don't want too much garden. Still, lovely day. Yes. Yup. At the moment ... Mind you, Mrs M, be no time till the leaves is fallin' and all this'll be withered and brown, dark at quarter to bleedin' four, us all bleatin' about the cold, then first thing you know, by crikey it'll be Chrismis. You mark my words, Mrs M and see if it ain't. Then before you know it,' he chuckled, 'I reckon it'll be time for poor old Johnny Tripp to deep-dig this ruddy bed again. 'Carse I know, I'm just a ignorant peasant, wouldn't presume to tell nobody their business. You may just be thinkin', why that damned silly old basket, and no doubt you'd be correct. I don't take no issue with no one, but *you don't want too much garden.* Nyaw.'

Harriet retched and spat out a vile yellow phlegm.

'Yeah, you gets fed up. We all gets fed up. But it don't do no good to moan. You want them green-fly sprayed today, Mrs M?'

'Tomorrow ... Mr Tripp,' Harriet gasped. 'Tomorrow, if you please.'

'Righty-oh, then. By the way, them bleedin' flea beetles is at your fuchsias again. Cheers, Mrs M.' He went off, humming loudly and chewing on the unlit stub of a cigarette, the human being on whom the future of her beloved garden would most likely depend.

Harriet collapsed, her face in the dirt. 'Oh good gracious!'

She had not realized the medicine would work so soon. Inexperienced as she was with drugs, she no doubt had miscalculated the dose. Was she paralysed? Would she never get to the bottom of the garden? Her brain seemed to have been freeze-dried – poor brain, probably so deficient in the

first place – and she feared that in another moment she might
not even care that she had not yet said goodbye to everyone
and heard what they had to tell her, that is, if she really were
'anybody worth talking to'.

Fuchsias, flea beetles? Harriet was seized by a sudden fit of
anxiety before everything went dark. When she awoke, she
was feeling better, in fact she was feeling fine, finer than she
had ever felt. Why hadn't Dr Berkowitz given her more of this
stuff? Oh what meanies they all were! Salammbo appeared and
rubbed against her hair. She tried to stroke the cat but could
not raise her arm.

'Goodbye, Darling,' she whispered and made little kissing
noises.

Salammbo was a white Persian, stupid, bad-tempered, and
a decorative addition to any garden. Harriet tried again to
stroke her, but she took refuge in the hedge at the approach of
Biggles, the Applebys' formidable ginger tom.

Biggles strutted up to a clump of delphiniums, positioned
himself with precision and sprayed, his ringed tail absolutely
vertical and vibrating with the lonely thrill of self-expression.

'So it *was* you,' Harriet murmured. 'I've suspected you for
weeks. Don't you know how bad that is for the azaleas?'

Biggles spied the cowering Salammbo, and in a single
bound was on her.

'Biggles! Salammbo! Pussies!' Harriet tried to shout. Salammbo
escaped by a whisker and fled across the back lawn into
the woodland garden (developed according to the tenets of
Gertrude Jekyll) from which could be heard dreadful shrieks
and yowls. Harriet was powerless to assist, and Mr Tripp, she
knew, would do nothing to interfere. Salammbo was for it.

'The violence,' Harried sighed. 'Dear God the violence.
"Exaudi orationem meam, ad te omnis caro veniet".' As she
prayed, a blackbird alighted on the grassy path to struggle
briefly with a worm which it bit in two, devouring one half
and leaving the other to be quickly smothered by glittering
flies. Harriet pulled herself to her hands and knees and crawled
forwards through the chincherinchee.

'My temple,' she whispered as she rested beside a trollius
europaeus. 'My Temple of Flora. Let me shelter myself in you
for ever.' She gazed at the flower, imagining what it would be

like to be hidden eternally in the depths of its butter-yellow safety. She separated the petals of its dense round head and inspected it carefully: calyx, corolla, stamen, pistil, anther, stigma.

'Stigma – female organ. I've wondered why, but never asked. Too shy, I guess.'

Suddenly the trollius seemed different, and disturbingly so. Harriet pulled herself closer to a day lily and bent it gently towards her. It too had changed. She looked round. All of them had subtly and horribly changed. They seemed to jut, to spread, to dangle and stretch themselves in the most lurid manner. She drew back. Something had turned very nasty. Was it the medicine? Was she imagining it? Drugs, she knew, could produce strange side-effects. But this –

Harriet's sense of alarm was not entirely unfamiliar. It was a kind of panic she had experienced before, especially that day at St Catherine's oh, it must have been twenty-five years ago – when her best friend had begun dramatically to menstruate and had been sent home crying. The scene came rushing back with the force and speed of some awful engine and ploughed into her like a vicious rapist. How shocked she had been. That blood, those breasts, had been lurking there all along and she had been so stupidly unaware of them. She looked at herself that night, for the first time, really looked, and saw how they were lurking also in her own body. She wanted somehow to escape herself, but of course there was nowhere to go. Then there had been that boy, the only one before David . . . Now here it was again, the same scary shocking thing, straining towards her out of this lily, like a tongue lolling from a mouth. Harriet felt appalled and duped. Why had she persisted in thinking of her flowers as innocent? Did she imagine that even in this earthly paradise, enclosed by its beech hedge and ten-foot wall, life would be any different?

'You whores!' She would have cried if the medicine had allowed her any tears. 'Prostitutes, shameless glamour pusses, hermaphrodite strumpets. It's sex everywhere, isn't it, nothing but sex and enticement and exploitation. And we arrange it all for you, we human pimps, we nice respectable ladies with our Garden Clubs, we arrange it all for the gratification of your lust. But I've known this for ages! I've read the books, I won the biology prize! If anyone should know your tricks and your ways, I should. The truth just never sank in. I relegated it to some lower drawer of my sub-standard brain. I didn't want to believe you're as sordid as we are.'

She watched a fat bee stumble about in the plant's extrusions. Swathed in pollen, it took to the air and made a reeling reconnaissance of some digitalis.

'What do you feel', Harriet addressed the day lily, 'when one of those fuzzy fellows slides down your landing strip? Do you care? Do you come? Or are you just cold, cold, and gluttonous? You're devious, actually, with your hair triggers and your coded messages and your infra-red light. There's one of you, isn't there, who closes tight exactly four seconds after fertilization. Bam, zip, and that's all folks. And that little pervert who, when all else fails, wraps up in its own corolla like Venus in Furs and fucks itself. Cleis . . . Cleist . . . Cleistogomy or something seedy like that. And you're even cruel. You lay traps, you sting, poison and paralyse. You can make cattle weep tears of blood. You devour creatures alive like any ravenous beast. How could I have thought you were the only things on earth that were wholly good?'

Harriet swallowed, with difficulty, the rest of the palfium and threw the bottle into the hedge.

'You're heartless. How could you do this to me? After St Catherine's, after David, after the worm in my brain – how could you?'

> Sed siquifer repraesentet eas in lucem sanctum:
> Quam olim Abrahae et semini ejus.
> Sanctus, sanctus, sanctus . . .

'Harriet! Yoo hoo!' A horrible familiar voice was calling from outside the gate. Fiona, of course, come to interfere with her death. She spied Harriet behind the Shirley poppies and bustled down the path, smiling, bleached-blonde and pregnant.

'Hello, dear. Just passing, thought I'd check on something with you.' She leaned forwards, hands on her knees, as though she were addressing a spaniel.

'*Poor* Harriet! Working on a day like this. You are mad keen, aren't you. Isn't the heat dreadful. Now, what I wanted to talk to you about was this. I know it's my turn to have the girls for the August meeting, but what with school holidays and my little bun in the oven – ' She patted her belly in what seemed to Harriet the most revolting gesture.

'Fiona, I'm dying.'

'Oh *poor* Harriet. Well, I'm not surprised. I did tell you just now, didn't I, that the heat is simply devastating. You oughtn't to be out here in the afternoon sun, you know you oughtn't.'

Was it afternoon already? The Golden Afternoon?

'So I thought – mind you as long as it's all right with you and Jean – I thought we might just this once, and of course I'll make up for it later – my dear, do you know you have pollen all over your nose and a very dirty face? Whatever have you been doing? Oh you *do* look funny.' Fiona giggled. 'I thought it might be easier if we – '

She was never going to stop. There must be some way to prevent her ruining everything.

'Whatever you like, Fiona. Fine with me. Just fine.' Harriet gasped.

'Oh good. Thanks so much, Harriet. I knew you'd understand. Now are you sure it's all right? You're absolutely sure?'

'Dear God, yes.'

'You know, Harriet, you have rather an odd way of putting things. But never mind. Try to stop working and get out of the sun. I know how dedicated you are and how committed and all that, but you're looking decidedly peaky, you know. Really you are. I'm quite concerned about you. You're sure our little arrangement is all right now. Absolutely sure? Oh thanks so much. Well, we'll talk tomorrow, how's that? Bye-bye, dear.'

Harriet lay full length in the dirt, exhausted, her head on her arm. Was the end to be here, now, like this with everything suddenly so muddled and no time to sort out her feelings? Perhaps it might have been better to have gone into hospital after all. At least they would have kept Fiona out and she could have *remembered* the garden instead of uncovering at the eleventh hour all this lurking malevolence. Perhaps directing one's own death was simply too ambitious an undertaking for a brain-damaged person.

Oh no, and here was someone else. The postman with a second delivery. She watched him from one eye as he shuffled up the walk and deposited the mail in the Millers' open hall. Half-way back to the van, he stopped and looked around. He did not see Harriet where she lay barely conscious in the dense foliage. Still checking furtively, he unzipped his trousers and urinated on the base of the acacia tree.

'Bloody cheek! I wonder how many times he's – ' Harriet passed out.

Mr Tripp had been absolutely right. The rain began at five o'clock, to the accompaniment of thunder and some dramatic flashes of lightning which caused Fiona to shout at the children that they must switch off the telly lest it explode, brought an end to Hugo's Rugby match, and spoilt David's golf, so that he and Dudley were forced to spend two hours in the bar.

When she had been struck by a number of hailstones, Harriet woke up. Her first concern was for the delphiniums. They had been ravaged two years ago in just such a storm. Then she feared for the greenhouse. Then she threw up. Her dulled senses registered that she was wet through, covered with mud, cold, aching and still, just, alive. She noticed the sodden missal beside her open to the words, '*Cum sanctis tuis in aeternum; quia pius es.*'

'Because thou art merciful,' Harriet snorted. She was weak but awake. Better get on with the ritual. It was all that remained. She guessed she would have to resort to the razor and the vodka after all. Thank heavens she had planned and protected her death against the Natural Course of Events with all its perfidious ways. She abandoned the missal and dragged herself as far as the arch in the hedge.

Hailstones still pelted her, and the flowers dripped as she passed. Why had she done so much for them? They didn't love her any more than David did.

The storm ended. The clouds rolled away to the east, towards Herstmonceux and Ninfield and Rye, and left behind a pale clean sky, replete with negative ions, and that yellow light in which all growing things look their best. How Harriet had loved to come out into the garden on such evenings and admire the subtle intensity of the colours, their almost electric glow. How it had filled her with well-being, left her with a pleasant ache of pride at what she had accomplished. Perhaps, in the end, she was glad to be seeing the garden like this, at its very best – even though nothing was nice any more.

She rested on the grassy path that led under the arch. She wondered if she would be able to make her way among the dahlias with their lush new growth. She would miss them this year. They would not miss her.

At the end of her strength, she crawled to the corner where the beech hedge met the ten-foot wall. From here she could see the house and all of the front garden. She crouched, shivering, beneath the Albertine rose which spread massively over the warm red brick. Birds called to each other. Rain dripped from the trees. Harriet found the vodka and the razor where she had left them wrapped in a plastic bag. She could barely lift the bottle, but managed to unscrew the cap and take three large swallows. She had heard them say that vodka and pills were the woman's way. Oh hell, who cared any more what they said. There was no pleasing them. They took exception to everything.

She looked up into Albertine's profuse and seemingly inno- cent pink.

'You're terrible,' she said. 'You're all terrible. You look so wonderful and you're so terrible.'

She suddenly felt a sensation she knew she ought to control, but the lower half of her body failed to respond to old commands. It was frighteningly relaxed. Something warm and wet was trickling into her trousers and running down her leg. Dear God, she was urinating. Pissing as freely as a baby. Now it really was all going to pieces. Well, she had known that the ritual would hold up only to a point.

Her hands and clothes were covered with mud. Her appear- ance, she realized, must be disastrous, and after she had worked so hard this morning to make herself attractive. She hadn't counted on being found in such a state. Why, why had she failed to consider this of all factors? Well, she would just have to die looking a fright, she supposed. She thought of David. A tear, her only tear, slid down her muddy cheek.

'You're so clever,' quite drunk now, she spoke to the

flowers again. 'You get everything you want. I'm jealous of you, that's what. All beauty and sex. You're so successful in your alluring. There was I with my clothes, make-up, jewellery, scent, trying to be like you – pretending I was you. But *I* never bloomed.'

Albertine rustled her foliage and drops of water fell on to Harriet's head and arms.

Harriet looked up. 'Oh, Albertine,' she whispered. 'It's been a dreadful shock, but I suppose I forgive you all.'

She was shaking violently, and the gnats were biting like mad. As she turned towards the wall, she saw an over-ripe blossom had fallen from the trellis and was being devoured by slugs, large and small, who were nibbling away at the tender rotting thing. Radiating from it in every direction were their trails of slime. Harriet vomited again. This really was too much.

She removed the razor from the bag and succeeded in making quite a neat slice through her left wrist. It hurt. She hadn't thought it would. She dropped the razor with a trembling hand, lifted the rose from the ground and brought it to her face. Despite three slugs which still clung to it, she pressed the flower to her mouth, inhaling deeply its odour of death. She let her blood drip into all its crevices, she crushed it, kissed it, and held it hard against her heart. She watched the blood staining her shirt and trousers. What a terrible mess it was making. Then she wrapped her arms around herself, pulled her knees up to her chest, and tried to huddle closer to the wall.

The evening was long and light. At nine o'clock David and Hugo returned. They found the house in darkness and assumed that Harriet had gone to bed with one of her headaches. They took what they wanted from the fridge, complaining that nothing had been prepared for them. Obviously, Mum had squandered another day playing with her flowers. They sat down to watch 'Sportsnight' and eat sandwiches. David was very drunk.

Through the open French doors the sound of the television reached every part of the garden. Salammbo, wet and dirty, slunk in by the cat door. Delphiniums bent under their wet weight. A moon rose in the opalescent suburban sky. In the corner between the beech hedge and the ten-foot wall, Harriet was curled up tight against the world, holding her rose. She was falling far away, falling vast distances through endless fields of glittering points. She was one of those points now. She was a pebble, a pearl, a seed, a star; potentized, exhausted, wind-borne, unique, dispensable. She was a grain of pollen.

Melusina

Half she drew him
Half sank he down
And never more was seen.

None of us can remember when it was exactly, that Adrian
began to lose his mind. Oh, I don't mean barking mad or
anything like that. He wasn't violent. He wasn't even difficult,
really. His personality did not undergo a violent transformation. We couldn't say what had changed, and I don't
think any of us spoke openly of it for some time, except to
comment on the amount he was spending on books and on
their accumulation in his tiny flat. But everyone sensed it.
Everyone knew. He was mad, all right – mad in his own
sweet way.

I think I first became aware of how far he had – how shall I
put it? – drifted, when I took Melissa to see him one afternoon
last April. Now that may have been a manifestation of *my*
madness. All I can say is that it seemed a good idea at the time.
So I marched her up to Lisson Grove (yes, literally, though I
made a joke of it), marched her up that narrow, dirty, twisty
little stairway and presented her to an abstracted Adrian.

I hadn't rung him to say we would be coming and, as he had
not seen Melissa in two years, it was not surprising that he at
first ignored her, though he gave me his usual enthusiastic
greeting – well, perhaps not quite as enthusiastic as usual. He
then stared at her in undisguised distaste. I was teasing him by
purposely neglecting to introduce her. After a few quizzical
glances, he offered us tea, and fumbled about the kitchen,

talking animatedly and rather incoherently to me. He stopped in mid-sentence and reappeared with a greasy tea towel slung over his shoulder and his wet hands dripping on to his shoes. He had recognized her at last.

'Good Lord!' he exploded. 'It isn't Melly, is it?'

She shrugged her narrow shoulders and scowled at him, though there was a hint of sparkle in her big black eyes. To her annoyance, he gathered her in his arms, laughing heartily and slapping her several times on the back, as though she had been a child choking on a rusk. She made a face and wriggled away.

'Heavens, what have you done to yourself?' He seemed not to notice her irritation.

'Melly's gone Punk,' I informed him. 'She's dyed her hair, as you may have noticed, been caught peddling pills, and expelled from Bryanston. Now she devotes her time to shaving her little brother's head and being thrown out of rock concerts.'

'Oh yes.' Adrian was kneeling before Melissa, smiling goodnaturedly.

'Well I'm fifteen, aren't I? I can do as I please.' She glared at me through layers of Ultra-Lash. 'Besides, what else is there to do?'

As usual, Jack and I had chosen to adopt a *laissez-aller* attitude to her most recent calamity, to speak of it frankly and to treat it with restrained good humour. I had taken her to see Adrian because I thought he might inject her with a little enthusiasm for learning. I believe in teaching by example.

'There, there, little rebel, never mind.' Adrian patted her leather-encased thigh. 'One doesn't learn much of importance at school, does one? Life's the great teacher, eh? . . . challenge, experience, the quest for individuality, the good old Unattainable . . . '

It wasn't exactly what I'd hoped he'd say.

Melissa regarded him with a fraction less contempt. 'Too right.'

Obviously, Adrian was no longer put off by her bizarre exterior. He had replaced it with an earlier Melissa, one he had last seen on a September afternoon in our back garden, during a quiet family picnic that had somehow become a mob of forty people. *That* Melissa was an undersized thirteen-year-old with beautiful limbs and chestnut hair to the waist, flapping about in shorts and my sling-back shoes, lavishing love on the creature she claimed was her only friend, Boots the cat, and telling us all what she didn't like; but exhibiting, as always, an arch affection for Adrian.

'I have a book you might be interested in, Mel, since you're that way inclined. Great stuff, you'll like it.' He scratched his head and went searching the bookshelves which enclosed three-quarters of the room. But the kettle began to shriek and he stopped to make the tea.

Now this behaviour may not seem particularly mad. However, he did commit one telling act which I have not mentioned but which I noted immediately. He had been reading when we arrived. Nothing unusual in that. He was always reading, seated at his fortress-like desk, volumes stacked mightily on three sides, boxes of file cards arranged in battle formation, papers and notebooks everywhere. But his response to our arrival was strange. Ordinarily, after a hearty greeting, he would have thrust The Book at me and commenced an enthusiastic precis before I had taken my coat off. That day, he put down the manuscript (it was a manuscript not a book), covered it with some pages of his copious notes, and said nothing about it. Such covert behaviour was totally out of character, the tell-tale clue that he was beginning to shut himself off from us. And this before he even had begun to talk of all those peculiar things . . .

But let me explain the network of relationships which linked Adrian and Melissa and me.

Melissa is my step-daughter. I have known her since the day she was born. When her father deserted her mother for her mother's best friend, that is, me, her mother attempted suicide. She was later caught stealing eight pairs of Christian Dior tights from Harvey Nichols. Clearly, she was craquée. Poor Diana spent the next six months in a rest home in Surrey, during which she relinquished custody of her child. I took Melissa to me, as they say, and raised her as my own. (Melissa's father and I had another child – Orlando – seven years later.) You have no doubt gathered that Melissa was a wanton thing, but not unintelligent, and attractive in a dangerous way. But I liked that. Almost everyone does.

Besides, I thought I understood her. Therefore, I have always adopted a light tone and a loose rein. Her father is a painter, a serious and irrational person, but with the conventional soft spot for his only daughter. So she has been indulged, perhaps disastrously so. She is an exquisite monster with, as I said, a brain, and we still believe her capable of some accomplishment.

That is Melissa. Adrian is pure soul. He is a scholar and, in his eccentric way, a gentleman. His mother Rosalind is my godmother. She has money but, as far as I know, has never given him much. Consequently, he lives like a cheerful church mouse. He is the one person I know who never complains of his finances.

Adrian has always been part of my life. He was my childhood companion and, at school, one of Jack's closest friends. (Incestuous, but you know what life in London can be like.) He has been the archetypal friend of the family, and has dandled Melissa and Orlando on his knee. My surrogate elder brother, he is an absent-minded darling whom I still adore despite the distance that now separates us, the distance of which I was, that April afternoon, only beginning to be aware. That is Adrian. Or an attempt at Adrian. It is so difficult to describe a truly good person. One has so little to refer to.

He brought the tea, which was served in miserable brown mugs and accompanied by half a packet of chocolate digestives. He leaned towards me, talking eagerly, unaware that he was eating all the biscuits himself. His narrow shoulders were permanently hunched, and his fine reddish hair flapped against his forehead. He was so poor. He didn't realize how poor he was.

We chatted about all the usual things: Jung, Nietzsche, Gothic art, Liszt, British archeology, Ancient Egypt, Dostoevsky, the piano, etc. We played a duet on his Bluthner, which he had bought when he worked for North Sea Oil and which was the one expensive item in the room. It was Ravel's *Mother Goose Suite* that we played. We had performed the piece with great success at a concert when we were children, and still remembered every note.

Melly said nothing and looked bored. She stirred three sugars into her lukewarm tea and leaned back on the rotting sofa, her legs sprawled out like a boy's. As we talked, Adrian's eyes kept returning to her dead-white face, her mouth like a purple tulip and the pink and orange streaks exploding from her spiky black hair. I thought how wonderful it would be if she were to come to love some of the things he stood for, or at least glimpse them, even briefly.

When I asked why he hadn't been to see us in ages, he said he was devoting himself to the study of Alchemy and spending most of his time in the reading room of the British Museum. All in preparation for his next work, a treatise in blank verse, the title of which he refused to tell me.

'People have such misconceptions about the old puffers, you know. Paracelsus, Michael Meier, Raymond Lully, Nicholas Flammel, Fulcanelli – they were really on to something, and I don't mean metallurgy. Lead into gold was only a metaphor for the Ultimate Goal.'

We continued to sit on the piano bench as Adrian stared at Melissa.

'But I thought you were about to sign a contract with Thames and Hudson to do that paperback on mazes.'

'Nope. Decided not to.' He watched her going through his stacks of records. 'It would have had to be so watered down, all colour reproductions and a compromised text. There's enough glossy rubbish on the market without my adding to the heap. So derivative. Appalling, really. I can't do that sort of thing, you know.' His smile showed no bitterness. 'Besides, they'll get someone else easily enough. Someone more – well, some – '

'Popularizer.' I struck a chord and played a series of modulations. 'You're too pure, *mon vieux*. You could have used the money. In this awful world one had to be a bit corrupt. Now how are you going to support your researches?'

'Oh I'll manage,' he winked. 'The gods will look after me.'

'They're known to be a bit arbitrary with their favours. You're a big boy now, and you should know that goodness is no guarantee of protection.'

'Yes I should,' he laughed. 'Even so, I won't do the book. I'm after bigger fish, and I have to tell you, Kitty, all this – ' he gestured towards the heap on his desk, 'it's great stuff. It's the most important – '

'Yes, tell me.' He was staring with such intensity at Melissa that I couldn't help looking at her myself. He watched her, I thought, like someone looking out of a window in the middle of the night watches a fire burning on a distant hill.

'You're impossible,' I pushed him gently with my shoulder. 'It's foolish to hide what you know. Sell it man! You're erudite and rare and you've worked hard. You shouldn't have to live like this.'

'Oh the old shop is all right.' He was suddenly serious. 'You know I don't want or need acclaim, Kitty. What I do, I do for its own sake and for the very few, for the wise.'

'Well, like most innocents you're occasionally very pompous. But I never thought you'd turn out a snob. What about the rest of us? We'd love to reap a little of the fruits of your labour. God knows, we poor benighted materialists need it. And would it really be so dreadful if we wanted to *pay* for our enlightenment? Don't be so uncharitable, my dear. Don't withhold yourself from us so.'

'I promise I shall do my best to make the spirit manifest.'

'Well, be sure to let me know when you do, in case I should happen not to notice, base metal that I am.'

Adrian laughed. 'Darling Kitty, I'm an awful bore. Why did you come?'

'Hadn't seen you in weeks,' I stood up, 'wondered how you were, wanted to chat to someone intelligent – you know how lazy I am about reading – wanted to pick your brains, and was hoping that by some crazy kind of osmosis my juvenile delinquent might absorb a bit of your virtue.'

Melissa gave a short grunt. She was flipping absently through a copy of A's single published work, a sprawling prose-poem of heroic proportions called *The Alembic*. Abstruse, fat, and unreadable, it has been ignored by critics and public alike.

'Now what about *that*?' I pointed to the paper-bound edition. 'What's been happening with *that*?'

He shrugged. 'Oh, I suppose they've been selling one or two, here and there.'

'You mean you haven't made enquiries? You haven't called your publisher, gone down in person to the Turret Bookshop? But my dear you must. Do you have any idea how often Jack

rings up his gallery or simply appears unannounced? He is
ever-present and menacing, and it's the only way to ensure
one's rights. You could be owed hundreds.'

I could feel him shrinking from me. 'Now Kitty, you know
that's unlikely.'

Only 1,500 copies had been printed, of which Jack and I had
bought ten and Ros fifteen. Adrian was right, and I could see
that I was being too much for him. I patted his cheek.

'You do as you see fit, A. I'm a busybody and very corrupt.
Trust in your innocence and be just as you are.'

He still looked a bit uncomfortable.

'I don't blame you for remaining a bachelor, my dear. Fancy
what a nightmare it would be for you, married to someone
like me.' Adrian's one extended relationship had ended nearly
a year ago.

'Oh well,' he laughed, 'that's what you ladies are for: to give
us men a good sorting out and force us to confront our
Unconscious. "The divine soul imprisoned in the elements,"
what?'

Melissa snorted.

'Do stop,' I said to Adrian and prepared to leave. I was
going to a dinner party at the home of a mutual friend. Adrian
had been invited, but insisted that he was too *occupé* for social
life. 'You're a silly old thing, and it's just damn lucky that I
love you.' I kissed him. He liked that.

We waited another ten minutes while he searched for
Melissa's book. It turned out to be *Songs of Innocence and
Experience*, with copies of the original engravings.

Melissa took it blankly. 'Thanks,' she said and gave him a
grudging smile. 'When do you want it back?'

'You keep it, Mel. Old times and all.'

'I'll return it. Old times are a bore.'

I could have kicked her, but Adrian was unoffended.

'Too right.' He laughed and saw us to the door.

'What happened to your cello? Don't you play any more?'

'Nope.'

She was a stubborn imp.

Two weeks later, Ros rang me. She is a nervous woman
who expresses love mainly by anxiety, and as a result has been
driven frantic by her only son.

'Kitty, have you seen Adrian? I've been ringing him for days and there's no answer. I call at two in the morning, at six in the morning, at eight in the evening — he's never at home. Is he ill do you think? Has he gone to Paris again? If you know, for heaven's sake tell me. But why doesn't *he* tell me? Is it such a terrible thing for a mother to ask? He knows I can't bear the worry. My only hope, my only prayer is that it's a woman at last. Is it a woman?'

'Ros, I don't know.' I was in the midst of a painting, and consequently a little abrupt. My most recent encounter with her had, I thought, been quite enough. (We met once a week, either for lunch at Meridana or to play backgammon and consume chocolates and port.)

'He's forty-two, Kitty. Think of it, forty-two. And still — well, as he is. He can't be homosexual, can he? Do you think he's homosexual? He's rather delicate. Oh dear, and that red hair, all those recessive genes. And then there was boarding school . . . '

I reassured her for the thousandth time. 'Ros, Adrian likes women, believe me. He fucks them whenever he can. If he had the opportunity he'd fuck them all the time, five or six a day at least. Besides, physique has nothing to do with — '

'Then *where* is he? Oh dear, what could have happened to him?' She began to cry and I softened a bit. I'm fond of Ros, really.

'Ros darling, he's all right. He's probably closeted in the BM reading room, lost to the world and to the likes of us. I'm sure he's happy.'

Nothing I said could comfort her and she moved on to the usual litany of complaints.

'Now he had a good job, Kitty, a marvellous job. Why he gave it up I'll never understand. A first in bio-chemistry, a first! Imagine, at forty, throwing it all away, and for what? *What* is it that he wants?'

'I don't know, Ros. Probably to be himself.'

'I thought at first it was for the piano, the Sacrifice, I mean. A career in music at his age seemed so improbable that, can you imagine, I was positively relieved when he told me it was for Poetry. Well, I said to myself, he's sacrificing a brilliant career with North Sea Oil for Poetry. Swallow it, Rosalind,

just simply swallow it. Perhaps it's safer in the end. One hears
such dreadful stories of people falling off those rigs. There was
one poor chap, and practically on the eve of his wedding,
utterly incapacitated, you know what I mean. Of course she
married him anyway, but it was all too awful, and then they
do tip over. So I convinced myself he was going to be a great
poet. I was sure of it, well of course we all were. Weren't you
certain he was going to be *known*, even in a modest way, even
if we had to settle for some dreary posthumous acclaim? (a
depressing thought, but let us be realistic, such are the perils of
beginning careers at forty). Well, I must tell you, Kitty, that I
find the Work incomprehensible. In-com-pre-hen-sible. *The
Alembic*. What does it mean? I can't imagine anyone buying it.
But then again, perhaps it *is* wonderful, that's the terrible,
maddening rub! Do you think it's wonderful, Kitty? You're
supposed to understand Art and Literature. Please be honest.
And if it is wonderful, how on earth could you tell? There
really ought to be a guaranteed apparatus for divining these
things, a device that would assure one with a simple yes or no.
Oh, what a relief it would be! Now he's on to Alchemy! Tell
me, for pity's sake, Kitty, what is Alchemy? Another of those
dismally ambiguous subjects about which nothing can be
known for sure. It may be real, it may be imagined. It may
exist or not. In my opinion, it only generates anxiety, and I'm
sure it's unhealthy. I've heard these people, these *Alchemists*,
perform diabolical experiments with dangerous chemicals.
Why Adrian may be blowing himself up at this very moment.
And for What? For what is he blowing himself up? For an
ambiguity! And just when I've been lulled into a false sense of
security about the oil rigs. Oh heavens, such a marvellous job
with North Sea Oil, a first in bio-chemistry . . . '

The loop cassette went round again. I must add that Ros
never used to be so impossible. She has been encouraged by
her psychiatrist to free herself of certain British restraints,
with, as is apparent, disastrous results. (There are excellent
reasons why our island race comes packaged as it does.
Liberation, as I believe Nietzsche put it, is for the very few.)

I was still trying to finish the painting, sipping an iced
vermouth and listening to some Fauré songs − so exquisite −
when who should appear at my studio door but Adrian.

My astonishment at the way he looked must have been plain. Never had I seen A. so shabby. His old air-force coat hung open, devoid of buttons, there was a hole in his threadbare cords, and he was wearing the cheapest kind of imitation leather shoes. My first impulse was to fuss over him, offer him money, invite him to dinner, make him laugh and forget his solemn preoccupations – all the things I normally would have done. But he seemed so remote (not unsympathetic, he could never be that), I suddenly felt it was no longer my place to mother or sister him. I would be exceeding my limit, or rather the limit he had just imposed on me. He was making me, for the very first time, uncomfortable.

All I could do was to pretend that everything was *comme d'habitude* between us. That is, I think, the best approach in these delicate situations.

I offered him the swivel chair and perched myself close-by on a paint-splattered stool. I asked if he wanted a sherry, which I knew he would refuse and he did. He said he was not taking alcohol but I have never known him to drink much anyway. I poured another vermouth for me and asked what he thought of the painting which was of a large blue bird. I have always painted birds.

He squinted at it. 'Birds are thoughts, you know.'

'Really? I thought butterflies were.'

'Nope. They're the soul.'

'Oh yes.'

'Yes. In the *Mutus Liber*, for instance, there's a sixteenth-century print of the *artifex* and his *soror mystica* in a boat. He's fishing and she's catching birds with a net – blue birds, come to think of it. You ought to have a look. Most interesting.'

'Fascinating. Yes, I'd love to see it.' I felt insubstantial and hollow in his presence. I had often seen Adrian distracted, but never depressed or distraught or whatever he suddenly was. The pale face and grizzled golden whiskers, the circles under his eyes and the dirty nails told me my friend was languishing, sinking even. I, practically his sister, ought to be able to read his heart and rest his mind, but all I could say was,

'Tell me, my dear, what *is* the *Mutus Liber*?'

At first I was relieved when he wanted to talk. He told me about his studies and about the long and difficult poem he was going to write. He seemed about to confide in me in the old way. But I found it hard to follow his thoughts. I wasn't sure whether this was the result of my ignorance, or if they were really in a terrible jumble. He kept hinting that there was much he couldn't reveal, and that what he did say must remain couched in the most obscure symbolism.

'I believe I'm getting jolly close to sorting out the Prima Materia, you know,' he said, addressing himself more than me and growing quite excited.

'Well, after all those years as a metallurgist,' I began, but knew right away that was *not* what he meant. He hadn't even heard me.

'Now it's down to the old Nigredo,' he shook his head and clicked his tongue quietly. 'Of course everything takes place in the Unconscious these days,' he said, inclining towards me by way of something like partial confidence. 'Laboratory explosions are a thing of the past, and – '

'You mean one sort of blows up *inside*?' He gave me an odd look.

' – among the greatest practitioners of Our Art, were unheard of anyway. They, you know, dealt exclusively with the highest spiritual essences. And the Philosopher's Stone is no ordinary rock.'

'I do realize . . . '

'The thing is, dammit,' back to himself now, his thumb pressed hard into his chin, 'to extract the supermonic elements.'

'*Super-manic*?' I hardly dared ask.

Adrian hesitated, as if deciding whether or not to let me in on it.

'Higher inspirations,' he gravely brought out.

'Ah-ah,' I whispered. There was a pause.

'Ros has been calling me,' I said. 'She's frantic.'

'Oh dear.' He sighed and tapped his foot lightly on the floor. 'But you know, Kitty, solitude is essential for the Work. All the tracts say so and it's true. If one is going to deal with these unconscious contents . . . '

'Adrian darling, you're alone too much, I think.' I smiled. 'You get no refreshment and you're growing tired, Adrian, tired in your mind.'

'No, no, Kitty, I'm being fed! And I'm getting closer every day to the Source, the Source of all nourishment, you might say.'

Why was he talking like this? Why weren't we discussing Liszt and Mahler?

'I'm beginning to *see*. From the *masa confusa* I've extracted the first essence, I really have, you know.' He spoke sometimes like a brave eight-year-old. 'That's why, well, I'm sorry not to see you, Kit, but other people – ' He smiled a little. 'You're thinking what a bore all my earnestness is.'

'It's just that I'm nonplussed by your earnestness, Adrian. I don't know how to behave in the face of such earnestness. But I've told you before I believe in you. I'm sure some reward, either material or spiritual, awaits all this patient labour.'

'It's not reward I'm after, Kitty,' he looked hurt. Again I had failed to understand. 'You said once that I was rare and erudite. Well if I am, I shall achieve something that those tainted with "the slimy filth of avarice" can never comprehend.' He went from eight-year-old to fanatic. Did he mean *me*?

'Well, if not reward,' I smiled nervously, 'then what?'

'Transformation. Into gold. And use of highest order.'

'I see. And Ros?'

'Parsifal did, after all, leave his mother standing on the bridge.' How suddenly certain he was. How he meant it. 'There are things more important.' Kind Adrian, how could he? 'There's the most important thing.'

'Which is?' I kept looking into my drink.

'The work.'

His poem? The Stone? Some internal Krakatoa? I longed for one of Ros's imagined devices for certifying Meaning.

'But she's driving me mad,' I said as calmly as possible.

Adrian stared at me, uncomprehending. Then he got up and walked about the studio, agitatedly examining the paintings. I was very uncomfortable. I realized there was something he wanted and that he hadn't come simply to see me.

'Adrian, I'm sorry,' I went to him, taking his arm. 'Adrian, let me do something for you. At least stay to dinner. Jack would love to – '

'No, no, my dear. Must get back to my mistress – to my

terrible mistress. I was only just waiting for them to find a
particular manuscript and thought I'd drop in on you for the
interim. Sometimes takes hours, you know. I once waited
three days for a — I say, Melissa isn't about, is she?'

'Melissa?'

'Well you see I brought her another book.'

'But I'm sure she hasn't read the one you gave her, yet. I
doubt you'll ever see it again.'

'Oh, but she's returned it.'

'She has?' I was stunned. Melissa had said nothing. 'When?
You mean she went round to see you?'

'Mmmmm. Last week it was. She said she'd enjoyed it
immensely and that she'd got a great deal out of it.'

'Melly?' My voice cracked with disbelief. 'My little Philistine?'

'You mustn't underestimate her, Kitty. That's one of the
things I wanted to say to you. There's a side to her nature
which she's often too shy to reveal. Beneath that admittedly
rather awful surface, she's a lovely little girl, really. A pure
essence.' Only Adrian could say something like that with a
straight face.

'Good gracious! Well, she's not here right now, but I'll
certainly give her the book if and when she comes in.' I put out
my hand to take it.

'Thanks, Kitty, but I'd like to give it to her myself.
Bye-bye.'

I stood with my arm still extended.

'Well blow me.'

I couldn't help it. I had to ask Melly about this. I probed her
carefully, but, being Melly, she was giving nothing away. It's
difficult to be delicate when one is compelled to shout above
the Boomtown Rats, so I gave up and left her alone. I told
myself I ought to feel chuffed, since *mon petit complot* had
worked so well, and it looked as though Adrian was exerting a
positive influence on our Melly-brat. But all I felt was
nervous.

We had done little or nothing to punish her for her disgrace.
She came and went as she liked and was not called upon to
account for her activities. She had been asked only to give her
word of honour that there would be no more drugs. But now I

began to be aware of whether or not she was in the house. If the door banged, I would run to the street-facing window. If there were footsteps on the stairs I would look up automatically from my painting and glance at the clock. That I should worry about her visiting Adrian when I thought nothing of her being out until three with her little gang of Punks made me almost ashamed. It was inexcusable of me.

I had said nothing to Jack who was working hard for his next exhibition and consequently incommunicado. How odd it all was when at first I had visualized myself boasting of my achievement.

Ros kept calling me. Her efforts had been partially rewarded by a glimpse of her son, but their meeting had only compounded her misery.

'Now Kitty, you know Adrian always used to sound sensible. Whatever he got up to in private, he was at least excellent company. I mean that one could talk to him and feel occasionally that he was listening. He *referred* to things, don't you know, topical things. One could tell he read the newspapers. But now! Everything he says seems disjointed and peculiar. I don't know how else to describe it. It's absolutely peculiar.'

'I've noticed.'

'Oh, and do you know who was there when I called on him? I could scarcely believe it, after all the times I've been turned away, told he was busy or couldn't find him and nearly went mad with anxiety, do you know who? Your Melissa! Lounging on his bed with those horrible big boots of hers, drinking tequila and blowing smoke everywhere.'

'When?'

'It was intolerable. I had to ask Adrian to open a window. Two days ago. Kitty, I do hope you intend doing something about her. I must tell you I'm seriously concerned for her future. And why Adrian encourages her visits, I've no idea.'

'She goes to him often, then?'

'Of course. Or at least it seemed so. Didn't you know? They're positively thick!'

'Adrian is a good influence on her.'

'Well, I'm sure. But you know he's a perfect innocent. What do you suppose *she's* doing to *him*?'

The thought had occurred to me.

'And the state of the flat. Kitty, it's a sty. And Adrian was always so careful with his things. Is this what he calls making the spirit manifest?'

That night, for the first time in months, I waited up for Melissa. When at one o'clock she had not come home, I did something unprecedented: I lost control – well, just a bit, but for me just a bit is a great deal. I needed to express and to share my anxiety. I knocked timidly at the door of Jack's studio.

'Melissa's not back,' I shouted above *Ivan the Terrible*.

'Oh yes. Want to call the police?'

'Don't be absurd, Jack. I just thought you ought to know.'

'Call them if you're worried. Let them do something for the good of the community instead of protecting the National Front or beating people's heads in at perfectly peaceful demonstrations, or selling their memoirs for more money than you or I shall ever see. Is it morning yet?'

'It's nearly one.'

'Only one? Look here, Kitty, it's a bit much. I'm working my arse off to finish this show and you're upset because Melissa's not closeted in her room doing needle-point or practising the spinet or something. I've told you before, the girl's no dunce, she knows what she's doing. Believe me, I understand her, and any interference will only escalate hostilities.'

'That's unfair, Jack. I'm the last person to interfere.'

'Then leave me in peace. Please. You know perfectly well that if I don't sell everything in this show, we'll be on the bank manager's shit list and there'll be no holiday in Corsica this year. Oh, and you can also forget your exotic little plans about Sri Lanka next winter. Come to think of it, why don't we move to New York or even Dusseldorf? London is no bloody place for an artist. Everyone knows the British don't understand painting. What the hell are we doing here, anyway? Meanwhile, if you're feeling so desperately maternal, have a look-in on Orlando. Your son seems a bit peaky to me.'

'Listen, Jack, I think – oh dear, perhaps I shouldn't say anything, but well, they may be having an affair.'

'Who may be?' He had gone back to work and was crawling around on his hands and knees, tipping tins of acrylic paint on to the seven by nine foot canvas.

'Melissa and Adrian.'

'Which Adrian?'

'Adrian your schoolmate, my life-long friend. Adrian the poet, the scholar, the gentleman. Adrian the mad genius.'

'Good Lord!' I finally had his attention. 'Kitty, are you sure?'

'Well I said they *might* be. They're both such queer creatures, I suppose it was inevitable they'd be attracted to each other. Now please don't be angry.'

'Angry?' He scrambled to his feet. 'Why in God's name did you tell me this if you were so afraid I'd be angry? Kitty, for someone supposedly blessed with an evolved social sense, you operate like the Ape Girl of Brundi.' He wiped his hands on a rag and went for his coat.

'Jack, where are you going?'

'Round to his flat, of course.'

'Whose flat?'

'*Adrian's*, you silly bitch!'

I felt a bit panic stricken, but quickly collected myself. I am not unequal to Jack's irrationalism. In fact, Jack in a mad mood has always been an inspiration to me to keep my head. I followed him to the front door, mentally rehearsing a smooth deterrent. At that moment Melissa walked out of the sitting room.

'Hi, Jack,' she smiled at him almost pleasantly. 'Are you off? Give us a ciggy before you go?'

'Melissa, where have you been?' Of course he just waded in, didn't he.

She tensed immediately. 'In the sitting room watching Hammer House of Horror if it's any affair of yours.'

'Since when?' Would he never learn the value of a light touch?

She looked from one of us to the other, scanning the frowns that must have been creasing our faces.

'Oh balls! I'm not going to take this. Just to satisfy your nasty curiosity I'll tell you that I've been here for the past two hours. But that's the last you'll ever hear from me, because I'm never speaking to either of you again.' She ran upstairs and slammed and bolted her door.

I couldn't have been so wrong about the time. I was certain

that she had not been in the house when I checked half an hour
before, but had come in quietly when I was in Jack's studio and
slipped into the sitting room then. But I could not bring
myself to call Melly a liar outright. Why had she done it? She
had never had compunction about coming in openly at whatever time she pleased. In fact she seemed to enjoy flaunting her
méchanceté. (Naturally, we have always understood such
behaviour as simply a means of provoking us, and so
judiciously have ignored it.)

Jack was saying something to me, only now it was I who
wasn't listening. I felt I no longer understood Melly. It was as
though a part of her had died and gone to live on another
plane. What remained with us was all dim and inscrutable.

'Well, I'm leaving this with you, Kitty. You're the dip-
lomat, after all, and I have to cope with the show. Apply that
famous light touch of yours and see what you can find out. It's
probably nothing, though,' he smiled. 'You always were
prone to hysteria.' An arm went round my waist and a hand up
under my jumper. 'Come and see me later when I've finished,
Ape Girl.' Not only was Jack a terrible tease, but he still liked
making love occasionally on that freezing studio floor.

I didn't go. After putting the duvet back on Orlando, I went
to my room and stayed there. I tried to think what the best
approach to the Melly-Adrian dilemma might be. I'm not a
stupid person, nor a bungler, nor a hysteric, despite what Jack
had said. I like to be just, to be delicate yet honest, to do the
beautiful, intelligent thing, and to combine, if possible, reason
with love. I saw that I was about to take the wrong tone. I
must try to see the situation in its larger sense, see its irony, its
beauty even. Yes, once one rid oneself of a certain vestigial
morality, there was a kind of beauty in the idea of Adrian and
Melissa as lovers, a balance of opposites, and consequently a
rightness. Perhaps instead of interfering I ought to encourage.
But I could do neither I realized, until their relationship was
clear, until I saw for myself what it was.

I *would* see them. I would be their friend. I would appear not
in the least worried or inquisitive. I would behave as if nothing
had happened, as if nothing ever could happen. *Ça, c'est la
meilleure façon, je crois.* Yes, it has been my experience that that
is always the best approach.

It took me several tries and many fruitless telephone calls and notes to catch Adrian at home. I was not certain whether the lack of response was because he was hunched over his cubicle in the BM, meeting Melly at a secret rendezvous, or right there behind his own door in his own bed with a naked Melissa, locked in some fabulous conjunctio.

Finally my timing was right. It was after six on an August evening, and the West End was lonely under a broad pink sky. I looked up from the street to Adrian's tiny window and imagined what it must be like to be him, to be round-shouldered and losing one's eyesight, to have nothing on earth but that room and those books, to live on Campbell's soup and Mother's Pride and McVitie's Digestives, to ride a bicycle instead of drive a car, to be always alone. Tears rose in my eyes. I missed Adrian terribly.

I was about to ring the bell, but someone came out of the building and let me in with a smile. People trust me I suppose. I climbed the four flights of stairs and stopped outside Adrian's door. He was speaking, not at his usual rapid tilt, but slowly and precisely. I knocked. There was no tell-tale scuffling or desperately polite Just a Moment. Adrian answered the door immediately, his finger clamped between the pages of a book.

'Kitty!' he boomed. 'How wonderful! Staying, I hope?' He hugged me hard. His warmth made me laugh with relief. He seemed the old Adrian again – frank, free, and hospitable.

Ros was right, though, the room was a bomb-site. Papers, books, records, and dirty dishes littered the floor. The bed was a heap of crumpled linen. In the heat, the place smelled of mice and blocked drains, and was made curiously sad by the rosy evening light. On the couch, beside which stood a bottle of Nicolas Rouge and two smudgy glasses, lay Melissa. She wore a pair of my high-heels and a pencil skirt pulled flagrantly up over her bare white knees.

'Hullo, Kit. Had an *intuition* you'd turn up.'

'Hello, darling. Lovely to find you here. Well, are you going to offer me a drink?'

'Yes, but you must promise to be quiet and not babble because A's translating for me. Sit down, why don't you? A, get her a glass or something.'

She pointed imperiously at a wobbly chair and I took it

without a word. Her behaving as if she owned the place was a bit irritating, but I had come, after all, to observe and not to react.

I sat in my straight-backed chair, my drink on my knees, feeling absurdly prim. Adrian resumed his reading. He was translating Meyrink's *Angel at the Western Window* directly from the French. The fantastic tale was being rendered into careful, though not unlyrical, English, and Melissa, sipping her wine and blowing clouds of smoke into the darkening room, was all serious consideration. I was touched. How sweet of Adrian, selflessly giving of his time and effort for the edification of my benighted little girl. And what an effect he appeared to be having! Never had I known Melly to focus so much attention on a grown-up, at least not without coercion.

At first I didn't listen. I was absorbed in their faces and in the atmosphere of the scene, trying to divine the secret link that existed between them, if it did exist. But I soon forgot about the two of them and all I had meant to discover, the thing itself was so beautifully weird and engrossing. How long we sat there I don't know but when the candle by which Adrian was reading went out, the room was in darkness.

'I'm tired anyway, A,' Melissa said. 'Can we stop now?'

I heard the book close. I thought I could detect the sticking and parting of flesh, the damp pressure of a hand on the inside of a – thigh? Then the light went on.

'Well, Kit, what did you think of that?'

'Marvellous. I had no idea your French was so proficient.'

'Ah, I've been practising, you see. Off to Paris next week, then Basle.'

This might mean relief. 'Oh yes, what for?'

'There's a manuscript in the Basle library, the Egerton 845; thought I'd have a look at it, then immerse myself in the Bibliothèque Nationale, for quite a spell, really. Wonderful things there, you know.' He was reassuringly crisp.

'Exhausted the BM then?'

'As a matter of fact,' he smiled at me, 'just about.'

'How long will you be away?'

'Not sure. A good while, I expect.'

How he intended to manage the journey financially I had no idea. Perhaps he had borrowed again from Ros.

'I want to leave now,' Melly announced. 'Will you drive me, Kit?'

Well, well. My fears were falling off like dead skin.

'Too bad we didn't have a chance to play.' I glanced at the Bluthner. 'Next time we really must.'

'Indeed we must.'

I held Adrian in a long embrace. Melissa didn't approach him but, from the doorway, waved the tips of her fingers at him with an enigmatic smile.

'Did you really like the book?' she asked me as we walked to the car.

'It's fantastic. As though it were written in another world, another state of being.'

'Funny. It seemed like real life to me.'

'Will you miss Adrian?' I had to ask, even as I imagined myself articulately laying all Jack's suspicions to rest.

'Don't be daft, Kit.'

Of course she ran off with him. At first I thought we had been burgled because £112 in cash, my amber necklace, and all of my make-up were missing. But when she had not appeared in thirty-six hours, we put two and two together and rang Sac Frères. Sure enough, a young lady answering her description had been in the previous morning and sold them a necklace exactly like mine. We raced to Adrian's flat, but, as we suspected, there was no answer. A neighbour confirmed that he had left the evening before with a suitcase and a companion.

For one awful moment we considered ringing the police. Instead I rang Ros. She knew nothing. Adrian hadn't told her he was leaving and naturally she was hysterical when I broke the news. She was spluttering so badly that I recommended an immediate phone call to her psychiatrist.

We tried to be calm and rational. We had to be. There were only ten days until Jack's show opened. To my surprise, he did not refer again to the subject of police involvement. ('Godammit, Kitty, I refuse to play Godwin to that aging Shelley.') He seemed prepared to take the larger view.

We drank a bottle of Jameson's and decided to do the Grand Thing: we would let them alone. Obviously, it was a necessary experience for them both, and no doubt a compensation for some terrible breach in their early development. We could not, we should not, deprive them of the opportunity for that compensation. After all, it was their business. Clearly *we* understood neither of them.

I imagined the incongruous pair trudging across Northern Europe, shivering on railway platforms (autumn was coming and Melissa had not taken her heavy jacket), and setting down their suitcases, exhausted, in bleak hotel rooms. Surely passion, if that's what it was, must pale under such conditions. And then what would Melly do for the six to eight hours a day that Adrian would be sure to spend in libraries? I already knew the answer to that: get into trouble.

Then I wondered if Melly really was different with Adrian? What if she showed him, and only him, a side of her nature that was secretly beautiful? What if he had extracted her pure essence, in a word, redeemed her? I suppose, for a while, that is what I chose to believe. Nevertheless, I was far from happy about it, and so was Jack.

As the weeks went by, we spoke very little of Melissa and Adrian. Whenever Orlando asked about his sister, we said she was on holiday. It wasn't really a lie; it was simply the way we were trying to regard the situation. Besides, how could we explain to an eight-year-old something we did not comprehend ourselves? Perhaps, as Adrian would have said, it *was* all taking place in the Unconscious.

Jack's show went moderately well. Quite good reviews, but not as many paintings sold as we had hoped. It would have to be Ros's cottage in Cornwall next summer, and not Corsica.

Melissa's letter arrived at the end of September. This single communication we had had from her contained only the name and address of a hotel in Amiens, the suggestion that in three days we all meet for dinner at the restaurant downstairs, and a postscript in red: we were not, under any circumstances, to bring Ros. We booked a place on the hovercraft for the morning of the second of October.

Now that Jack knew Melissa was on her way home (that was the only conclusion one could draw), he turned nauseatingly benign. He'd had time to rationalize, and was positively flooded with realizations which he expanded upon, without a break, all the way from London to Boulogne.

'You know I've been giving the matter a great deal of

thought, Kit. People can so easily go off the deep end with things like Alchemy, especially a chap as sensitive and ungratified as Adrian. Potentially dangerous, these so-called voyages of self-discovery, and bloody boring for us uninitiated. Same with Astrology, Yoga, ESP ... Remember Julia and Stuart and their greasy Rajneesh? Dressed up in those awful plastic malas with pictures of the old boy – Ugh! And Charlie Platts – he spent a fortune on EST and became insufferable.'

'Adrian takes seriously things that other people only play at. You can't compare him to Charlie Platts – he was born insufferable.'

Jack ignored me. 'Adrian's lonely, correct? He's cerebral, mother-dominated and needs a woman. Melly re-enters his life. Bam! She's perfect: familiar and strange, accessible and remote. *Young*. And she's naughty as hell. Nothing could be more guaranteed to appeal.'

'You mean goody-goody Adrian, nasty-nymphet Melissa? Compensation for Ros and all that? I'd say it was a bit too neat and Freudian.'

'What's wrong with Freud? He was a perfectly pleasant man and his ideas have done excellent service as far as I can tell. Look, Kit, you may regard the whole affair as some "Education Sentimentale," but it's cunt pure and simple.'

'All that thought and this is your conclusion?'

'Besides, the way you and Ros fuss over him, I expect he's damned pleased to meet a woman who'll treat him rough.'

It has never ceased to amaze me what Philistines artists can be.

'You seem to have trouble perceiving shades of meaning, my dear. I don't in the least regard the affair as simply romantic, though it would be a mistake to exclude that influence completely. No, I think Adrian sees Melly as the feminine aspect of himself, as something from the depths of his own unconscious that he has to confront and grapple with. It's himself he's after, not Melly.' Jack had to be made to realize that he wasn't the only one who'd been giving the matter some thought.

'Kitty, you're tossing around an awful lot of concepts you don't understand. Just because you got half-way through

Archetypes and the Collective Unconscious, you don't necessarily
have the key to the mysteries. *You* may think and *he* may think
he's extracting her pure essence, but all he really wants is a
good fuck. I certainly can sympathize with that!'

I was tempted to ask why he assumed Melly to be so
exceptionally qualified in that department. But I was not
going to argue with Jack. Best keep him in a good mood, since
there was no telling what might happen later. Just then I was
rather wishing that Adrian had opted for the plastic malas.

He didn't say much until we reached the outskirts of
Amiens. Neither of us had visited the place for years, and we
were confounded by the one-way system.

'I'm sure we passed this square ten minutes ago,' I said,
putting the Michelin guide face down on my lap and flipping
the cassette tape over.

'We mustn't blame him you know,' Jack suddenly said, as
though he had just invented compassion.

'Who on earth is blaming him?'

'So much of his problem is loneliness. The saddest thing is
that if A had talked to us more about how he was feeling, we
might have avoided this.'

I was inclined to agree with him there.

'Pity he shut himself off that way. So unnecessary. Melly's
had enough, obviously. He'll have to face it. I'm sure there's a
great deal he'll want to get off his chest now – are you paying
attention to the street signs? I don't know about you, but I'm
certainly prepared to stay and hammer it out with him, talk to
him as long as he likes, do whatever I can for the poor chap,
you know.'

As if I had ever, for a single moment, considered aban-
doning Adrian.

Having at last found the street, the hotel and the restaurant,
we arrived forty-five minutes late for our meeting. The place
was situated on a narrow old rue that gave on to the cathedral,
which in the deepening twilight, seemed to engulf us all in its
great Gothic shadow.

The restaurant, a family business, was brightly lit and
already crowded with locals plus the last few tourists of the
season. Beethoven's Seventh was being piped repeatedly
through a loud speaker bristling with static. Near the entrance

to the kitchen a waiter in evening dress was attempting to catch a trout from among a dozen or so swimming in a tank. He fished uncertainly with a small white net, his free hand clutching a plastic bag. But even in such a confined space, the creature eluded him. The diners watched with lively interest as the embarrassed waiter made one futile attempt after another to land his prey. Among the onlookers was Adrian, seated alone at a corner table, his chin on his palm, gnawing at the nail of his middle finger. He seemed, unlike the others, to find the spectacle not at all comic. He was so absorbed that we were seated opposite him before he realized that we had arrived.

'Oh, you're here.' He turned in his chair. 'How was the journey?'

He looked quite anorexic. They had been living rough, obviously.

'Not bad.' Jack unfurled his napkin and cast about for the Carte de Vins. 'Channel was smooth. Dreadful one-way system here, though. Positive maze. Uh, where's Melly?'

'She got a bit bored waiting, I'm afraid, and went for a stroll. She's probably looking at the cathedral.'

I leaned over and kissed him and he smiled weakly. I wanted more than anything in the world to do something for him.

I felt a kick under the table: my cue from Jack to disappear. Apparently he had decided to launch straight into his man-to-man with Adrian. I resented his taking over like that. Adrian was my friend, my brother almost. I had always understood him better than Jack did. But I got up, announcing that I was going in search of Melissa.

As I walked out, the whole restaurant suddenly burst into applause. I stopped, startled and very self-conscious. I could feel my shoulders tense, and I may inadvertently have clutched my bag to my stomach. Then I realized what had happened. It had nothing to do with me. The trout had been caught at last, and the waiter, smiling and blushing and holding up the plastic bag with its wriggling victim, was bowing hurriedly to his little audience. Then he raced off to the kitchen, no doubt to plop the fish into a waiting court-bouillon.

I walked to the end of the deserted street and turned right. I saw Melly by the dingy glow of a lamp. She was standing beneath the South Transept Door looking up at the statue of the Virgin Mary over the entrance. (You may know it – the one with the funny little smile, like a young girl with the most delightful secret, the culmination of fifteenth-century French sculpture, and sometimes referred to as 'La Soubrette Picarde'.) On the opposite side of the road was a smoke-filled café where boys played pinball machines and space invaders. As I approached, I saw that her hair had grown out, that it was no longer spiky but lay flat and straight with only traces of the pink and orange streaks. Despite the chilly evening, she wore just a print dress over her black fish-net stockings and gold espadrilles. She caught the sound of my footsteps and turned. She smiled a little. She seemed different, but I knew better than to make any big display of affection.

'Hullo, Kitty. What kept you?'

'I'm pleased to see you, Melissa. Are you all right?'

'Yes.' She looked up at the statue.

I thought of a dozen things to say, all inappropriate. But there was an awkward silence to be filled. I stood beside her.

'Wonderful, isn't she? I haven't seen her in years.'

Melissa didn't look at me. 'Adrian says that Melusina is the snake-woman, that she's a mermaid, cold and terrible, but that when she's married to the Sun she's redeemed and crowned like the Virgin Mary and that she leads to all knowledge like Sophia.' Her voice was sweet and far away. Something *had* changed. 'Do you think that's true, Kitty? Do you believe that?'

I touched her lightly on her bare arm. 'Darling, if Adrian says so, I'm sure it's true. After all, he's the expert.'

'Oh really?' She did not alter her tone nor look at me. 'Then you must be as daft as he is, because it's all a crock of shit.'

I thought of Adrian's pale face and his nails bitten down to the quick. I couldn't help it. All of a sudden I blamed her. I desperately wanted her to feel guilt, or at least the infliction of some punishment.

I meant to slap her as hard as I could, but half-way to her face, the movement disintegrated. As in a dream, my hand seemed to travel not through air but mush, and there was no real force to my blow. Melly barely flinched. Her eyes were black and hard in the lamplight. I felt, just briefly, afraid.

'I always knew you were an interfering cunt, Kitty. But I

didn't realize until now that you were a fool as well. I'm going back.'

I followed her to the hotel.

Jack and Melissa devoured a four-course meal plus wine, coffee and copious cigarettes. Adrian and I scarcely ate anything. I could not get over the way I had bungled what might have been a beautiful denouement. Never had my diplomacy so failed me. As for Adrian, he was thoroughly gloomy. He said nothing and stared at his untouched food, and when he looked at me, his eyes seemed big with damned-up tears. Jack was holding forth as usual, about wine, about art, about money, about the French. He seemed to be one enormous opinion. It was obvious that he was hugely pleased with himself and considered that he had "hammered it out" satisfactorily with Adrian. His insensitivity appalled me.

Melly, meanwhile, was managing everything. She made it clear that she wanted to leave that very night and was not prepared to wait another hour.

We paid for the meal. We paid their hotel bill. We paid a week's rent in advance for Adrian. (Another demonstration of Jack's largesse. Oh he was grand, alright.) Then we all went upstairs to collect Melly's things. She threw her few belongings into an old rucksack and two plastic bags and surveyed for the last time the mess they had made of the room. Adrian sat on the bed watching her, making no effort to hide his misery.

'Well A, I'm off now.' She stood before him.

He did not look up but raised his hand to her. She took it and pumped it gently.

'Don't be depressed.' Her voice was almost kind. She waited, but he said nothing. He clung to her hand. Melly's patience was limited, and she seemed to consider that he was taking far too long to cheer up. She snatched her hand away, bent down, and kissed him quickly.

'Bye-bye, Babe. Hope you find your rock an' all.'

He didn't speak. Melissa turned, picked up her plastic bags, and walked out.

I let her and Jack go on ahead while I had one last minute with Adrian. I couldn't bear to leave him like that.

'Adrian,' I pleaded, 'why stay in this place? Come with us. We'll drive you back to London. Please come.'

I had hoped that when we were alone he would break down and confide in me, let me into the whole mysterious thing.

'Can't, Kitty. It's back to the Bibliothèque Nationale.' To my astonishment, he appeared to be gathering strength.

'Back to my terrible mistress. She's saving me a chair and my corner and some manuscripts I've waited a long time to see.' He half-smiled. 'I'm nearly ready to start writing now.' It was terrible the way he was being so brave.

'Your book will be superb, Adrian, divinely inspired, I know it. But how will you live?' I held out a roll of notes I had been keeping for him. 'At least take some money. I insist.'

He pushed my hand away.

'Oh come now,' I tried to be light. 'It isn't exactly "the slimy filth of avarice".'

'I don't want it. I can't take it.'

His resistance, I sensed, was impregnable. I gave up.

'Adrian,' I said, 'I'm so sorry.'

'Why are you sorry, Kitty?'

'Melissa — I don't know how to put it. Don't try to tell me she hasn't made things difficult.'

'On the contrary,' he seemed surprised. 'I'm for ever in her debt.'

'Indebted to that — oh Adrian, you don't know what you're saying.'

'Quite honestly, Kitty, neither do you. You judge only by appearance. You don't understand that now I can move on to the next stage of the Work, and she,' he made some noise I didn't know how to interpret, 'she can go back to Nymphidida.'

I would sooner he had said she could go back to hell.

'Adrian, you don't know how funny you're talking. You're exhausted, my dear. Come back with us. Come back and rest.'

'"The Stone will be found when the search sits heavy on the searcher." Which means that if it's not difficult, it's not worth much, and that the nearer the truth one gets, the greater the difficulties become.'

'Adrian, please . . . ' I took his hand. He squeezed it kindly.

'I'm in difficulties for good, Kitty. Don't imagine you can rescue me.'

'Rescue? Oh Adrian, I wouldn't dream – '

'Then why don't you go now, Kitty darling. And you won't tell Ros where I am, will you?'

'How can I when I don't know myself? Will you at least tell me?'

'I'll drop you a line.' He let go of my hand. He hadn't let me into it after all. He'd never let me in.

'Adrian. Adrian, erudite and rare, don't abandon me. Don't send me back alone with those two – ' I hadn't meant to say it. It just came out.

'Run along now, Kitty, there's a good girl.'

Desolation overwhelmed me. Half-way down the stairs I stopped to press myself into the corner of the landing. I didn't want the others to see me cry.

Just after Easter, Ros found him in Paris. It had taken her months and I don't know how she managed it. He lives in a wretched place four floors above the sex shops, whores and fast-food stands on the Rue St Denis. He says he is writing.

Of course she called me immediately she got back. I rather dreaded talking to her, but was hungry for news of Adrian.

'He looks awful. He's worn out and run down. He's developed a dreadful cough, and he desperately needs glasses which he refuses to buy because they'll keep him from "truly seeing". Well, it's not surprising he's deranged, living in that place, spending six days a week at the Bibliothèque Nationale, reading those crazy books and not knowing a soul, as far as I can make out. When he's not in the library he's at Notre Dame or St Chapelle or – oh, what's the other one called? Paris is such a rude, dirty city, I'm always confused there. You have no idea what this has done to me, Kitty. I feel he's going to die and that I shall die too.' She began to cry, but not long enough to give me a chance to say anything. 'I told him he was ill, but he insists he's *happy*. I begged him to return. He wouldn't have it, nor would he take money. I ended by hiding some in one of his books. Thank God he hasn't sent it back, at least not yet. Kitty, I'm sorry, but I have to say this: if it weren't for that terrible depraved Melissa this would never have happened. But he won't hear a word against her. He even asked where she was, though he swore to me he has no plans to see her again. I should think so too, after she so effectively ruined him.'

'She's at school. They took her back at half-term. I almost never see her.' It was true, and I was glad of it.

'What did she *do* to him, I ask myself over and over. Was he in love, or was it just sex, or what?'

'I don't pretend to know, Ros. She hardly speaks to me. *Nous sommes aux antipodes, j'ai peur.* Jack's the one who – well, she told him, I guess, that sex had nothing to do with it. It's my opinion that she's lying again, but then whatever she said now I'd think she was lying.'

'Poor Kitty. She's made life difficult for you too, hasn't she? You've been awfully brave.'

'Really, Ros, you didn't think I would ever – *break down* or anything, did you?'

'Well, no. But somehow I feel we're in the same boat, you and I.'

'I'm only sorry Adrian felt he had to go away from us, that's all.'

'Oh Kitty, you have no idea what this has done to me.'

She calls me nearly every day. It makes me rather *fatiguée* at times, but I humour her and try to console her. Ros is one of those people with whom it's important to use a light touch.

A Parma Violet Room

(a tale of ruin)

Letter One

March 10,1978
Los Angeles

My Dear Sylvie,

It has not been easy to find you. I wrote first to Marlowe's
mother who informed me that the darling boy has fled to
Singapore, no doubt in quest of more illicit plunder, or
possibly just to die like a Conrad hero beneath that burning
sky. (Tell me please, how is your old love?) Then I met
Caroline in a bar in West Hollywood. She looks eighty and
can't be more than forty-two. Years of self-abuse will leave
their mark, n'est-ce-pas? She said Ivor had seen you in London
last September and that you were looking for a flat in N1 – and
you a confirmed SWer. Accordingly phoned Ivor. He lives on
the dole and is married to that aging speed freak, the one with
the Alsatians and no teeth who had delusions of herself as some
West Coast Dorothy Parker. He invited me to tea, and
reluctantly I went round. Flat and female both appalling. He
told me that Linda committed suicide at Christmas – all to the
good; the poor lamb had had leukaemia for years – and that
when last seen you were staying with Pauline who is still
trying to be an actress and weighs eleven stone.

At last I had an address. Pauline actually replied, saying that
you had bought a flat in Barnsbury. You are, it appears, in
hiding. Is this true? You certainly must be among the last of us
in London. Strange that you and I should swap countries like

this. Anyway, I had recourse to International Directory Enquiries and here I am!

By now I am sure you have heard the tragic news. Not unexpected. But I am also sure that you, just as I − we knew her best, did we not? − were aghast when confronted with the bare horror of her end. It is too dreadful. It is unendurable. It is a deep long look into the eyes of the Dweller on the Threshold. What can one do with such awfulness but transform it into Art? In reference to which I enclose an obituary which I wrote immediately I was informed that she was no longer with us. (Sadly we are old enough to perform these functions for each other now.) It has been published already in an arts magazine of some repute. *Rolling Stone* almost took it, but the *LA Times* refused on the grounds that she isn't known here. What rubbish, when she was a seminal influence for what may have been five of the most culturally critical years of this century.

There can be no doubt, however, that she is known in London. She did, after all, establish her reputation, artistic and otherwise, in that city. If you still maintain any of your old contacts, do please submit this for me. It is so important that her achievement be recognized, especially given the dismal circumstances of her last years.

Of course I wanted you to see the piece first.

I have been living quietly since she died, not in mourning, you understand, but in temporary retirement, working on a new collection of poems called *The Burning Bush*, dedicated, of course, to Her. I rent a charming house in Santa Monica with a piano and avocado trees. Arthur has converted what was once a chicken coop in the back, and stays here when life with Umburto has become umbearable. The neighbourhood, however, is crawling with gays who use the next-door garage as a trysting place and wake me in the middle of the night with their carousals. All nature conspires against the struggle to create. 'One must be strong in order to become strong.' Well Amen to that.

The bookshop prospers. I have an excellent assistant to whom I entrust business matters when the Muse is beating on my walls or has me by the balls or whatever.

Oh, I have been to the grave. The funeral was, of course, out of the question. You will be pleased to know that the

atmosphere around that sad new mound was at least serene. I
went alone and left but one token: a bunch of Parma violets.
Associations were rife: George Sand at the grave of Chopin,
Adrienne LeCouvreure, my first ecstatic days with Georgia. I
wept. Would, I thought, that I were Orpheus and that the
earth would open and show me the passage to the Under-
world. How I should employ all my arts to charm Perse-
phone's seducer. *I* should not fail to bring Eurydice back to the
light.

Do write me, my darling. I have been deprived too long of
the sweet solace of your personality.

Yours in resignation,
Miles

PS You might try *Thera, A Magazine of the Arts.* The office is
in South Ken, I think. Best contact them straightaway while
interest is high.

Enclosure

Georgia DeBellis – A Death for the Time of Our Life

Debauch, Balzac said, is not for craven spirits. Our
darling Georgia must hold a high place among the practitioners of that dangerous art. Her macabre indulgences
were legion and legend. She led a life that few would dare
and had a charisma few could equal. But like some queen
or courtesan out of the fabulous past, she no longer suited
this tame time. She burst upon the scene as prodigy and
prodigy she remained. For reason, repose and the settled
advancement of a quiet middle life she was not created.

She is gone, as of February 8, 1978, gone like youth,
glory, love, and the frenzy of creation. The dark god has
claimed her, and we are all diminished thereby. He was a
god she knew, a god she sought and worshipped openly.
She consecrated her life to him, and in return he granted
her the power to create, out of darkness, a rare beauty.

Happily, Georgia's works have survived her self-destruction. They speak for her. They will always speak for her.

Her collages couple daring simplicity with veiled menace. They are sensual, witty, mystical, and reveal, on closer inspection, many occult and cabalistic references. She was, among other things, a learned hermeticist, some say witch. If so, her real witchery lies in these little masterpieces. They are invocations, invocations that work. They call forth daemons and are themselves daemonic. Their queer juxtapositions afford a glimpse of an exotic inner world – a place voluptuous, sophisticated, malicious, and whimsical. The world of dreams. Looking at her works, absorbed by them, one feels that this is what lies behind our seemingly ordered reality: the terror, the joke, the weird beauty. In the way they surprise and manipulate the viewer the pictures are Surrealist. They have their origin in the two great periods of collage making, the 1920s and the 1960s – both exuberant, rebellious, and anarchistic decades, both influenced by the findings of psychoanalysis, and both politically extremist.

Georgia openly acknowledged her debt to the Surrealists, especially Max ('Hundred Headed Woman') Ernst and Man Ray. The same deft manipulation of the imagery of the unconscious is common to all three. In the wider sense she is part of a tradition whose aesthetic pedigree is traceable back to the great French super-Romantics, to Theophile Gautier and Gustave Moreau. But she is unique, in that her pictures are imbued with an exclusively female libido. They glow with genital fire; they are consummately sexual. For Georgia was among the first of those outlandish blooms to flower during the so-called 'liberation' of the early Sixties (a term so universally taken up as to have become sadly trite, and whose original impact has been virtually forgotten). She was artist, satirist, rebel, but above all, woman. She was an original, and frighteningly free. (Admit it, brothers, we all took cover when she shot from that delectable hip.) Society did not know how to account for her. It simply was drawn to her, irresistibly drawn, by an attraction undeniable even to those purists — both the aesthetic and the moral variety — who normally scorn such allurements.

Georgia DeBellis went the way of many great artists and all great voluptuaries. Nothing could tame that insatiate spirit, to her damnation and our loss. Depravity and despair led to illness and isolation. The flame was quenched. It was inevitable.

From our position in this saner, more sterile time, ten years past the peak of her notoriety, we mourn her. We mourn ourselves too. For with her, it seems, have gone the appetites and aspirations of our youth. We who survived that sensational era have life and a pale reason. Georgia has death and our regrets. She also has fame and a place for ever in the temple of art. She has, above all, our love.

Miles Plowright
February 13, 1978

Letter Two

Belitha Villas
London, N1
March 17, 1978

Miles! You!

Out of darkness and despair. After five years. Your letter! A miracle. Thank you, Miles.

Before I say more, let me tell you that I have delivered your beautiful piece into the capable hands of Sarah Debden, now an editor at *Thera*. Together we wept over it.

As to Georgia, I am unable to voice my distress. I cannot, like you, transform grief into art. I am simply paralysed. If only I knew how it happened. Her last letters were incoherent and barely legible. It was so confusing. There have been no reports in the papers. There has been no one to ask, no one who would understand. So your article fills a great gap for me and, I am sure, for others who knew her and who now regret their lack of compassion. It is incredible that she could have been forgotten like this. I have never forgotten, and I never shall forget. My memories give me no peace.

The most poignant of my memories is the last visit I paid to the Parma Violet Room. It was eleven days after I had put Georgia on a plane to LA. (Even then, as she disappeared behind the passenger barrier, I had a premonition that I would not see her again in this world.)

I cannot tell you how I felt as I opened that battered door again and saw the dirt, the squalour, the sadness. I shudder to describe what I found under the bed. Oh that room. When one thinks how Georgia consecrated it as a kind of temple to love and art and lavished on it all her taste and enthusiasm. Perhaps she should never have left it. Perhaps I'm wrong. I only know I was afraid of it and of that sinister apartment with its long dark hallways and closed doors. And I was afraid of those three women who were once her friends and flatmates and lovers. They had rung me to ask me to clear out her remaining possessions. They said they were anxious to rent the room. But it seemed impossible that any soul could exist in peace in that haunted place.

The women were glad to be rid of Georgia. They hated her, with some reason I suppose. Her paranoia did become impossible. In the end, she would unbolt the door only to me. She was convinced the others were trying to poison her. So she took her meals alone into that infamous room. There she ate them like a hunted animal, vomiting almost immediately into that silver bowl she kept by the bed. You know the one – it served as an ashtray in better days. I can still hear her shrieking at Marlowe when he miscalculated and flicked his joint on to the Chinese picture rug.

I found old syringes, dirty needles, yellowed underwear, colonies of insects. Georgia had left behind several books which would not fit in the trunks. These I kept, according to her instructions. The rest I would not have touched. I told the three they might keep it or burn it. It was straight out of Edgar Allen Poe.

Oh Miles, I thought of you so much that night in that room

where once we all listened to Fauré and Mahler, read poetry to
each other, drank the milk of paradise. I wanted you with me.
But that is selfish. Better you never knew the final state of the
place: the oppressive heat, the smell, the lurid half-light.
Better you never saw the patches on the wall where the
collages used to hang, the odious stains on the satin sheets, her
old silks and velvets, the broken bed, the Odeon ceiling lamp
covered with dust and cobwebs, the floor dismally bare of the
scattered Oriental rugs. (She got the idea from a photograph
of Sarah Bernhardt's room, remember?) I tell you, Miles, it
was as though Georgia were dead already.

The evening left me with a permanent sense of oppression.
Georgia was my dearest friend, Miles. I loved her. I tried my
best to help her. After she left London I sent her some
homeopathic remedies, but she was too far gone for them to
be of any use. If I knew then what I know now − perhaps
radionics could have saved her. Maybe not, since she was her
own worst enemy. And proved it. One by one, every friend,
every lover deserted her. She used drugs to smother the pain of
rejection, but the more drugs she took, the more erratic her
personality grew. The more she alienated people. Then when
illness struck there was no one to save her. No one but me, and
it seems I failed.

But you know about this. In your heart, Miles, I'm sure you
really loved her, in spite of what happened. What you have
written proves it. For her sake and for mine, do please tell me
the circumstances of her death. It is dreadful to be cut off like
this, knowing nothing. I am treating myself with Ignatia, but
the effects are minimal. The only cure for me is the truth.

As for us, we've calmed down, haven't we. Life is no longer
tumultuous. Sometimes I think, oh those old raucous days,
the 'Arch Angel' days, the Georgia days . . . Yes, we've
calmed down.

I too live quietly since Marlowe and I separated. There is a
small income, deaths in the family, you know. I seldom go
out, except to my violin lessons or to a book shop on Upper
Street. I have been studying radionics for the past three years. I
have some machines you would find interesting and even a
few patients with whom I have had encouraging results. It is
nice to be able to do everything at home and to feel that one is

helping – but that is hubris, an illusion of the ego.

Please Miles, if you know, if you can bear it, tell me what the End was like. I sleep very badly.

Yours,
Sylvie

PS Marlowe is in the Far East. We do not correspond.
PPS Do you still keep the Archives?

Letter Three

Los Angeles
June 7, 1978

Dear Sylvie,

Excuses are superfluous and ignoble. We move in and out of each other's lives. Brahma wakes and sleeps. I am aware that it has been three months.

Suffice it to say that my fallow period has ended and that I have risen like Osiris from the netherworld – and not without an inspiration or two to show for my sojourn.

My dear little girl, I know that Georgia, upon her flight from London, left many of her things with you, partly in gratitude, partly in haste. Were there among them any collages, prints, sketches or personal effects? I'll tell you why. It strikes me that now is the time for a DeBellis retrospective! I have already contacted the parents at their hideous home in Burbank, and they have agreed to loan me all of the collages in their possession. Naturally their enthusiasms were doubled when I hinted that the value of the pictures will have skyrocketed since the demise of their only daughter.

Because Georgia almost ceased selling anything or creating in the real sense once she returned to LA, there are limited sources to mine on the West Coast. But England must still be rich. I have written to her old gallery and to one or two other people. Have you any suggestions?

I am most excited about the prospect of resurrecting our

mutual friend. It's time she was re-evaluated and her influence examined in its true perspective. Avery Little at 'Schnabel' thinks we might do the show there, most likely in October. I am devoting all my energies which, as you know, are considerable, to the project. I am already at work upon the catalogue and would appreciate any biographical goodies you might send me. (You are the only person of my acquaintance, by the way, whose photographic memory is also lyrical.) Of course you'll fly over for the opening. It will be heaven to see you. Can you imagine the reunion?

On a more sombre note, I confess my motives are partly selfish. I want so much to *do* something for her. Unlike you, I had no opportunity of assisting once she had, as it were, hit the skids. Of course circumstances prevented, I was in LA by then, et cetera, et cetera. But I would like to redress the balance. I feel I must make a gesture, a gesture the nature of which our relationship precluded when she was alive. At the point when I might have done something I was spent, dried up. She had exhausted me. My sensibilities were shattered. Whatever I tried would have been wrong, and so it seemed kindest to avoid all contact.

Which brings me to the distressing part of this letter. Sylvie, what follows is written solely because you ask it. I have given an account of my last meeting with Georgia to no one else. It is for your eyes only.

The encounter took place at Umberto's New Year's Eve party. I was aware that Georgia was in town. I had been dreading a meeting and counted myself fortunate at having avoided her for more than two years. Of course she hardly went into society. She was closeted with her parents, supposedly kicking the habit. Skint as she was, she hadn't much choice. (I've heard the cold turkey drove them half insane, what with tantrums, the covert dealings with pushers, the attempted suicides, the stealing, even.) So she had been tucked more or less safely away until that fateful occasion. Moreover, since I often go to Monterey and San Francisco, I don't suppose it is surprising that we never met. In a word, I had been lulled into a false sense of security, the most perilous of conditions.

Imagine my horror, therefore, when she appeared at

Umberto's alone, apparently straight, and dressed like something out of Bertolt Brecht. Half an inch of pancake, plus her formidable artifice, and all that Max ever Factored were inadequate to conceal the ravages of illness and depravity. She could not have weighed much more than seven stone. Her hands were like talons. One eye bulged grotesquely, while the other, by comparison or in fact, receded into the skull (a not uncommon symptom in thyroid conditions, as I'm sure you are aware). Layers of mauve and silver eye shadow and a pair of false lashes exaggerated rather than concealed the deformity. Her hair had been hennaed, unsuccessfully. The skin looked dead, as though the capillaries had ceased to function and brought no fresh blood to animate it. Her once marvellous breasts were barely discernible, and I noticed when she smiled that a couple of teeth were missing. I had to concentrate hard to remind myself that this piece of withered eroticism was once a voluptuous woman of mystery who was barely thirty-three years old. (Amazing. She was a prodigy, wasn't she? Is this what comes of losing one's virginity at eleven, I wonder.)

She was at first reserved, even shy, and refused everything but a glass of champagne. Could this be Georgia, La Divina, whiplash of my emotions, my heroin heroine? For one awful moment I realized why Cheri killed himself. Despondency, however, quickly gave way to panic. She hadn't changed. One drink was sufficienct to roll back the years and restore that ravenous glint to her now protruding eye. I saw her glance longingly at a mirrorful of cocaine.

It began.

'Come home with me, Miles. You'll love my new apartment. It's in a 1920s building and has an Art Nouveau fireplace. William Randolph Hearst built it as a hotel for his guests. I'm doing it up. It's going to be all white wicker and plants. Even the cat is white with one blue eye and one green eye.' (This seemed an unhappy resemblance.) 'When I was in London I kept out the light. Now I'm going to let it all in. All, all. I've got so many new collages to show you. You'll love them. Maybe you'll even love me. Please come.'

Clearly she was fantasizing about a Return. I had visions of Gloria Swanson in *Sunset Boulevard* and wondered if the apartment house boasted a swimming pool.

'I recognize that look in your eyes, Miles. That old fear. Put it away, Angel. All I want to be is friends.'

I admit I was as curious as I was repelled. She had been important to me. She was a great artist. We had *influenced* each other. And she was, as always, damned persistent. She tried another approach.

'Take me home, Miles. I feel so weak. I'm not used to crowds any more. Let me rest on you a little. You don't know how ill I've been.'

She said she was going to faint. I could hardly believe that after so many years this woman was again exploiting my good nature and the fact of which she, more than anyone, is aware: that I am a gentleman. The thought of a scene either there or at her flat appalled me. I made the stipulation that I would come provided Tony, whom I think you may know, accompanied us. Georgia agreed.

I watched Umberto reverently assist her, as though she were still that duchess of yesteryear, into the monkey fur coat she used to wear and which seemed badly in need of a visit from Rentokil.

The moment we got into the car I knew I had made a dreadful mistake. Her recovery was immediate. Somewhere, somehow she had dropped, inhaled, God knows even shot something. I am, as you know, a keen observer, but one is forced to concede defeat in the face of such practised genius. She talked incessantly in that cracked and whining tone which was always Georgia at her worst, and kept gripping my knee with those bejewelled claws in the most alarming fashion. Tony is a quiet person whose presence I had intended as a balm to any agitation. But I realized that he was scared to death and would be of absolutely no use. He had never met Georgia and was nonplussed by the extravagance of her persona. She complained about her illness, her parents' rejection, her chronic financial difficulties. How she had managed the flat I've no idea, but I am certain that thereby hangs another tale. It couldn't have been Arabs this time. She said she missed London, and I could understand why. She had been seduced by Europe. But she never learned how to behave towards it, and in the end it ruined her. Another turn of the screw of Daisy Miller. Part of a great American tradition, I suppose.

She must not have been long in the flat, because there were still boxes about, scant furniture, and an as yet undecorated room. And you know Georgia's impatience to impose the unmistakable stamp of her taste upon the environment. (Remember when she moved into the Parma Violet Room? It was painted the dreaded purple and furnished within a week.) She had managed, though, to infuse the place with some of the old style: still the Fauré and the Scriabin, still the green grapes lamp. But one sensed her failure to recreate the magic of the original, a magic that would never be again. Am I horribly negative?

I felt negative. She pressed jasmine tea on us with trembling hands and rattling saucers. (She was suffering from a mysterious paralysis of the right arm. Do you know anything about this?) Then the assault began in earnest. Off came the monkey fur coat and out came the collages. She left a stack of them with me and disappeared into the other room to ingest more heinous chemicals and to emerge twenty minutes later in fresh make-up, a silk dressing gown, and Turkish slippers. I noted that her ankles, at least, were still exquisite.

Clearly she wished me to enthuse over her new accomplishments. I felt as though I were choking on a fish bone which I could neither swallow nor spit up. My larynx was paralysed. In a word, the pictures were awful – empty parodies of her once brilliant creations. They were amateurish, trite. She even had made a botch-up of the cutting and pasting, but that may have had something to do with the afflicted arm. They were dated, feeble, meaningless, stuck together mainly from old jewellery ads – a pathetic contrast to her penury. I was sick at heart and on the verge of being physically sick.

She knelt beside me on the floor, squirming closer as we talked. Out of old habit I looked for that fold of flesh in her neck that had always reminded me of an early Greek sculpture. It was gone. In its place was an awful declivity which terminated in her stark collar bone.

She opened a new front.

'I knew you'd turn up, Miles. The cards said so.' She gave me a meaningful look and drew out the tarot deck she had made years ago and tried without success to publish. How many times had we pondered over it, alone together in the

Parma Violet Room while the rest of the world slept and we
mused on our high destinies. The cards were worn now and a
bit faded, but still lovely, still charged with the Georgia magic.
They made the new work seem all the more absurd.

'Knight of Swords, Miles. You remember?' She held the
card before my face. I could think of nothing but escape.

'Georgia,' I managed to speak at last. 'You've been working
hard. It's so difficult to regain one's momentum, isn't it?'

'Still deft and difficult, Miles. Still attractive. Not run to fat,
still all your nice brown hair. A beautifully engineered mean
little gentleman, that's what you are. Knight of Swords,
Miles.' Suddenly her eyes filled with tears. 'It's been so hard,
Miles. I've been so ill. The thyroid condition doesn't get any
better. I've had no friends or lovers or money. You have no
idea what it's like to live this way. No one ever calls me. I'm
just so fucking *lonely*! You hate them, don't you? I have to get a
girl to do the cutting and pasting. My arm is partially paralysed, couldn't you tell? They don't know why.'

She intended to spare me nothing.

'Georgia', I tried, 'Georgia, my dear ... '

'No, you hate them, I know you do. I know they're not as
good as my early work, only I've been so ill, so scared.' She
seized my hand with her good one which still had a grip of
iron. She meant to ask me for money, I felt certain.

'You know sometimes I feel as though I've lost my soul.
That's why I can't work and why these are – like they are. But
I can't really have lost my soul, can I? All the drugs in the
world couldn't kill my soul, I know it.'

Who did she think she was, Billie Holliday?

'Of course not, Ma Belle, you're eternal.'

'I'm not. I'm dying and you don't care.' She sank back on
her haunches and looked at me with red-hot hatred. 'You just
say the same correct things, don't you Miles. You play the
gentleman.'

She flung the pack of cards at me. Tony made for the door.
Next thing I knew, she was on the floor in the midst of that
scattered deck, clasping my knees and weeping hysterically.
Suddenly I saw the whole scene from above, as one is meant to
do on one's death bed: the richly coloured anarchy of those
doom-laden cards, Georgia's long dark hair streaming over

her back, a shadowy Tony lurking in the corner. It might have
been a bad Caravaggio.

'Please don't leave me, Miles. You can't leave me alone on
New Year's Eve. Stay with me a while. Have another cup of
tea. I'm so afraid to be alone. I go searching for my soul. I
mean really search for it in drawers and things and then I start
to go mad.' Her dressing gown had fallen open, and I could see
that she was naked underneath. I was filled with revulsion and,
quite suddenly, anger.

Swifty I extricated myself from her grasp. You know how
physically strong I am when piqued.

'Georgia, I must go. I advise you to see a doctor, keep
working, it's your only salvation, and for God's sake stay off
the barbiturates and the DMT − whatever it is you're taking.
Otherwise you are beyond my assistance. Or anybody's.'

'I thought you were my friend,' she wailed, lying full length
on the floor.

'I thought so too.'

'But if you're my friend you can't abandon me.' She
crawled towards me, her make-up smeared, her mascara
running all over her face. She looked like something out of one
of her own pictures.

'Then I recommend you cease to think of me in that
capacity.'

'But we were − we were so − oh Miles!'

She sobbed uncontrollably. Would she be unwise enough to
dredge up our intended marriage? Why not. When was
Georgia anything but unwise? I must, I thought, flee this lurid
Los Angeles Gothic. By now my hand was on the door knob.

'Come back just one more time. Promise me you'll come
back, please, oh please, honey. Just to have tea. Just for twenty
minutes. It would help me so much. It would let me live.'

'Georgia, I'm sorry, really sorry for you. But I cannot see
you again.'

'Never?' She rose unsteadily.

'Never.'

She leapt at me. But years of intimacy had made me
anticipate her deviousness. She meant to lock me in, I knew it.
My adrenalin was up. I was quick as well as strong, and
slipped out, slamming the door before she could reach me. I

raced to the lift where Tony was waiting, pale as a ghost. I expected her to follow, hurling imprecations like Kali Durga, but everything was quiet. I checked my wallet, and we drove away without incident. That was the last time I saw her. A month later she died. Suicide. Maybe, you tell me. No note, overdose of barbiturates, as I suspected, needles too. The usual series of incidents led to the discovery of the corpse, found several days after death occurred, landlady, et cetera. Not pleasant. Now you know as much as I of her demise.

Sylvie, I can write no more. I am spent. Kindly burn this letter.

Your devoted
Miles

PS Have you any idea what might have become of that Tarot deck? She didn't send it to you, did she? The parents don't have it. Heaven forbid she destroyed it. Please post photocopies of letters, pictures, whatever you feel would be appropriate for the catalogue or the Archives. Yes, I do still keep them.

Letter Four A

Belitha Villas
June 14, 1978

Dear Miles,

I've been doing the garden, planting the fuchsias in old stone pots. I am trying to recover my sanity after reading your letter. The day is excessively warm. Reminds me of New York. The thought makes me want to weep with gratitude to be living in a civilized place. I do intend to live and die here, you know. Someday, perhaps, you will come and see me. But not yet.

Sylvie

Letter Four B

June 15
2.30 a.m.

Adored Miles,

How brave of you to tell me. Such candour is rare. It cancels everything. Because of it I forgive you everything.

You're right, Georgia could be impossible. But her excesses came out of a great longing for joy. They did, you know. Thomas Hardy said, in a way, that humanity is like that. Plato said, in a way, that humanity is like that. Her longing was bigger and stronger than other people's. That's all. And look where we were living. London was a banquet of vices then. Anything one wanted, anything. All available, all cheap. How could our precious, voracious Georgia resist? Big Livers seem also to go in for death in a big way. That extraordinary energy which made her a creative person also made her require such bizarre and dangerous amusements. Can sex, drugs and art all be linked somehow?

She was tragic, Miles. The fall of a great person is tragic. You understand what I am saying.

It was a long time before she realized how far gone she really was. She believed she was special and that nothing could touch her. Almost as though she were under supernatural protection. In a way it was true. The dark god you spoke of was holding her on a tether all along, and in the end he just reined her in like a sacrificial animal. He made her vicious and pathetic. He made her ill. She became bitter, a parody of herself, then a total wreck. It was too cruel.

She began to ring people in the middle of the night and abuse them for no reason. She went to parties and dinners and openings and insulted everyone. She complained, she shouted, she overdressed. She took every available drug and all available breathing space. Like the mistral she blew and blew and set everyone's nerves on edge. For a while she was still turning out her 'little masterpieces', but her relations with the gallery director were strained. He was tired of her temper and her arrogance. And all because of that wicked drug.

Of course everyone we knew flirted with it. You did, and in rather a big way. It was so good then. Besides, as Georgia once wrote, 'Nothing in the universe is evil. There is nothing a strong will may not attempt, nothing it may not risk. One must discover oneself through every available experience in order that one may not die and may be afraid no longer.' The road of excess, in this case, did not lead to the palace of wisdom. But who am I to say such a vile thing? Who knows what she found in the end? Perhaps ruin was necessary. It's all so mysterious.

You see I am obsessed with her this warm London night when the Devil himself seems to be abroad. I burn Dittany of Crete in my room. I light the correct candles and protect my threshold with holy water. I was always a little in awe of her, you know. I still am, even of her ghost.

I was the last to stand by her. When panic set in she clung to me like a drowning person, calling me every day, begging me to come and see her, to buy food for her, to accompany her on those dreaded visits to the doctor. I devoted myself first to her rehabilitation, then to saving her life. I felt I could, somehow. It was the time, it was destiny, and Marlowe was away so much. Though she horrified others, for me it was simply all right. I felt it my duty, and truly not an unpleasant one, to take on this deformity no one would touch. It was not easy, but for some reason, I was impervious to her selfishness, her harsh words, her indulgent laments. She was grateful; we became very close; we believed in each other's loyalty. I held her to me. I consoled her in her heart of darkness.

Things got worse and worse. All the money was gone and no one cared. She was so ill and weak that she couldn't leave the room. The thyroid condition seemed incurable. The rent was due. Her flatmates snarled at her and shunned her as though she were the carrier of some hideous contagion. Everything was finished. It was then we decided, in mutual despair, that she must return to her parents in Los Angeles (she ran away at sixteen, I guess you know), and that she must beg them to have her back in order to recover her health and start a new life. A curator who wishes to be anonymous paid for the ticket. Reluctantly. Together we packed up the collages, what remained of the books, the tapestries, the rugs, the once-glamorous clothes. I got her somehow to the airport. The rest you know.

Letter Four C

4.15 a.m.

I have been sitting outside in my little garden. The stars have disappeared. It is dawn, that disturbing early summer dawn which makes sleep impossible. I have been thinking, Miles, looking up into the pale sky and wondering where Georgia, like the stars, has gone. Such fire could not have been extinguished. She was right when she said that all the drugs in the world could not kill her soul. Somewhere, as Georgia, she exists. It makes me want to cross myself. Such certainty is a holy thing.

We, her dearest friends, have been treating her unfairly. We have been speaking of her only in negative terms. But she was a great talent with an energy that nothing and no one could suppress, not, I tell you, even death. And how wonderful her collages are. I have my three before me now. And how prolific she was. It all just came pouring out of her, didn't it? And she lived what she believed: that the will is sovereign and the individual divine. The denouement of her story does not negate that.

She could be so sweet and funny and affectionate. One felt almost honoured by the attention she lavished on one. Wild as she was, she was loyal to her friends and very generous. Do you remember how she paid for Penny's abortion, sent Steve to Italy when another month in London might have killed him, gave her emerald ring, her most treasured possession, to Delia as a birthday present? And those dinners whenever she sold a picture – no wonder she ended up broke. No one who went to her in distress was ever turned away. If she could do nothing else, she would make you laugh till your sides ached. Or she would read to you out of some occult treatise or from Jung or French or Chinese poetry or one of her 'perfumed novels', as she called them, exactly the right passage which would lift you above your despair and clarify everything. She had a genius for it.

When I first knew her, I thought her the most effervescent female I had ever met. Not beautiful in the usual sense – her nose was too prominent and she was a bit plump. She had wonderful black eyes and very long lashes, though, which she used to great advantage. Her teeth were large and white with that front gap one somehow envies. One imagines forcing a tongue into it, what do I mean. She was seductive, absolutely seductive, that's it, and very witty. She always wore a mischievous expression, and moved in an air of complete self-confidence, as though she had just put one over on you. (Perhaps seductiveness *is* nothing more than complete self-confidence.) Despite certain vulgarities, she possessed the unmistakable marks of refinement; delicate wrists and ankles, tapered fingers, well-formed ears, not to mention her cultivated tastes, her wide reading, her own formidable accomplishments.

I remember her first one-woman show. What a crowd of people and how brilliant she was with them all. She was dressed in purple and silver and black with a small veiled hat that rested in her exotically coiffed hair. She had a sort of bizarre chic, didn't she?

Such a success: reviews in *The Times* and the *Guardian*, articles about her in *Nova* and *Art News*, even *Woman's Journal*, which she thought very funny. She was a queen, she was on a cloud, she had hundreds of friends, all her lovers were famous. She hardly noticed me then. I think she was more interested in Marlowe. It was later, after she had moved into the Parma Violet Room, that we became close. At first she just enjoyed the contrast of the simplicity of my surface, though she was often contemptuous of it, and I was the brunt of a joke or two. But when she discovered how much I had read, that I played the violin, was interested in Homeopathy and worked for such a notable alternative weekly as the *Arch Angel* – edited by you – she invited me more often to tea or to her soirées.

You know how she delighted in that room, Miles. She had been planning the purple environment for months, and that small corner of a Victorian mansion flat with its fireplace and ornate period features suited her to perfection. She adored her *objêts* and enthused like a child over each new acquisition, driving amazing bargains with the dealers in Camden Passage, Portobello, and Bermondsey. Empire clocks, Art Nouveau lamps, Lalique vases . . . and the first editions – of course she eventually sold most of them for smack. For Georgia the place really was 'a room of one's own': temple, sanctuary, womb,

parlour, study, drug den, brothel. It was her world. She could
not compartmentalize. (Is that a particularly feminine trait, do
you think?) She ate, slept, created, loved, and nearly died
there. She devised elaborate entertainments for her friends and
lovers. God, the wild fun, the revels that went on in that
room. And then the high talk, the music, the poetry. It was a
distillation of the cultural climate of London at that time.

Remember the many visits we paid to her after working all
day and half the night at the *Arch Angel*, not bothering to ring
up, just certain she'd be there, awake, either alone, cutting and
pasting into the small hours of the morning, listening to
Mahler and Strauss; or entertaining accomplished, witty,
frightening people from her central position on the big
wrought-iron bed. They were like something out of Balzac,
those carousals. The lighting was somehow the same, and the
talk, alternately intense and careless. Depending on what
substances were being dispensed (she usually managed them at
someone else's expense) we would talk of Rilke or Crowley or
all make love with each other. That was how it began with you
and Georgia, wasn't it? Until then you had been with Arthur
or Edward, anyway the one who went to Eton whose mother
became so incensed and threatened Georgia with a law suit.
Until then you had been only the best of friends. But perhaps
you were always in love and didn't know it.

You were the most dashing couple I've ever seen. So much
in love, feeding and inspiring each other, yet both such
individuals and retaining your independence. I think we were
all a bit envious, and astonished, especially when you began to
talk about marriage and even a child! Perhaps such affairs are
fated to end in tragedy.

Truly, Miles, I don't believe Georgia loved anyone as she
loved you. That is clear from the effects of your desertion. She
felt your rejection as total. She was crushed by it.

I know she was difficult. But she was a great artist. She
needed and deserved more patience and understanding than
the rest of us. Of course I don't blame you. You did what you
had to do. You followed, as always, your true will. But oh
Miles, if you had seen her despair, if you really had felt how
she loved you, I cannot believe that you would have abandoned her. I must tell you, my dear, that on the day you left for

New York she began her long downwards spiral. You didn't know, did you, that she took an overdose of sleeping pills. (Her comment upon returning from hospital: 'Death is not a religious experience. It is purely scientific. Ugh!') A week later she was shooting up with the heroin you had given her.

'I'm going to take his baby and flush it down the loo,' she screamed at me over the telephone. Of course she wasn't pregnant. I don't think she ever could be. There was something wrong, I don't know what. Oh Miles, dear Miles, please don't think I'm blaming you. How could I blame you. You were only being yourself. We can, all of us, be only ourselves. But thwarted desire kills. It really does. The ego is destroyed and then the body. Your leaving was the turning point of her brief existence. It was the suddenness of your departure, I'm sure, that devastated her. The way she carried on, it was incredible I tell you. We all thought she would lose her reason there and then in the middle of the Parma Violet Room.

If only you hadn't taught her to shoot up. No, that's unfair. It may have been Steve or even Patsy. But you know she thought she could do anything, get away with anything. You must have known she would make no attempt to regulate her intake. Miles, why am I saying this to you, why am I still so upset by events of five years ago? I'm sorry, Miles. I don't sleep well, it's the time of year. I shall go and take some Rescue Remedy.

Letter Four D

6.00 a.m.

I am better now. My pulse is normal. My temperature is 98.8°. Daylight drives away daemons. Now I know why I have said all these things to you. It is because I am certain you want to know the truth, just as I want to know the truth. It is no platitude, is it, that the truth makes one free. I am calm again. Thank you for allowing me this small catharsis. You are a man of understanding. I have always recognized that in you. You follow your own high nature. How could I have blamed you? Only I didn't blame you.

Write to me, Miles. Let this be the beginning of our

correspondence. It is so important that we say everything, make everything clear. That is why you keep the Archives, isn't it? I will send you some items about Georgia. There was a psychiatrist, by the way, in Highgate, whom Georgia saw for a while. She might have something. I'll call her.

Again, I feel our correspondence is so important. Everyone we knew is scattered, stagnant, in gaol, or dead. You and I seem to be the only functioning, creative members of what was once a very naughty but interesting group of people. The Children of their Time, I guess you'd call them. Miles, we did some silly things, but we have survived, we have been saved for a reason, don't you agree? For our work, it must be for that.

There comes a point where the raving must stop if one is to continue simply to exist. Drink makes me ill. Drugs nearly kill me. Is it so with you as well? (You should see our once handsome Marlowe. You would weep.) One has only a certain quantum of energy: this must be the realization of the survivor. Perhaps I am wrong. I am struggling to see. I need your beautiful cutting mind, like a glass-cutter, like a sword, Miles, to help me clarify.

I enclose a copy of the obituary which was printed in the Spring issue of *Thera*, and some photographs of Georgia. I am shipping my three DeBellis collages for the exhibition. I feel, however, that I cannot release Georgia's last letters, even to the Archives. They are too heart-rending. The risk of publication is too great. It would be a foul betrayal. You understand. Of course you do. Friendship and sensitivity do not permit. As to the cards, I have no idea.

All good luck with the retrospective. Do let me know how it progresses. I am with you – in spite of everything and because of everything. This is the longest letter I have ever written.

Sylvie

Letter Five

Los Angeles
July 10

First of all her real name was Wendy Perlmutter. Pathetic, isn't it? I once caught a glimpse of her birth certificate while rifling her drawers in search of an onyx ring of mine which had gone, so she claimed, 'missing'. How do you think I found the parents? She'd have died if she knew I knew. I have kept quiet about this only because I am a gentleman.

Wild fun! She thought she was fucking Sally Bowles, a regular cauldron of animus possession. (Which reminds me, I knew that shrink in Highgate. Gave up in despair, she did. What can one do with a patient who does not wish to be cured? *Is* there such a thing as a cure?) Anyway you were correct when you implied that some poor chump was invariably landed with the bill for those Balzacian Bacchanals, not infrequently myself.

Yes, she was prolific. She made a great many *things*. That does not mean that a tenth of them were of any artistic merit. Her spasm of true creative effort was brief, to say the least. Upon this I and most other discerning critics have always agreed. Such extravagant affluxes of the female libido usually do produce questionable results. You see, she never succeeded in purging her work, or herself, of an inherent strain of vulgarity. As is the case with all junkies, something was basically rotten.

To proceed. Apparently you are unaware that she was Marlowe's lover, or at least went to bed with him on several occasions, not only when she had become bosom friends with your dear self, but while she was my, for lack of a better word, betrothed. (The narrowness of that particular escape still causes me to break out in a cold sweat.) In addition, I have been witness to several dirty little dramas wherein she burnt, amidst some quite revolting occult paraphernalia, vile imprecations and obvious relish, the hair, photographs, nail clippings, even bits of skin of her nearest and dearest. She collected the specimens, don't you remember, and kept them in a locked lacquer box. We, naively, attributed the aberration to sentiment and her amateur coiffeuserie. Well, she was stockpiling the gory gewgaws for use on such occasions as evoked Dragon Lady's displeasure. Her revenge was implacable. Even I was shocked. When I reminded her of the boomerang effects of such *Malleus Maleficarum* high jinks, she haughtily affirmed that She was no coward. 'I do as I please and I am prepared to take the consequences for my actions. Whom I love I slay. The Devil doesn't scare me.' And so on. Now this may confirm your image of Georgia as some sort of psychic stormtrooper, but where, I wonder, does it leave that interesting collection of misconceptions about her touching loyalty and her eternal friendship? I suppose she might have been nice to you. You were certainly no threat, and Georgia was always happy to add to her platoon of sycophants. Her own flattery verged on the cosmic if she sensed the proximity of a free meal or a free blow.

Now you seem to be saying — mistakenly, let me hasten to add — that it was I who corrupted Georgia by introducing her to smack. Nothing, repeat nothing, could be further from your precious truth. She had been snorting cwts for months before we began our *liaison dangereuse*. You are correct on only one point. It was Steve who originally produced the poison, and at Georgia's insistence. They hoovered it up together at every conceivable opportunity. (The only time she would allow Steve out of bed was to pay a call on his connection. Otherwise the poor boy was a sex slave pure and simple.) By the time I had been lured into her purple parlour, she had downward spiralled to at least the Ninth Circle. So there.

On to the next misapprehension: my callous rejection which perpetrated, so you seem to think, her ultimate ruin. Just *why* do you think I fled if not for my very life? Do you think I *like* New York? I do not. But it was *far*. LA was even farther, hence my current address. (Thank heavens I'm rich.) I find it difficult to imagine that even you, dearest Sylvie, could be so simple-minded. Nevertheless, here's to clarity. I shall tell you why. One or two examples from Georgiana files should suffice.

Lunch at San Lorenzo one April day, making the last of several efforts to knit up the ravelled sleeve of our *amour*. She had ordered, naturally, the most expensive items on the menu,

and was expostulating clamorously about art, money, furniture and sex, flashing those jungle-red nails at me to emphasize
every other word. As always on such occasions when she was
at her most purposefully purple, we were the object of a good
deal of gaping and *sotto voce* commentary. I was wondering
whether I would be able to last the meal when suddenly,
before my eyes, she disappeared. I had drunk only half a bottle
of champagne and hadn't been in the neighbourhood of an
hallucinogen for more than a week. Nevertheless, she was
gone. Somewhere I heard her scuffling with her handbag like a
demented chipmunk. There was a peculiar smell. I lifted the
white tablecloth that hung to the floor and found her crouched
at my feet, her silk scarf wrapped round her upper arm, a
syringe poised in her right hand.

'Georgia, for God's sake,' I hissed.

'With you in a sec, darling. Don't start the lobby without
me.'

She reappeared, glassy-eyed and swaying. I was speechless.
Within five minutes she had vomited her dozen oysters on to
the fresh hot dinner plate that had just been put before her.
(She usually, at least, managed to do it into a napkin which she
would leave discreetly folded next to her cutlery.) Need I
describe the ensuing chaos?

I escorted her home, finding it difficult, I confess, to
maintain my gentlemanly façade. The afternoon ended in a
brawl with a taxi driver who had misinterpreted some slurred
remark. I remember what it was. She was anxious for me to
return with her to the PVR for more blood-sucking, and I was
anxious to be off and free. We sat arguing for some minutes in
the back seat.

'Make your mind up,' growled the driver.

'Mind your make-up,' was Georgia's instant reposte.

He did not take the witticism kindly – one of her better ones
considering her condition at the time. Insults flew. She hit him
with the great sack of hers and he went straight for her jugular.
With Georgia's shrieks, the local PC quickly materialized. At
that moment I loathed her thoroughly and, I admit, fled in
horror. I did pay the fare, however, otherwise God knows,
she would have offered herself in recompense. A blow job at
the very least.

It is extremely painful for me to recall these scenes which grew alarmingly frequent. Restaurants were her speciality, as is the case with many psychotics. Whenever she failed to engage my total attention, she turned to the public at large. There was the time I invited her to meet my parents. Even now I groan inwardly at the recollection. Unbeknown to me, she had been dropping barbiturates all day with Steve and consequently went face first into the profiteroles with chocolate sauce. Dead faint. But I can't go on. You must take my word, you must know yourself how intolerable were her excesses. No, my dear, Georgia's disintegration did *not* commence with my plane flight.

How I became involved with Georgia emotionally is a question I put to myself every day of my life. Which brings me to the most agonizing part of this letter. (Why are you making me tell you these things? Who are you, I am beginning to wonder, and what is your goddam function, psychic or otherwise?) To continue. Of course we had known each other for years. I adored her long before that fatal encounter in the Parma Violet Room. As a friend, you understand, as a some-time lover, and as an admirer of her work. Well, didn't we all. No one can say I was alone in my delusions. Then there was that gaudy Jewish attractiveness you already have described, rather well I thought. Yes, she had hundreds of admirers, dozens of lovers: that creature from the Tate, the New York minimalist, the curator from Chicago, the *Guardian* journalist (come now, how do you think she got that review?), the plumber, even, and of course Steve. And that estimate covers a period of only thirty days.

It was during one of those orgies, you're right. We were together in a corner of the PVR, closely coupled, nymph and satyr amidst a sea of writhing bodies. (See Yeats, no, 'Faust II'.) I believe someone was making a film. Someone was always making a film then. More cocks and cunts, ho hum, thought I. And then, and then . . .

I looked into Georgia's eyes, really looked right through those multiple layers of mascara. It is difficult to describe my reaction. I can only imagine that it was similar to what a blind person experiences when sight is miraculously restored and he or she sees for the first time the moon, the ocean, a tropic sunset. I looked again. The usual mocking expression was gone. She was all invitation, all, dare I say it, surrender. (Christ this is awful, but how else does one describe true love?) I kissed her and realized that the world, my ambitions, my very nature were changed for ever. Precisely then, a minute and artful daemon, a beautiful little green viper, a chthonic creature that lived deep inside Georgia, that may well have been Georgia, something, I tell you, licked and tickled and sucked away at my penis and it swelled up, galvanized like I have never known, no , not with anyone before, nor with any lover since, male or female.

We could not stop; we refused to be separated; we refused to change partners. The others were furious. They all wanted us, but we wanted only each other. The camera was on us, in close-up, churning away to a soundtrack of the 'Dies Irae' from Verdi's *Requiem*, which made it all the more thrilling somehow. (Just think, somewhere, someone, a bevy of people for all I know, may actually be seated comfortably in their living room witnessing that fatal coitus. The mind boggles.) We made love for hours, until everyone had left. Finally we slept, a damned doomed sleep it seemed. I felt as though I had embraced a succubus, Melusina herself. We awoke, I don't know when – perpetual darkness reigned in that place – and it began all over again. We had appointments; we did not keep them. People banged on the door and went away. We could neither eat nor sleep nor defecate. We could only take each other over and over as though possessed, our rapture shot through with a greed that was almost agony. That afternoon I discovered her great secret: she could not stop coming. The spasms went on and on, it was terrifying. I realized that I had found the Great Cunt of man's dreams (don't laugh, don't even snicker. You or anyone. Ever.) The arch seductress, Circe, Cytheraea. I then felt blessed, magically endowed like some mythical hero. I could not tell Georgia this. I could barely speak, my thoughts were in chaos. I experienced surge after surge of power. We would reach new levels of unbearable exhaustion only to switch, like a great symphony, into an even more brilliant key and be revived all over again in our lust. How can I explain? How does one explain death and resurrection? It was then, in my delirium, that I scrawled

upon the wall over her bed those lines from Faust which you
may have noticed if you looked closely and which I suppose
have long since been painted over in Magnolia or Alpine
Green by some anonymous Philistine.

> Hail the breezes' gentle blisses
> Hail mysterious abysses.
> All things let all adore
> And the elements all four!

I meant it, I tell you. I had discovered the most highly-sexed
human being I have ever known. We could not let each other
alone. She surpassed – I admit it – even myself, as I then was,
in lasciviousness. But more. Not only our fucking, but our
talk, our shared learning – neither of us had ever communi-
cated like that before. It was the meeting and merging of true
wills. She was the woman in me, I the man in her. We were
exalted, raised above common humanity by a divine passion,
fated for each other since the beginning of time.

Enough of this rubbish. Nothing in life is more deadly or
more absurd than the combination of lust with what one
misinterprets as destiny. As I realized to my eternal chagrin.
You can imagine how, in this state of dementia, I allowed
myself to be lured into the prospect of marriage. That we
produce a child seemed inevitable and imperative. During
those months she might have convinced me of anything.
Clearly what was in her mind, beyond the destruction of my
body and the enslavement of my soul, was the acquisition of
my inheritance. In short, I began to realize that she would be
the undoing of me, that my individuality, which she was so
fond of extolling, was, in fact, deeply threatened, and that if I
did not guard my sex, my psyche and my wallet, I would be
Vagina Dentata's next victim.

My work suffered. The *Arch Angel* was in a bad way, as you
recall. It needed a strong hand, and mine was constantly
between Georgia's thighs. *She*, on the other hand, was churning out *Kunst* and selling it as if there were no tomorrow. And
I found her sexuality more and more *outré*, no longer intoxi-
cating but suffocating. Not for nothing did she venerate the
Marquis and Maldoror. She persuaded me to perform and to

watch acts of the most decadent perversion. At first I was
enthralled. This, I thought, is how a great woman entertains a
great man. Then I grew sated and finally nauseated. Her
demands became more extreme. I felt like a prisoner in that
room. To employ a tired but apt metaphor, I was being
devoured alive, Orpheus thrown yet again to the maenads.

When the *Arch Angel* finally did go under, I was almost
relieved. I saw in its collapse a golden opportunity and decided
to bolt. I am sorry and ashamed about not saying goodbye to
everyone, but surely you must understand that you had no one
to blame for your months on the dole queue but Georgia
DeBellis.

She got wind of my plans in her witchy way, and there was a
dreadful scene. It was then she realized the stuff of which my
will is made. The composition of hers does not bear comment.
I put my possessions in storage, gave the flat to Steve, hoping
he too might extricate himself from the influence of that
daughter of darkness, and booked a ticket to New York.
Suffice it to say I have no regrets.

In closing may I suggest that we are not merely survivors.
Surviving implies a kind of passivity which is not the case with
you and certainly not with me. (By the way, what do you
mean by 'the rest of us', as though Georgia's misguided libido
were the hallmark of towering genius.) I remind you, dear
Sylvia, of the dichotomy which exists between what Nietzsche calls the Apollonian and the Dionysiac. Surely you are
familiar with this idea from Humanities One or whatever your
American university offered in the way of first year pabulum.
If not, I strongly recommend a re-read of *The Birth of Tragedy*,
Kaufmann translation. But you read German, do you not?
Many of our former friends, especially Georgia, were committed to the orgiastic deity. Yes, in the superabundance of
our youth we hailed him. But his exclusive worship brings
destruction and death. Through him Georgia sought the
ecstasy of oblivion. Well, we all know what she found.

We have become Apollonian, and that is as it should be. We
restrain ourselves, govern out libidos and channel our energies
into work. We *do* 'swallow the call note of depth dark
sobbing'. All She did was curse and moan. Damned un-
dignified, if you ask me. The function of displacement *is*

necessary for the growth of the individual. Dread words, but absolutely true. My dear Sylvie, you have much to contribute. Do as I do. Get on with it. Abjure the past, and for God's sake live.

I hope this little matter has been sufficiently 'clarified'. If so, just add a squeeze of lemon and dip your artichoke in it. I have now corresponded with you. Satisfied?

M.

Letter Six

Belitha Villas
July 16, 1978

Dearest Miles,

Pardon me if I say that not only are you bi-sexual, you are bi-everything. No doubt this is the source of your power and attraction. But you have misunderstood me. You have confused me.

Your letter has put me into such a state of agitation that I have been forced to treat myself with argent nitrate in a very high potency. Truly, Miles, you frighten me. What have I done to deserve this outburst?

Many of the things you told me I did not know, and I cannot pretend that they have not hurt me. You have made Georgia suddenly a stranger. I feel quite insecure. It was cruel of you, Miles, not only to speak ill of the dead, but to torment the living with doubts. But then I asked for it. I wanted the truth and I got it. Now I must live with it.

Of course you are right about her behaviour. How such refinement and such vulgarity could co-exist in the same nature is very mysterious. She was like the moon with a light and a dark side. With that dark side I was, like yourself, all too familiar. And the types that dark side attracted! You can't imagine, but perhaps you can, the company she kept during those last London months. Artists, writers, and occultists were replaced by drug dealers of the worst sort, prostitutes, assorted rough trade, and a few toadies from the old days out of whom she wheedled money to support her habit and pay the rent. She even tried a bit of whoring herself but never had much luck with it. When she was destitute she paid off the dealers with her own frail flesh. I was asked to leave the room on more than one occasion while she entertained them for twenty minutes. The Arabs you know about, it seems. But by the time of which I write they wouldn't touch her. A tart with tracks is not attractive to Islamic gentlemen. And the tracks were everywhere: both arms, thighs, even hands. First the left hand then the right was constantly bandaged. It was so bad, Miles, that sometimes I had to help her to shoot up. She had run out of everything, even veins.

And she stole. Once a black girl, Marcia Kinsey, came round to deliver a small quantity of the stuff, barely enough to get Georgia off, given the scale of her habit. We sat in the dim light of the green grapes lamp, the curtains drawn as usual, the purple walls gloomy as a crypt. The room was suffocating. She had stopped cleaning or changing the linen weeks ago. Georgia, who was always so fastidious. Anyway she paid Marcia and we all had a little of the drug. (I confess it was impossible for me to be with Georgia without taking some of it myself, though I never shot it. I even gave her money when the withdrawal was driving her to insanity. I simply could not deny her. No aspect of our relationship was more horrible for me than that one. Please God, I would think, don't let her miss and hit an artery.)

Marcia went out to the loo. The moment she was gone, Georgia was into her handbag. She removed a larger packet of heroin and poured most of it into her own little bottle, making up the loss with the milk sugar she kept handy for such occasions. She then opened the zippered compartment of the handbag, removed all but a few pounds, and stuffed the bills under her mattress. All this accomplished quickly, efficiently, soundlessly. And she was high out of her mind! She never lost a kind of diabolical resourcefulness.

As I consider these things again, I see how she must have made life for you insupportable. I begin to understand your desperation, you need to save yourself. Forgive me if I implied that your act was brutal or your motives selfish. You are an understanding person. I know you, I worked for you, we were friends. You would not have hurt Georgia intentionally. As you rightly state, she was bent on self-destruction. Then of course there was fate.

Oh I want to think of better times. Of the cameraderie of our years on the *Arch Angel*, of a dear Marlowe, a glamorous and successful Georgia, a beautiful, funny Steve, and of course you. There are so many things in the past that are good and that I do not wish to forget. Like our holiday in France. You and Steve and I, remember? You had just come into an inheritance and invited us both for two weeks of pure hedonism. Touring châteaux, eating in four-star restaurants, looking at, surrounded by nothing but beauty. It was like something out of Scott Fitzgerald. And Georgia loaned us Steve to keep us both happy. (You see, she could be divinely generous.) But it was you, Miles, who made it possible, your largesse, your energy, your endless good humour. It was a magic time for me, for all of us. I don't think such times can ever be again.

Now I have made myself sad. You are right when you tell me I must forget the past. Yes, I am haunted by it. It has cut me off from the world. It has turned me into a melancholic. I need your irrepressible gaiety, Miles, to save me.

Write to me, my dear. Tell me if the pictures have arrived. I am hungry for news of the DeBellis exhibition and of your progress on Georgia's book. I wish I could be with you to help with the organization as in the old days, but such things are no longer my forté. I must close. I am expecting a patient. Write, write, write.

Always,
Sylvie

PS Am re-reading *The Birth of Tragedy*, Kaufmann translation.

Letter Seven

August 20
San Francisco

My Darling Sylvie,

Glorious news! *The Burning Bush* is to be published by *City Lights*, probably at Christmas. It will be a limited edition, one hundred of which will be signed by the author – on the finest paper and using the very best designer. Naturally, I am ecstatic. I feel the collection represents a turning point in my life and career, a distillation of all my experiences and painfully acquired realizations over the past decade. It was, I know, intended as a monument to Georgia's memory. I am now beginning to question the appropriateness of the dedication. Though important, she was but one of many influences out of which this book has been born. The child, after all, is mine. And of my time. I have created it by my will, my talent, and my persistence, and I wonder if there might not be a more fitting dedicatee; if, indeed, the poems are meant for a single individual. Are they not rather representative of an entire generation?

At any rate, I have just received confirmation of the project and am in San Francisco negotiating the particulars. I wanted you to be among the first to know of my success. You have been a source of consolation and support throughout the aftermath of Georgia's suicide – which nearly, if the truth be told, shattered my sensibilities. How sweetly you have compelled me to confront my role in the affair. You have helped to free me. For that I thank you.

You are right, my darling, our correspondence is vital. Think of it. Almost no one writes to anyone any more. The epistolary style, once so assiduously practised and so highly regarded among cultivated people, has ceased to exist. I can't help feeling that you and I, double-handedly, are reviving it. How can it be, how miraculaous it is that after so many years apart we are beginning to affect each other this way, for we are affecting each other, you know. What is afoot, I ask myself. What delicious mystery?

I fly back to LA this evening. I am working diligently on the catalogue and assembling the collages. This occupies a great deal of my time when I would like to start work on a novella (you see how you inspire me, my little muse. I am simply brimming with ideas). The shop is very busy and demands my continual attention. Oh yes, the collages have arrived safely, but the exhibition has been put back until February. Thank heavens, I can barely cope with my present burden of responsibilities.

I must close, Sylvie dearest, as I have three appointments before leaving for the airport.

Yours in haste, happiness, and a mountain of details,

Miles

Letter Eight

August 26
Belitha Villas

Dearest Miles,

'I had a dream, what can it mean?' In the small hours of the morning when the summer light is so disturbing. I sleep badly and have enervating hallucinations during my brief lapses into unconsciousness. I have put myself on the machine, but so far no improvement. I shall try an acupuncturist in NW3.

I am sorry to go on about my little problems. They are simply aspects of one's evolution. That is how I try to regard them. Don't you think that's right? Oh but this dream, Miles. It was of Georgia, and on the very date of your last letter, August 20th. What can such a piece of synchronicity mean except that we have made a psychic link with her? She is with us still. She is all around us. It makes me glad, yet it frightens me. Sometimes I feel she is here in the room searching for her soul. Can it be? You must help me, Miles. You must analyse all this and help me to see it clearly.

Here is the dream. I was walking down the Marylebone Road. It was one of those bright cold windy afternoons in March, the sort that make one so nervous, I'm sure you know what I mean. All the daffodils flattened in Regent's Park. One can't help a certain depressive agitation. Sorry. Ahead of me I saw a dark-haired woman in a plaid coat which swung about her gracefully as she walked. She wore a peaked wool hat at a jaunty angle and black pumps. She gave the impression of light-hearted self-assurance. She seemed familiar. We both stopped at the traffic lights on Baker Street. The woman turned to me and smiled. It was Georgia! She was healthy again, plump, blooming as we would wish her eternally to be. I said what one stupidly says when meeting a ghost: 'But you're dead!' I cannot remember her response, except she implied that she often 'came back', that is, returned to the world, almost as one would go for an afternoon stroll, for a breath of air, a little break. She took my arm in a kindly way, and we crossed the road. She suggested I accompany her on the bus she was about to catch.

'Aren't you taking the underground?' I motioned towards the station. She did not reply, but stepped on to the bus outside Madam Tussaud's, motioning me to follow. We climbed up to the upper deck and sat down. She never ceased to smile that lovely close-lipped smile, half indulgent, half mischievous. Nor did she let go of my hand. We were headed towards Euston. I couldn't help it, I had to ask her about the afterlife. She said calmly that oh it was all right in general, but that occasionally she got tired straining her neck to look up at those great tall beings. By this I assumed she meant the upper echelons of the immortals, who must be enormous in size as well as in soul. This all seemed perfectly normal.

The seventy-three bus came to a stop at King's Cross. Georgia looked at me significantly, and I knew that I must get off. I also knew that she was not coming with me. I felt pain, loss, loneliness. I felt like an abandoned child. I knew I must not ask if I would ever see her again. She pressed my hand and I stood up. I couldn't bear to leave her. Oh Miles, I'm crying uncontrollably. I must take some Rescue Remedy.

To continue. When I stepped off the bus, I turned to look up at her once more. She waved the tips of her fingers at me with that enigmatic smile, only there was nothing mocking in it, nothing sardonic as in the past. Then I glanced into the window of W. H. Smith and saw you. You, Miles, reading a famous and once-suppressed Victorian novel about sexual deviation among the upper classes. *Walter*, isn't that the one? The cover was purple and black. You were very absorbed. I knocked on the glass. You looked up and I pointed urgently at the seventy-three bus which was pulling away from the curb. I mouthed the word Georgia, but you didn't understand. I looked again towards the Caledonian Road. The bus had disappeared into the traffic.

In tears I rushed into W.H. Smith and described to you, incoherently I suppose, what had just happened. Somewhere I could hear the Frank violin sonata.

'Don't you live in Barnsbury now, my dear?' you interrupted my story.

'Yes, I believe I've been living there for several months.' Everything was very through the looking glass.

'Then shall we go home for a cup of tea?' You glanced at your watch. 'Or are they open yet?'

I woke up. The birds were singing. It was quarter to six. The bedlinen was in chaos, and I was sweating profusely, not knowing whether to laugh or cry. I wanted only to return to the dream, to walk with you through the back streets to Ripplevale Grove, to go with you into The Rising Sun and sit by the fire and drink Jameson's like we used to and can't do any more, and ask you to explain why Providence should have ordained that my life be entangled for over ten years with a woman named Wendy Perlmutter. I have some thoughts on the matter, but they need distillation.

I am so happy about your book. No one could more deserve the accolades I am certain will follow its publication. You will send me a copy, won't you, and you won't mind if I say that I think it *must* be dedicated to Georgia. How could it be otherwise?

You are overworked, my dear Miles. I prescribe Cherry Plum and Star of Bethlehem. Shall I put you on the machine?

Your mystified
Sylvie

Letter Nine

Los Angeles
September 1

My Darling,

Your letter arrived this morning. I have just read it for the fifth time, sitting at the kitchen table in a silk burgundy dressing gown, barefoot, eating an archetypal avocado, and listening to Arthur's matutinal rumblings in the chicken coop. (How can people lay abed after eight a.m.? It must signify something deeply degenerate in their nature.)

Your letter. Your letter has provoked a divine afflatus. I burn and freeze. I am all awareness. And all love.

First the awareness. Never in my long and varied experience have I understood so well the beautiful way in which the Unconscious directs the lives of those who open themselves to its influence. The clarity with which I see the meaning of your dream is profoundly gratifying, not only in an intellectual but in an existential sense. Your dream is both macrocosm and microcosm. It is, my dearest Sylvia, real life. It is all that one hopes to achieve. And do you know why? Because it signifies a change in consciousness, an enantiodromia – for you, for me, for Georgia. I also must say that I have been trying for years to have this dream. You have succeeded where I have failed. You have, as it were, dreamed it for me.

In the first place, your emotions have been divided over the past months between Georgia and myself. You are full of guilt. You blame yourself for what happened; you blame me; you blame yourself for blaming me. Give it up, my dear, for I tell you that you are free – free of your obligations to a dead friend and free to love me as you have wished to love me for a very long time.

It is clear that Georgia is attaining peace at last. Her visits to the 'real world', her rather lowly position in the hereafter, suggest a lengthy, though necessary, sojourn in Purgatoria. Her disinclination to use the Underground is proof that, metaphysically speaking, she has kicked the habit. (Underground equals trains equals *tracks*!) She is healthy, well-dressed,

though not, it appears, in her 'bizarre chic'. Sounds even
remotely respectable. Pumps!?

She takes you on to a bus. What bus? The seventy-three.
Seven and three, the two most perfect mystical numbers,
which when combined gematrically, make ten, the number of
completion, of Adam Kadmon, of the Tree of Life. Yggdrasil,
Darling. A most powerful sanction, if I may say so. And where
does the bus go? King's Cross. This is rich indeed. First of all,
the cross refers to my suit, Swords, that is Intellect. Only now I
am elevated from Knight to King, signifying that I have
attained maturity at last through an acceptance of my
responsibilities and the realization of my potential. King's
Cross also gives you away. You obviously fear my displeasure.
Calm yourself, my pet. King adores you. Most important,
Cross equals crossroads, turning point, decision, the taking of
a definite step, embarking upon a new direction. In a word, and
what a word, enantiodromia! Of course there is a link to
Georgia herself, especially to her dark side. The goddess
Hecate presided over crossroads, *trivia* in Latin, that is tri-via,
three ways, symbolizing the three paths of our three lives and
linking back to the number of the bus. *Voilà*, Georgia-Hecate
has led you to the crossroads and to the King — me.

My dear, don't you see? Georgia has given you to me and
has blessed our union by disappearing for ever. I am the
reward for all your devotion. You are the exoneration of my
(supposed) betrayal. She has left us in peace at last to pursue
her own mysterious destiny. May her next incarnation be a
saner, kinder one.

As to the Victorian paperback — yes, clearly *Walter*, and a
journal, by the way, not a novel — it is in Georgia's colours,
purple and black, and is concerned with a depraved sexuality,
once covert, now commonplace (though I do not think you
will find *Walter* on the shelves of any W.H. Smith. Try Soho if
you wish to pursue the reference.) I am absorbed, you say, but
only through a detached, humorous curiosity, my wish to
explore all aspects of human nature. I show you the book and
smile. It is a topic to be discussed, no longer a compelling and
destructive reality. It represents both a dead morality and a
dead immorality. One must pass through and beyond both.
Such is my interpretation, but perhaps there is more to be

uncovered here. Your sexuality, for instance. Consider it. That you and Georgia were never lovers seems to me incredible. But since you always claimed the negative, I accept your word without question.

Let us proceed, my dear, with this most intriguing dream. You are close to Barnsbury, near to home, within walking distance equals nearly returned to your true self. But you seem uncertain ('I believe I have lived there,' etc.) An atmosphere of unreality still surrounds you. But then who invites you to return 'home'? Who will escort you? Yours truly.

Now for the love. Sylvie, do you not see that there are no limits to what we can do for each other? Can it be that after all these years of friendship, separation, and grief we discover that I am the man in you and you are the woman in me? When I consider that holiday with Steve, the hours of tête-à-tête at the *Arch Angel*, the orgies, it seems inconceivable that we have maintained a chaste relationship. Why have we never made love? *Have* we ever made love? Surely we cannot have been saving ourselves for each other in the medieval sense. And yet you are medieval somehow. You remind me of the music of that era: clear, pure, resonant with suppressed ardour, an ardour for something not of this world. Perhaps we have always loved each other and were unaware. Yes, it may be as simple as that. All great things are simple.

But let us see. Let us see. It has only just begun. It is so marvellously new. Don't you feel it? Haven't I made you feel it? I must end here, my love, only because I am burning to begin a long new poem, a poem inspired entirely by you and, of course, dedicated to you.

Your dream — let me say it once more — shows a great capacity to see beyond the grotesque muddle of appearances straight into the true nature of things. You have honoured me. You have made me unspeakably happy. Dare I say that I am beginning to long to see you? No, no. We must proceed slowly. Slowly equals deliciously. We shall talk first, and then ... *Shall* we talk?

Yours sempeternally,
Miles

PS Do remember that every person in one's dream is in fact oneself.

Letter Ten

Belitha Villas
September 7

I don't know what to say.
Yes, call me.
No, don't.
 I'm afraid. One becomes so guarded as one gets older. Grief
and repeated injuries nurture a despicable paranoia. One
protects oneself in a hundred little ways. Gradually one
becomes deformed. One is barely conscious of this process
which is called growing up but which is really the loss of
spontaneity. Change, any change, is a threat to one's already
shaky security.
 Our relationship is perfect. I fear that any alteration would
destroy the balance we have created. I know you understand
me. But when I think of how strong and brave you are, I know
it is I who am wrong. I must climb above my fear, climb out of
it entirely and for ever. Risk is renewal. Not to go forward is
to regress. And you and I must go forward. Only help me
Miles, please. You have gone so much further than I, dared
more than I, and therefore learned more than I. Of course you
have made me see that I love you and that I have loved you for
years. Perhaps I even loved Georgia as a way of loving you.
But that is a complicated thought, and just now I wish to be
simple. Only to feel and be simple. So I say yes, because this is
love, and love can never say no.
 Call me. Though I tremble at the thought of hearing your
voice. Call me, call me. I am always at home.

Letter Eleven (Telegram)

Sept. 13 LOS ANGELES CALIFORNIA USA MS SYLVIA LAKE 131
BELITHA VILLAS LONDON N1 KINGS CROSS CONTINENT KINGS
CROSS OCEAN SEVEN PLUS THREE CAST OUT FEAR UNTIL SEPT. 16
7.30 PM BST THE GODS ARE WITH US MILES WITH LOVE.

Letter Twelve

My Darling,

I know many things. I know that your nature is open, that you are without rancour, that you are charitable. Too charitable to prick me with petty recriminations. I know that to beg your forgiveness would be to cast aspersion upon that impeccable nature.

What I do not know is why I never told you before about my telephone phobia. My eagerness to express my feelings in the most direct and unmistakable terms caused me to over-estimate my requisite quantum of brute energy. Make no mistake, the act of telephoning, especially transglobally, is a brutal act. Nothing less than a de-sensitizing of one's entire nature will make it possible. First one must overcome one's revulsion at simply picking up the odious object. Then one's eardrum is tormented by varieties of static, shrieks, and whines reminiscent of the special effects department of *Star Wars*. Then the entire operation, for which one has geared oneself to such a pitch, utterly misfires, and one is forced to begin all over again. The operators are, without exception, surly and incapable of either speaking or comprehending English. Misunderstandings ensue, then arguments and insults. Receivers are slammed, telephones destroyed. Then comes the inevitable poor connection which forces the parties involved to shout inanities at each other in unison. Victims of a three-quarter of a second delay in voice transmission and a nervous debility generated, in the first place, by the abortive business. For this torture and frustration one receives, a month later, an astronomical bill. No, no, and again no. My sensibilities would have been shattered long before the first anguished hello, your sweet voice having been transmuted into something out of a laser disco. Ugh!

Of course, you saw well before I that recourse to technology was not only premature but potentially harmful. Perhaps if you were to call me . . . but then what would be the effect upon you of having to assume the role of instigator? I feel I cannot, much as I selfishly long for contiguity, ask you to submit your sensitive psyche to such an ordeal. I am certain that the shock of coming so blatantly, barbarously crash together would be more than either of us could endure, and might endanger the exquisite balance we have achieved. In a word, let us have patience. The alchemists did insist, after all, that it is the only virtue.

I was about to say come (oh please come, there I've said it anyway) for the opening of the DeBellis retrospective. But that proposed fête is at present nothing but the source of acute vexation. On all fronts I meet with apprehension, misunderstanding, and lack of co-operation. None of which is my doing, you understand. DeBellissima's flagitious influence extends beyond the grave, thwarting my selfless efforts to raise her from her muck of obscurity to the aesthetic heights where I – perhaps mistakenly – believe she belongs. Her bad mouth and worse behaviour cast a long shadow. (Atrocious metaphor, do forgive me; it is only that the umbrage taken falls upon *me*.) Many of those who were once in a position to help her, who wanted to help her, now hesitate. One does not easily forget the slanderous remarks, the cruel jests, the perfidious betrayals. My entrepreneurial efforts are constantly hindered by the necessity to explain, to rehabilitate, in some cases to reconstruct her character. What misguided impulse of generosity impelled me to this undertaking I now cannot imagine. (It all began with that visit to the grave. Parma violets, humph!)

So disheartened have I become over the project that work on the catalogue has ground to a complete halt. It is difficult to persuade critics and historians to write or even talk of her. It is difficult to persuade owners to lend their collages, especially the English. (I must say, however, that I have managed to extract a sizeable quantity even from them.) One person who shall be nameless had the temerity to enquire if I knew the whereabouts of a certain first edition – very rare – which disappeared several years ago from the library of her country house shortly after our mutual friend had paid a weekend visit, to inspect the installation of one of her mini-masterpieces, I'm told. Well, her ladyship was mad to ask Georgia in the first place. One can hardly expect otherwise if one invites Baby-

fingers to tea. And what has all this to do with me? It is making
my task, undertaken in the spirit of true friendship, in fact of a
pretty damned exalted altruism, if I may say so, wellnigh
impossible. Could She not have learned at least to curb her
tongue? If She was not employing that organ to extol herself
or deprecate others, She was thrusting it into every available
orifice, human and otherwise.

Forgive me, Sylvie, this will not do. Georgia's power over
me is gone. That has been established. I must not allow her to
poison my life any more. I shall persevere with the retrospective for the cause of Art and because I am a man of honour. The
world needs to see these pictures, of that I am convinced.

Meanwhile there are technical problems over the production of *The Burning Bush* with which I will not bore you,
but simply reflect once more on the way in which all nature
conspires against the creative individual. Gurdjieff put it so
well when he said oh fuck, what did he say, even my memory
is failing, and all because of this tiresome exhibition. Your
poem has had to be put aside. *Your* poem. Have you any idea
how it pains me to tell you that? Nevertheless, my will shall
prevail. Say you adore me.

Your bel-let-trist,
Miles

PS Are you sure you are right in withholding Georgia's
letters? I do not wish to pressure you, of course the decision
must be yours. But do give the matter further consideration,
there's a good girl.

Letter Thirteen A

Belitha Villas
September 27

Six a.m. In the garden.
I adore you.

Letter Thirteen B

Ten thirty a.m. Rain. Nice rain. Intermittent rain. Lots of
gentle dripping. Some sun. Butterflies on the Michaelmas
daisies.

Re-reading Georgia's letters. On second thoughts, perhaps
they belong in the Archives. Especially important once the
retrospective has become a reality. And when that happens,
poor Miles, you will be relieved of a heavy burden, nobly
assumed and carried alone. I wish I could be of some use to
you. Am I really your Muse?

As for the telephone call. Please, my love, don't think about
it. I also fear the disembodied voice. While I waited in anxiety
for seven thirty, I realized that our relationship, which
depends so much on distance, was suddenly threatened. We
are romantics. We long for beautiful longings. Better to wait
and heighten our sensibilities through waiting.

Perhaps you are right, perhaps there is something medieval
in my nature. For me, the physical presence of the loved one is
not a prerequisite for passion. Longing is passion, and longing
is generated by absence. Therefore, Miles, do not trouble
yourself on my account. All that you do or do not do is
perfect. Should I be embarrassed to say that I love you with a
higher love? No one says things like that any more.

You see, I am not like Georgia. Love, physical love was the
most important thing in her life. More important than her art.
At first I did not believe this, but it was true. She could not
exist without a man, not for twenty-four hours. (Women
were always considered poor substitutes.) We had a conversation about this once, not long before she left London. She

was in a morbid mood, bemoaning the lack of male companionship and reminiscing about past affairs. Despite the drug, she still felt the need of lovers. Any kind. Even the basest sort.

I said I was astonished. I could not understand why her art was not sufficient gratification. To me, at that time an uncreative person, a late developer still looking for my identity, nothing could have been more wonderful than the practice and perfecting of an art one believed in – especially an art that brought with it the degree of success that Georgia enjoyed. Surely it should be all the world, everything and everyone else of secondary importance.

'It's not enough,' she replied flatly. 'It doesn't give me enough. Only love and sex and knowing that a beautiful, talented, special man adores me give me something like enough. Failing that, that *any* man adores me. Women are all right. I mean you're cute but you're not my type.'

'I can't believe this, Georgia. I'd give anything to do what you do.'

'Oh really?' she snorted, but there were tears in her eyes. 'Wait a while. Just you wait, my dear, sweet, fucking naive Sylvie. If you ever do become a poet or a homeopathetic doctor or a violinist or one of those eight hundred super-refined things you think you want to be when you grow up, you'll find out what it's like, and fast. You'll be all alone with this thing you can do, and no one will understand why it's tearing you apart. Art breaks your heart, honey. Take it from me. And no one will care about your struggle. Because of it they'll hate you and run away from you. If you force them to love you it will frighten them. They'll be envious. They'll tell you you're a freak. They'll see you as a challenging object. They'll treat you mean and make you bitter in your isolation. And no matter how hard you work you'll never have enough money, and that's the worst part.'

I was frightened. It was as though she was attacking me personally.

'Do you think art can compensate for love and pain? Do you really think that if you wrote a brilliant novel and it sold 50,000 copies that you'd stop letting Marlowe make you miserable, that you'd stop trembling and worrying and crying whenever he curled his lip at you? Your art wouldn't make a damned bit of difference. I'm telling you the terrible truth: when there's no love, there's no nothing. The pictures are good when the love is good. It's as simple as that, at least with me it is. Otherwise I might as well be dead.' She gave a short, hard laugh and looked at her bandaged hands. 'Well I'm a junkie and that's as close as you can get, I guess.'

Once she rang me in a terrible state. Truly, Miles, I thought the end had come, she sounded so weak and hysterical. I dropped my violin and spent my last three pounds on a taxi to Chiltern Street. To my amazement, I found her not only out of bed, but prancing about in a red satin body-stocking and three-inch mules. Her face had been lavishly made up, her nails lacquered, her hair coiffed like Dolores Del Rio's. She seemed almost annoyed that I had come.

'Reinhold's just arrived from Berlin. He called me from the airport. He's taking me to the White Elephant and wants to stay here. I haven't seen him for three years. More to the point, *he* hasn't seen *me*.'

She was in an agony of nervous anticipation.

'God, oh God, three years! Will he think I'm hideous? Christ, how am I going to hide these tracks? Reinhold doesn't approve of drugs, any drugs, just the occasional schnapps. He'll never buy one of my collages if he thinks I'm a junkie. Even worse, he won't go to bed with me. He'll think I'm a depraved monster, he's so clean and good-looking and rich. I've just got to hide these tracks!' She screamed the word and frantically began applying layers of pancake to the blue-green bruises on her thighs and arms.

'I'll just have to invent something about my hands. I'll lie, that's all, there's no choice. He'll have to believe me. Sylvie, find me a long-sleeve blouse. There must be a clean one somewhere, one without a stain or a tear or a smell or all the buttons missing. Please find me something *quick*, what about that St Laurent knit dress. That has long sleeves. I've got to cover these tracks and do my eyes still, and he'll be here in twenty minutes. Maybe if I just keep the lights as low as possible, one black candle. But what will I do when we go out? He'll see everything, how ugly I am, every little . . . no, no, I can't think about it. Please, please, Sylvie, be an angel and put

on the Gina Bacchauer recording of the Brahms waltzes, no,
not that, the Rachmaninov Preludes, and *go* as fast as possible.
Go. I know Reinhold, he won't want anyone to be here, he's
so private and mysterious and German. I can't risk anything.
Oh you're fantastic, Sylvie, thank you, my love, you're my
only friend. We'll always be friends, eternally, I know it. Only
please hurry up, will you? Jesus, do you think I can get away
with this?'

The transformation was total. She looked five years
younger. The bizarre chic was back, and with it her old pert
tone. How she managed it I've no idea. What was she
expecting that could restore her to life like that? What she was
expecting, I guess, was everything. The twist of fate, the
miracle, the key to the mysteries. But the key was eternally in
the pocket of some male. The male was money, fame, the sale
of a picture, a new dress, a new beginning. Perhaps the male
was just eternal youth. Georgia DeBellis born again.

The outcomes of these encounters were always the same.
The man involved would leave half-way through the evening
if he were in any way cultivated. Of course these were the ones
guaranteed to break her heart. (Georgia worshipped that
particular brand of English refinement exemplified by you and
Marlowe.) If he did take her to bed, he was the sort to be
brutal and to exploit her vulnerability. One stole money,
another beat her up, a third humiliated her because of her
habit. Yet she never relinquished that mad, touching expectation. It was tragic to watch her in her expectation. It made my
heart ache. It also severely damaged my image of her as *the*
liberated woman.

She loved love in every form. And she loved to talk about it.
She would show me the bruises on her thighs, the gouges on
her shoulders, the teeth marks on her neck. She would describe in detail the penis, the testicles, the style of kissing, the
manner of penetration, everything that was said. She adored
it. Remembering all this makes me realize how terrifying an
insatiable woman can be. Was she a nymphomaniac, do you
think? From where else could that desperation have come? Yes
Miles, I do understand. She exhausted even you.

I will tell you another story. It touched me deeply at the
time. It still does. I arrived at Chiltern Street one afternoon

with the customary bag of groceries. I found her alone in
semi-darkness, though it was a bright June day. She was
half-dressed, propped up in bed crying. Not an uncommon
state of affairs, you are no doubt remarking. My dear, do not
be cynical. If you had seen her – but I would wish to spare you
any painful encounter, even imaginary. She was reading by
the glow of the green grapes lamp. She was reading a packet of
letters. They did not look familiar. I was surprised, for by that
time she had shown me just about everything that belonged to
her. She was obsessed with her past. Understandably, when
the present was such a nightmare.

I sat opposite her on the bed and took a little of her smack. It
was absurdly generous of her to offer, considering the horrors
she suffered when supplies ran out. I was ashamed, but I
accepted. I suppose that I, too, was taking more than was good
for me. But I was so depressed about Marlowe, so worn out
with worry over Georgia. One must, from time to time, have
a little happiness if one is weak – and even if one is not so
weak. The heroin was exceptionally good. For an hour we
laughed and talked and listened to music and took pleasure in
each other's company like two ordinary women who have
confided in each other for years.

She told me that the letters were from a boy named Billy
whom she had met when she first arrived in New York and
with whom she had shared a dismal apartment on Elizabeth
Street. He came from Indiana and was struggling to establish
himself as a journalist. He cared a great deal for causes and
humanity, neither of which held much appeal for Georgia.
She, at the time, was manipulating her way into an avant-
garde theatre company on Second Avenue. Being Georgia,
she succeeded, and in a few months was en route to Europe for
a tour with the troupe. Billy begged her to stay, but, as usual,
she knew what she wanted and gaily kissed him goodbye at
the airport.

He wrote to her frequently and passionately, and she sent
him the odd postcard from Positano and Delphi. Two years
later when she had settled in London and her work was
exhibited in a group show, he arrived unexpectedly, having
given up his job and followed her colourful trail across the
continent. He caught up with her in that little place she used to

rent on St Peter's Street. Georgia found him naively American and thoroughly square about drugs. But he was still good-looking, cheerful, and very generous. He lived three happy weeks with her until she got bored and sent him packing.

Europe held nothing else for him. He went back to New York but continued to write to her for another two years. She showed me the letters. They expressed the most tender sentiments, a bit awkwardly, but without any pretence. He was a genuinely nice person. He loved Georgia and would have married her in a minute. In fact, he'd have done anything for her, including leave without a fuss when she told him to go.

You can imagine the way that Georgia, in her self-pity, had come to regard these letters.

'I'll never part with them,' she wailed. 'I'll keep them all my life, so that when I'm old and ugly I can read them and say to myself that once somebody really loved me.'

I timidly suggested she write to Billy and describe her predicament, but the idea horrified her. No, he must never know what had happened. He must remember her always as glamorous, successful, sought after. That way, she said, the Georgia DeBellis who was would always be. She would exist unchanged in the memory of Billy Glazer. Amazing, isn't it? That was her conception of immortality. But in one respect she was right. True love is the love of the mind, or rather the love in the mind.

I could weep when I think of the difficulties you are meeting so courageously. I shall never add to them. Not even the smallest demand. But my thoughts and feelings are always with you. You are a constant preoccupation. Oh, sometimes Miles I wish I could see you. What am I saying? You are here before me. Of course I see you. I see nothing but you.

Sylvie

Letter Fourteen

Los Angeles
October 14

My Own Sylvie,

What follows is a love letter, or might best be described as a love letter. A wholehearted effort, though I cannot guarantee the results. I shall attempt, with unaccustomed humility, to describe my feelings for you. They are deep indeed.

Thus far I have played – and this *is* customary – the selfish and self-indulgent male. Without remonstrance you have made me realize how stranded in myself I have become. (Much of this was Georgia's work. My flight from her was a flight from everything.) I have unscrupulously, though unconsciously, made use of you as muse and amusement. What I have given in return seems suddenly little. I barely know where and how you live, or what you look like. Your life, what glimpses I have had of it, seems terribly isolated. (Are you depending on me *very* much, my Sweet?) How could I not have enquired, offered, suggested? But let me begin.

Tell me, do you still have your beautiful long hair, or do you think the style unsuitable for a woman of – there, you see, I don't even know your age. I have forgotten your birthday. Virgo? Libra? You're younger than I, of that I'm sure. Are you forty yet? Have you cut your hair or do you wear it up? In little plaits? Have you permed it? How, how do you wear it, I long to know. You have pierced ears, don't you, but never wear those large, vulgar earrings.

You were very beautiful, a pale, frail beauty with barely discernible eyebrows. Are your limbs as delicate as ever? I can't imagine that weight has been added to your years. And you were graceful – the loveliest attribute in a woman, a quality which cannot be lost, damaged, or stolen. A quality which also can never be acquired. It lives in the fibre of the being. (Our mutual friend could have done with a little more of it.) Yes, you are graceful still. Of course you are. And your eyes. They are light blue, aren't they, flecked grey, intelligent, but without a trace of irony, wide open and guileless. I can see you now. I am concentrating all upon you. I see your wise round little face, like a cat's. Oh cat woman, serious, gentle, self-contained. You have still, I am certain, I can hear it in your letters, that air of innocence, that refinement so extraordinary in an American. (God, think of Georgia.) You are a Daisy Miller who has learned decorum, an Isabelle Archer who had the sense to spurn Mr Osmond. (Marlowe is at heart nothing but a semi-cultivated scoundrel. He impressed you. You outgrew him. Besides, he preferred men. It must have been hell for you.)

I need you, Sylvie. I need your combination of elements. In you they are so finely mixed. They suit me as nothing has ever suited me. I love your delicate stoicism, your prettily deflected libido. You behave well; you retain your dignity – a rare attribute. It is the most refreshing thing. I know I can rely upon it. And you have multiple interests like me, like all truly civilized people. You are not obsessed.

Oh wonderful one, we must meet. Somehow. Somewhere. Our eyes must see, our fingers touch, our limbs embrace. But how? I ache to come to you, but I am so damned damaged, if you see what I mean. Still, still . . . I *will* rise up and come to you. Soon.

Meanwhile I labour like Atlas under the responsibilities which have been laid on me. The retrospective crawls forward, still a possibility, but kept alive only by my unceasing efforts. *City Lights* postpone and prevaricate. I fly to San Francisco once a week to argue with the editor and drink too much bad Chablis. The matter remains unresolved. I return to LA, exhausted. The plague of telephone calls commences, exacerbating my nervous irritability. In a fit of pique I throw Arthur out. We make it up forty-eight hours later, and he is back in the chicken coop, waiting for an inopportune moment to pester me about Umberto. My perfidious assistant has run off with a stunt person, and so I must go and sit half the day like a common shopkeeper while am bursting to commence the novella and longing to return to your poem. I am falling behind with the Archives. The irony is that I continue to make money. (With the exception of one who shall be nameless, I have been haunted by good fortune. It pursues me like a host of benign Eumenides.)

There, you see I have failed to keep up this love letter after all. I knew I should lapse. My mind wanders continually back to debilitating trivia. Forgive me. You can imagine the vast expenditure of vitality which these projects demand. I long for peace and an end to this LA life and an ocean of eternity with no one but you. You and you alone require nothing of me. What more can I say except write to me, come to me. Can you come?

Miles

Letter Fifteen

Belitha Villas
October 19

Darling Miles,

Are you sure? Wouldn't my presence only add to your responsibilities? Wouldn't I, too, become another demand? I couldn't bear that. Perhaps it is selfishness on my part to wish to protect the image you have of me. But I feel I can best serve you by my letters and my absence. Of course you must be assured of my spiritual presence. I am with you, Miles. That is where I am. That is all I am. Let us consider complicating the matter when your period of entanglement and frustration is over. Then I'll come to you.

Trusting and relenting, I enclose all of the letters I received from Georgia those last two years. I feel now that their rightful place is in the Archives. Aside from certain passages which I know you will suppress, use anything you think may be relevant for the catalogue.

I am also enclosing Argent Nitrate in powder form. It should help to balance your nerves. Write to me, adored Miles, when your busy life allows. I am here in my room.

Sylvie.

PS Plaits. Up. Virgo. Eyes hazel. Thirty-eight. No earrings. Sorry.

Letter Sixteen

Belitha Villas
October 20
2.00 a.m.

Miles, Miles, should I come? I could come. I could send my patients away or treat them from California. Would I be able to get the machine into America? I could be with you by Christmas, that soon. Wouldn't it be beautiful? Perhaps I might help you with your work, like the old days. Perhaps I might be of use after all. Really Miles, to be honest, and I haven't dared say this to you before, there is very little here for me. I burn Dittany of Crete and treat myself with the machine and see the NW3 acupuncturist, but nothing improves. I think this is because I belong with you and am not fulfilling my true function. Must we be apart, or am I having a weak moment? Miles, I have so many weak moments. I love you, Miles. Tell me please what you think. I need to know.

Sylvie

Letter Seventeen

Belitha Villas
November 1

Darling Miles,
Forgive, forgive my silly letter. Of course I would only be in your way. Of course I am happy here. I am helping others, I mean I am trying to help. And there is you. You for me. What could be more satisfying? You see, it was a lapse. I am myself again. Only please write and tell me where you are and how your work is progressing and what is going to happen to the DeBellis exhibition. I long to know. The days are so dark and the nights so long. Miles, where are you?

All my love,
Sylvie

Letter Eighteen

Los Angeles
November 30

Darling Sylvia,

As usual I shall spare the apologies. As usual they are unworthy of you. I am, however, faintly surprised by the last sentence in your letter of 1/11. Where *am* I? Where else, my dove, but with you? Having mutually agreed that physical proximity is a dispensable factor in our passion, should the occasional letter be any less so? I was under the impression that you and I were secure in our thoughts of each other. I shall say no more on the subject, but suggest you give it further consideration.

Of course I should adore you to come to Los Angeles. It would be heaven to see you. Perhaps after the New Year. Perhaps in March. The weather can be so divine then. Just now a visit would be impossible. You see, I am going to Mexico for Christmas. But I haven't told you!!!! Dear God, how could I not have burst the news upon you straightaway? *Steve is here*! Our lost adorable *puer aeternus*. Yes, here with me, in my house. (Arthur has been evicted from the chicken coop once and for all. Henceforth he must sort out his love life and his finances without me.) You can imagine my inexpressible joy at the miraculous appearance, our ecstatic reunion, how we talked and talked of you and Georgia, our adventures in the inner and outer worlds, and the strange beauty of fate that holds us all together and intertwines the threads of our lives.

I shan't keep you in suspense, my blossom. Yes, he is well – as fresh and funny and superhumanly beautiful as ever. He has been – can you believe this – four years in Minneapolis, too embarrassed to write, and understandably so. He was nearly ensnared by some piece of corn-fed gaol-bait, but thank heavens he escaped her and her Daddy's metaphorical shot-gun. Naturally he is broke. But yet again we are the victims of a benign synchronicity. (I think I am beginning to understand the expression Children of God.) I mentioned that my assistant at the shop had deserted me, thereby doubling my already insupportable work load and almost shattering my sensibilities. I was, I confess, at my wits' end. Other developments have contributed. Of these later. Then who should appear like a *deus ex machina* or, more appropriately, an angel from heaven, but Steve. Yes, I thought, yes! I saw it all immediately. Fate, inscrutable delicious fate, had brought us together again to save each other. He has rescued me from the shop (he manages it beautifully), and I have provided him with a home, a job, and an income. Above and beyond this, we have the virtually uninterrupted pleasure of each other's company. All that is needed to make our happiness complete is your dear self. But, as I said, I am shattered. I have been nearly prostrate for weeks. Heavens, hypoglycaemia, I thought. Nonsense, says Steve.

His suggestion that we spend two weeks in Mexico in order that I might have a well-earned rest and begin to recover my faculties so that I may take up my true work again was most welcome and insightful. (Forgive the run-on sentence. It is symptomatic of my relief and enthusiasm.) We will swim, read, and carry on our beautiful, endless, inimitable talk. Meanwhile Steve will be treating me. He has learned a marvellous new massage technique in Minneapolis, strange as that may seem. (He always had wonderful hands, didn't he?) He says my problem is my malfunctioning ileo-cecum which he can correct by applying exactly the right pressure to the corresponding spot on the sole of my left foot. Excruciating but effective. He has explained the technique so delightfully. I am thinking of writing an article on the subject, with his help, of course. But first I must begin my novella. All this needs time and space, and *I* need to recuperate. My dear, I can't tell you how necessary this holiday is. I shall simply close up the shop for two weeks. Take that, LA!

By the way, *City Lights* is going ahead with *The Burning Bush*. It will be out in the spring. The dedication, I feel, must be Steve's, considering all he's done for me.

And now I must deliver a piece of what I suppose qualifies as bad news. I hope it will not distress you, but things have come to such a pass — oh well, here it is: to be brutally brief, I have given up the retrospective. Not only did the mechanics become more than I could manage (due entirely, as I have explained, to the past misconduct of DeBellis), and the paper-work insurmountable, but my rapidly deteriorating health has made it imperative that I relinquish responsibility for the project immediately. Avery Little may take it over, with trepidation, but a good deal more positive energy than I can muster. My work has been suffering; my work calls – a summons that may not be ignored with impunity.

Not without regrets, I assure you, do I abandon the enter-prise. But, as Steve so aptly pointed out, I have been regarding the exhibition as a debt of honour which was never commis-sioned. My guilt, like all guilt, is self-generated. Besides, how could I have foreseen the way Georgia's spirit would thwart me? How could I have known the extent to which this act of friendship would sap my creative energies and threaten the functioning of my true will? Perhaps the retrospective was never meant to be. Fate seems against it. Indeed, Georgia herself may now wish to rest her troubled soul in calm obscurity. Perhaps we should let her lie down in darkness once and for all. Then again, it may be that the time is wrong and that the whole undertaking may one day blossom afresh and prosper. Perhaps, *au fond*, it is a job for the Whitechapel. Meanwhile, fear not. I know what you are thinking, my dear. I have all the collages. They are here with me, safe, and will remain with me until something can be sorted out. Georgia's letters, thanks to you, have been incorporated into the Archi-ves which now occupy five shelves in my study. One day they will be the source material for the history of a generation.

But the exhibition. Frankly, Sylvie, I cannot tell you how relieved I am to be rid of it. It was draining my very life blood. And the thought of the opening itself: the lower life-forms it would attract, the creatures such a reunion would lure from the woodwork, can you imagine. Wraiths and lamias. The last thing I need just now is an evening in a smoke-filled room with a bunch of seedy has-beens getting drunk on my liquor under the auspices of aesthetics and auld lang syne. Ugh! Besides, I am a man of letters who secretly has despised the art world for years. It is frivolous and corrupt, and everyone makes far too much money. Moreover, it has nurtured a superstar mentality among artists which is unhealthy and very unattractive. Let me out!

My darling Sylvie, we think of you so much. We long to see you. We have even entertained the idea of a trip to London upon our return from Mexico. We both confessed that besides the sweet solace of your personality the visit would afford, we expatriated Englishmen are just a weeny bit homesick. But as yet it cannot be. I know that with Steve to help me – how much we have to learn from each other! – my work will go well and I shall wish to carry on in seclusion for several months. Perhaps in the spring. It would be divine to stroll with you through Kensington Gardens the last week in April or the first week in May when London is the most beautiful city in Europe. We could all three go down to my parents' country house. But I am fantasizing. Steve is right. I must learn to live in the present, to know myself in the here and now. Had I done so previously I would never have been saddled with the DeBellis retrospective.

I do know myself well enough to know how haunted London would be for me. Even you could not dispel the ghosts, especially that one ghost who has been the subject of so many pages of our correspondence. I could not bear Regent's Park, Baker Street, the whole vicinity of Portman Mansions. Yet they would draw me like a magnet. I should be at Chiltern Street within an hour, risking a psychic assault, the consequences of which make me shudder in advance. My sensibilities would certainly be shattered. Steve is in complete agreement, and says that under no circumstances should I expose myself to Georgia's influence. For, let us face facts, it is a pernicious influence and still a pervasive one. You yourself have felt its effects. It is this influence which is disturbing you. Steve agrees. We think you must come to California – not to LA itself, you are too sensitive, but to meet us somewhere beautiful, the desert maybe. It would be so wonderful. Perhaps in June, what do you think? If money is a problem, please do not hesitate, out of pride, to tell me. All I have is yours, my precious, and vice versa I am sure. I'll gladly send you a ticket. Of course if you could manage your own spending money, so much the better. But even so. Do not fret about finances, ever. Among us they are irrelevant. Only please do give me plenty of notice if you intend to come – a month or two at least. Meanwhile, call whenever you like if you feel you can manage the phone. We are always here, except when we will be in Mexico. I shall stand on the shores of the Pacific and think long long thoughts of you. Prepare for a deluge of postcards.

Honour us with one of your exquisite epistles. We look forward to it with impatience.

All our love,
Miles

PS Guess who had the Tarot deck after all? Our Stevie! It seems the darling little sneak paid a surreptitious visit to LA and to Georgia just after I had seen her. She must have known the end was near. She was threatening to destroy the cards, to destroy everything, including herself. So, unbeknown to her, and on a high impulse of generosity and belief in Art, he pocketed the deck and rescued it from Georgiadammerung. It is here with me. I believe the DeBellis collection is now complete.

Letter Nineteen

Belitha Villas
December 10

Dearest Miles and Steve,

You probably won't receive this until your return from Mexico. But I wanted to send you a Christmas card and tell you how I love and miss you both and that I wish you a happy new year. How can the new year fail to be happy when friends are together? Well, I am with you in spirit, as it seems I never tire of saying.

Yes, I am very sorry about the collapse of the retrospective. I can hardly believe you are giving it up. Of course I'm not blaming you. But if it is true, would you please, dear Miles, return my collages. I love them so, and I feel their absence. They are all that is left to me of Georgia. I need to have them by me. And dear, dear Miles, the letters: promise me you

won't ever publish them. Ever. I know this is a tergiversation
and that I am behaving badly like a vacillating female. But
please don't publish them, even extracts from them. And
don't allow anyone else to do so. And don't show them to
anyone. It would cause me the most dreadful guilt. You
understand what I am saying. Of course you understand, you
are an understanding person. I trust you absolutely.

I shall spend Christmas alone. A patient invited me to her
country house, but I said no. I think I should find all those
family festivities depressing and besides, there is much I want
to think over. Christmas is a good time to think. London is so
quiet.

Yours in solitude,
Sylvie

Letter Twenty

Belitha Villas
January 28, 1979

Dear Miles,

Forgive my impatience and my anxiety. I had to write to
you. Are you all right? Are you working and shut away from
the world? If so, all is as it should be. Perhaps you are still in
Mexico. Perhaps it was too wonderful to leave. I miss you,
Miles. I am so selfish, I need the support your letters give me.
I am often agitated and depressed. I am trying a higher
potency of Ignatia, but Miles, sometimes I wonder what we
have done. It is difficult to have had so much liberty. What
did we live through that has made us so strange? What is this
grey effusiveness we cultivate between us? What am I saying?
I am saying have the drugs done something irreparable to us
do you think, or is it just human nature and being thirty-
eight?

I realize I am behaving badly like a paranoid woman. I lack
faith. Of course you are thinking of me. You are wishing me
well. You are here, naturally, I can feel you now. I only need

to write to you, to concentrate my thoughts, and everything is clear again.

My dear, if you are in LA, do you think you might please send me the collages. I would so like them here to keep me company and see me through the awful anniversary of Georgia's death. Then there is the London winter. I am sorry to put you to the trouble, but you are so understanding, I take advantage like everyone else. Only do send them, please Miles.

Write if you have a moment. All my love.

                                             Sylvie

Letter Twenty-One

                                             Belitha Villas
                                             March 8

Dear Miles,

The terrible day has come and gone. Of course I felt you here with me. And Steve too. I felt Steve, I'm sure I did. Was it too dreadful for you? I hope you are well and that your book is progressing. I should so like the collages. I know you must be very busy. Perhaps Steve could pack them. Shall I call you?

                                             Love,
                                             Sylvia

PS You won't publish the letters, will you?

Letter Twenty-Two

Belitha Villas
May 25

Dear Miles,

I wanted to tell you how much I can feel you all. You are here with me in my room, you and Georgia and Steve and Marlowe – everyone, oh just everyone. So good of you to think of me. I wonder where you are, but of course it doesn't matter. Except Miles, dear Miles, if only I could have the collages. If you could please send the collages. Please.